Slocum ducked low behind the boulders and thumbed cartridges into the loading port of his Winchester. He had one chance. That was to take out the sharpshooter on the west canyon wall, then break for cover while the big man with the Springfield was reloading on the bluff above to his right. With luck and one clear shot, he might make it . . .

A heavy slug hammered into the receiver of Slocum's rifle and ripped the weapon from his grasp, the shock numbing Slocum's hands. He tried to pull the spare Colt from beneath his belt; the fingers of his stiff hands refused to close on the revolver grips . . . Slocum twisted around, trying to will his hands to close on the Colt—and found himself staring at certain death . . .

# JAKE LOGAN

## SLOCUM AND THE SCALPLOCK TRAIL

JOVE BOOKS, NEW YORK

SLOCUM AND THE SCALPLOCK TRAIL

A Jove Book / published by arrangement with
the author

PRINTING HISTORY
Jove edition / March 1998

The Penguin Putnam Inc. World Wide Web site address is
http://www.penguinputnam.com

ISBN: 0-515-12243-2

A JOVE BOOK®
Jove Books are published by The Berkley Publishing Group,
a member of Penguin Putnam Inc.,
200 Madison Avenue, New York, New York 10016.
JOVE and the "J" design are trademarks
belonging to Jove Publications, Inc.

PRINTED IN THE UNITED STATES OF AMERICA

10  9  8  7  6  5  4  3  2  1

# SLOCUM AND THE
# SCALPLOCK TRAIL

# 1

Slocum let the mountain-savvy sorrel pick its way through the narrow notch between peaks overlooking the Rio Chamita and the town of Chama a half mile below.

He reined the gelding to a stop in the shade of a tall pine, dismounted, and loosened the girth so the horse could breathe easier. Slocum knew it wouldn't take long for the sorrel to get his air back. The horse with the spotted rump was barely winded from the long, twisting climb. The Nez Percé Indians bred tough, smart horses. Slocum idly patted the gelding's muscled shoulder.

In the shade of the pine, the air felt a good thirty degrees cooler than it did in the hot summer sunshine of the thin air out in the open, Slocum thought. It was just one of the reasons he had always liked the high country.

Slocum pulled a thin Mexican cheroot from his shirt pocket, lit the smoke with a sulphur match, and studied the town below.

It was a routine he always followed. Especially when the man he had come so far to kill could have friends down there.

From this distance, it didn't appear that Chama had changed much over the last few years. It seemed more a sleepy village than a town, dun-colored buildings clustered on the valley floor north of the confluence of the Chamita and Chama Rivers.

Most buildings in Chama, like those in other northern New Mexico towns, were made of adobe, a concession to the varied high-country weather. The mud-and-straw building blocks kept the interiors surprisingly cool in summer, yet warm in winter's bitter winds and deep snows. All but a couple of the buildings were low, one-story structures.

Narrow streets that once had been mere cart paths ambled between haphazardly spaced buildings. The only two roads wide enough for big freight wagons and six-horse-hitch stagecoaches ran to and from the four corners of the compass, intersecting in the center of town. A community water well with native stone walls and horse trough stood at the convergence of the major roads, in what would have been the town square of a larger settlement.

The streets of Chama were all but deserted. The town looked peaceful, quiet, almost as if it had shut down for siesta time.

Slocum knew Chama was anything but quiet.

Unless it had tamed considerably since his last visit, it was one of the wildest, most wide-open frontier towns between the Mississippi River and the Pacific Ocean. A place where a careless man could get himself killed over a couple of dollars. Or maybe just for fun. The kind of place a cold-blooded killer with the unlikely name of June Deschamp would be drawn to, like a fly to a rotting carcass.

Slocum studied the horses hitched along the main street, and the others that stood hipshot and half asleep in the livery corral on the northeast edge of Chama.

He saw no sign of the dozen or so spotted horses, which the Nez Percé called *palouse*, that Deschamp had stolen—four of them Slocum's—in the bloody raid on the Indian settlement almost three months ago. Slocum took that as a good sign. The shortcut through the rugged, heavily timbered San Juan Mountains had saved a few day's travel from the normal route through Cumbres Pass. He had gained enough time on the outlaws to feel reasonably sure he had beaten them to Chama by at least couple of days.

Still, he sensed Deschamp was nearby. Slocum could all but smell the stocky, aging outlaw. The end of the long and twisted trail was near. The thought was some consolation. Deschamp was about to pay for the blood he'd left behind on the Lapwai Reservation in northwest Idaho, where a once-proud people who had fought one of the most intense military campaigns in history had settled into a peaceful way of life, accepting their fate and trading with the white man.

Slocum had been fifty miles away in search of high-country elk when the bloodied, exhausted young Nez Percé boy reached him with word that Deschamp and his gang had left the Indian village in charred ruins, a dozen burned and mutilated bodies in their wake, the prized horses stolen.

The loss of the horses was secondary to Slocum. The rage that smoldered in his gut was because two of the dead were special to him.

Deschamp now carried the scalps of Joe Summerhawk and his daughter, Quill, tied to his saddle. For that, Deschamp would die. If not here in Chama, then wherever the trail led. Slocum couldn't—and wouldn't—rest until he had Deschamp in his sights.

Memories chased the sense of satisfaction of that vision from Slocum's heart, replacing it with a heavy tightness.

Memories of days spent smoking, trading yarns, and training young palouse horses with Joe Summerhawk, Slocum's jovial host during a long winter and a late but spectacular spring that painted the mountain valley in more colors than Slocum could count. And the days and nights shared with the strikingly beautiful and gentle Quill, she of the coltish, dancing eyes and quick wit by day—and an honest, lusty passion Slocum had never before known in any woman. The dark eyes would dance no more. Her laugh would no longer sing like cold water along a mountain stream, bringing a smile to Slocum's lips.

Slocum had had many women. He had never had one like Quill. She was more than just a supple, lusty, and beautiful girl, wise beyond her twenty-two summers. He couldn't say that he had been in love with Quill; Slocum was a man who had not known love. But there was something about her that left a man relaxed and happy, with a warmth in his breast, just to be around her. It was, Slocum figured, about as close to the undefined sensation called love as he had ever known.

Deschamp had taken that from him. Now he would pay.

Slocum dropped the stub of cheroot, ground it beneath a boot heel, and slipped the .44-40 Single Action Army revolver from its cross-draw holster. He thumbed the Peacemaker's hammer to half cock, turned the cylinder, and fed a sixth cartridge into the chamber he normally left empty beneath the hammer. When he was headed into a possible fight, Slocum found comfort in that sixth shot. He lowered the hammer, holstered the handgun, tightened the cinch, mounted, and let the spotted horse pick its own way down the mountainside.

He reined up at the edge of the cool, clear river water and

let the horse drink its fill. As the palouse drank, Slocum slid the Winchester .44-40 rifle from its saddle scabbard. There were rifles with more reach and a harder punch than the .44-40, but it put the slug where a man pointed. And carrying a rifle and handguns of the same caliber simplified ammunition needs.

The spotted gelding, its thirst quenched, lifted its head, ears perked toward the town. The horse snuffled softly, then lifted into an easy trot toward Chama at Slocum's gentle knee pressure against his ribs.

Chama, Slocum thought with a touch of disgust, was as trashy in appearance as it was in reputation.

The southwest breeze stirred bits of paper and refuse along the main streets. A scraggly mixed-breed dog nosed through the rubbish in an alley between a two-story clapboard hotel and a shotgun-style adobe general store. The dog's ribs showed through its gaunt brown hide; the mongrel looked up as Slocum rode past and whined, then trotted after Slocum's palouse. The sorrel backed its ears, but at Slocum's soft word, didn't kick at the dog.

Slocum's gaze swept the streets and alleys, noting potential ambush sites. He had learned from long experience that a town held more bushwhacking opportunities than any mountain trail. He saw nothing unusual.

He reined the gelding to a stop before a long, low building with the word "cantina" printed in crude letters on a weathered sign that creaked in the wind. Four horses stood hitched at the rail. Slocum studied the horses for a moment. A man could often tell what he was about to walk into by paying attention to the animals outside.

He frowned in disgust at the sight of two horses, each wearing a Walking T brand on the left hip. Their flanks were gaunt from lack of water. Flecks of lather and dried streaks of salt-sweat stained unbrushed hides. On both animals' backs were heavy, double-rigged stockman's saddles. Slocum marked them as working cowboy mounts. A third, a deep-chested, leggy bay, carried an ornately carved single-cinch rig, the saddle skirt leathers carved in ornate floral patterns and studded with silver conchas. A dandy's rig, Slocum thought. All three horses were still tightly cinched and bitted, the marks of men who cared little for the animals they rode.

It was the fourth horse that stood out in Slocum's eyes.

The sleek black gelding bore the stamp of carefully bred Tennessee racing bloodlines. The long-legged black was well tended, fresh marks of curry comb and brush tracing swirls in its shiny black coat. Unlike the others, the black's flanks were smooth; the animal had been watered, the long-shanked cavalry style bit slipped from its mouth, the bridle headstall draped behind the horse's trim throatlatch. A lightweight halter, its single rein tied in a slipknot, tethered the black to the hitch rail. The man who owned this horse knew how to treat a mount.

The saddle on the black's back piqued Slocum's interest as much as the horse did; it wasn't often a man ran across a Mc-Clellan rig this far west. The cinch was loosened, the leather well worn but supple, with a sheen of neat's-foot oil. On the off side, beneath the right stirrup, rested an unusual rifle boot, a good two feet longer and a handspan thicker than Slocum's own Winchester scabbard. The rifle boot was empty.

Slocum reined his sorrel palouse past the four mounts to the next hitch rail, one that stood before a combination saddlery and gun shop.

He dismounted, loosened the cinch, and heard a low whimper from nearby. The half-starved cur lowered its head onto its front paws and stared at him with hopeful brown eyes. Slocum hated to see an animal suffer, and somehow, the dog sensed it. Slocum reached into his near-side saddlebag, pulled a couple of strips of jerky from a cloth bag, and tossed the dried meat to the cur. The animal whined again, but made no move to pick up the jerky.

"Go ahead, boy," Slocum said softly. "It's all right."

The dog snatched up a strip of dried elk and settled down to chew on the handout meal. Slocum loosened the cinch on the spotted sorrel, looped the reins over the hitch rail, and turned toward the cantina. The dog stopped chewing and rose, as if to follow.

"Stay, boy," Slocum said.

The cur plopped down and started gnawing the jerky again.

Slocum instinctively loosened the Peacemaker in its holster before he stepped into the cantina. For the couple of seconds it took for his vision to adjust from bright sunlight to near-gloom, Slocum stood inside the doorway, his back to the wall.

The cantina smelled like any frontier saloon. The scent of sawdust floor, stale beer, smoke, and whiskey mingled with the nostril-biting odor of man sweat. Dim light filtered through the single dingy front window. Dust motes danced in the narrow ray of sunlight that spilled through a spiderwebbed bullet hole in the glass. Behind the bar, a pair of oil lanterns guttered feebly.

Slocum's eyes quickly adjusted to the near-gloom. He had little trouble matching up four of the customers inside with the horses at the hitch rail. Two cowboys leaned against the far end of the rough pine bar, nursing beers and smoking roll-your-owns. A third man, young and smooth of face, sat at a table in the near corner, a bottle and shot glass at his right hand. The dim light danced from silver conchas that studded his black vest and snakeskin hatband. He'd be the one with the gussied-up rig on the bay outside. Slocum paid little attention to the dandy.

The fourth man was little more than a shadow in the far corner of the cantina. Slocum could tell the man was tall and lean, but little else; his features were indistinct beneath a narrow-brimmed hat pulled low over the eyes. The long, heavy tube of a big-bore rifle barrel leaned against the wall near his right hand.

Somehow, the shadowy figure seemed familiar. Slocum shook off the notion. When a man had ridden as many trails as he had, someone in every town looked vaguely familiar.

At the end of the bar to Slocum's right stood a doorway draped with a heavy curtain that looked to be canvas. Slocum figured there were other rooms, either for gambling or prostitute's cribs—or both—in the back. Chama's cantina, he thought, had the answer to a man's needs. For a price.

Slocum picked his spot and strode to the end of the bar. He chose the spot deliberately. There, he had his back to the coarse adobe wall, and the door and window in plain view.

The bartender, a slightly built man with bushy mustache and weathered features and wearing a stained apron with an obvious bulge in a front pocket, limped to Slocum.

"What'll it be, mister?" the barkeep asked.

"Shot of Old Overholt, if you've got it. And a beer," Slocum said.

The bartender nodded, turned away, and a moment later placed a shot glass and full beer mug before Slocum. He showed Slocum the label, then poured the shot glass full of Old Overholt. At least, Slocum thought, a man got his money's worth for a drink. If it wasn't watered down.

"Thirty cents," the bartender said.

Slocum fished a half dollar from his shirt pocket and put the coin on the bar. He lifted the shot glass with his left hand and took a sip. The undiluted rye went down smooth and raised a pleasant warmth in his belly. He chased the liquor with a swig of beer and nodded his approval to the barkeep.

He nursed the shot and beer, savoring the smooth richness of each as the drinks cut the dust of a long trail from his tongue. He became aware that he was being watched. His gaze locked for a moment with the young dandy at the table.

Slocum was accustomed to being stared at; a man who stood a lean six-one, with jet-black hair and green eyes, and wore his handgun cross-draw-style, was a sure bet to draw attention. That didn't mean Slocum had ever learned to like it.

The dandy—clean shaven and barely out of his teens—tried to hold Slocum's steady gaze for a moment, but finally lowered his head and slowly refilled his shot glass. Slocum noticed that the kid had a black leather gunbelt around his hips, the holster tied down, riding low on his right thigh. The distinctively curved grips of a Bisley Colt protruded from the holster.

Slocum let his gaze drift away, but kept the youngster at the edge of his vision. Something about the kid spelled trouble. He studied the two cowboys at the end of the bar, saw nothing out of the ordinary about them, and dismissed them from his mind. He still could make out little about the tall, lean man in the shadows. That bothered Slocum a bit. He liked to know who and what was going on around him—and he couldn't shake the tickle of recognition from his gut.

Slocum's interest drifted from the shadow man as the curtains at the far end of the bar swung aside. A woman stepped through.

In the light of the guttering lantern, she could have been any age, Slocum thought, but there was no question about her being a woman.

She was taller than most women, possibly five-foot-eight. She stood with her back straight, head erect. Long, dark hair fell almost to her waist. The low-cut dress she wore revealed an impressive swell of full breasts. A slit high up the side of her gown showed a firm and muscular, yet long, leg—full thigh and calf, trim knee and slender ankle above her low-heeled shoe.

The woman spoke quietly with the bartender, then glanced

at Slocum. Her quick initial once-over glance turned into a long, speculative stare. She held his gaze as she strode toward Slocum, hips swaying beneath a waist that was not quite small, yet still trim.

One of the cowboys reached out, put a hand around her waist, and said something.

"Not today, Coy," Slocum heard her say. "Move your hand."

The cowboy's face flushed in disappointment, perhaps a touch of anger. But his hand dropped from her waist.

The woman stopped at Slocum's right side. Up close, she was even more impressive than at a distance. Slocum was no authority on the age of women—a man couldn't tooth them the way he could a horse to determine how old they were—but he guessed her to be in her early thirties. Her wide-set, deep brown eyes were flecked in gold that caught and held the flickers of lantern light. Her full lips parted in a smile that showed even, white teeth, and painted small crow's-feet wrinkles at the corners of her eyes. Her skin was dark, almost a Spanish tint.

She fell short of being a raving beauty, but she came close enough. Her nose was a bit long and slightly humped, but she was far from horse-faced. A faint dusting of dark hairs on her upper lip hinted at a dense thatch between those long legs.

She stood silently for a moment, staring into Slocum's eyes, then leaned an elbow on the bar, her right shoulder cocked slightly forward. The movement let the deep blue cloth of her dress fall away enough that Slocum could easily see the nipple rising from the near half-dollar-sized ring of pigment at the tip of her breast.

Slocum made no attempt to shift his gaze from the dark, full breast. The growing warmth in his crotch reminded him it had been a long time since he had had a woman. Since his last night with Quill more than three months ago.

"Care for another drink, stranger? Or maybe something even more relaxing?" As she spoke, she shifted her weight. Slocum felt the warmth of her body as her hip and thigh pressed against him. "A man like you could turn a girl's knees to butter, I'd bet."

Slocum stared into her eyes for a moment. The lack of true warmth there hinted that the buttery-knee comment was likely a practiced sales line. She might not be truly interested in anything but his money, Slocum thought, but he'd grant her one thing. She was one hell of an actress.

He smiled at her. "I'd like nothing better, miss," he said with genuine regret, "but it'll have to wait until I've taken care of some business."

He halfway expected her to stomp off in a huff, being turned down like that. It probably didn't happen often. Instead, her smile widened and she made no attempt to move away from him.

"Any time, mister," she said. "I can wait."

"Thanks. I'd be pleased to buy you a drink in the meantime."

"I'd be pleased to drink it." She nodded to the bartender. "The usual, Sam."

Slocum halfway expected the barkeep to reach for a bottle of colored water, or tea, in the frontier tradition of saloon girls hustling drinks from customers. Instead, Sam handed her a shot glass and filled it to the rim from the bottle of Old Overholt he had served Slocum with. "Two bits," Sam said.

Slocum paid. The woman lifted the shot glass and took a small sip. Slocum noticed for the first time that her eyebrows were naturally thick, her lashes long, and that she apparently wore no makeup.

"What brings you to Chama, if you don't mind my asking?" Her tone was pleasant, the voice throaty, almost musical. It blunted Slocum's usual irritation at people who poked their noses into places they didn't belong.

He shrugged. "I'm looking for a man, miss."

"Call me Lisa. On account of that's my real name. Well, actually, it's Lisolette Barnes, but I go by Lisa. What's yours?"

"Slocum."

At the corner of his vision, Slocum saw the dandy in the black vest stiffen, the bottle in his hand poised motionless above his glass as he stared at Slocum.

Lisa took another sip of her drink. "First name or last?"

"Just Slocum will do."

Slocum glanced up as the cowboy Lisa had rebuffed strode up. He stopped an arm's length away.

"What the hell's this feller got that I ain't, Lisa?" The challenge was clear in the cowboy's tone.

Slocum gazed steadily into the man's eyes for a moment,

then said softly, "For the moment I have her attention. I'd suggest you leave her alone."

"Listen, mister—"

"Coy," Slocum interrupted, "let me explain something to you as simply as possible. Go away."

The young man flushed and sputtered, his right hand balled into a fist near his side. For a moment, Slocum thought Coy might push his luck and reach for the worn .38 in his belt holster.

"Don't try it, Coy," Slocum said calmly, "I'd sure as hell hate to waste a cartridge on a man I didn't come here to kill."

The cowboy stared into Slocum's eyes. The anger faded from Coy's face, washed away by a wave of confusion and apprehension. He swallowed hard, then forced a defiant shrug. "It ain't worth my trouble right now, feller," he finally said. His voice wavered a bit. "I'll settle up with you later."

"Fine by me, Coy. But you're going to have to get in line if you want to try me. There's a few men in front of you."

The cowboy tried a cold glare, failed, and strode angrily out the door. After a moment, his companion downed the last of his beer and followed Coy outside.

Lisa shook her head, a faint smile tugging at the corners of her mouth. "Looks like Coy got the message. Sometimes, he's a little hardheaded. Jealous type." The smile faded. She lifted an eyebrow at Slocum. "Would you have shot him? He's just a kid."

Slocum shrugged. "A kid can pull a trigger just as easy as a grown man."

"Are you that cold, Slocum?"

"Not cold. Just careful. Anyway, it doesn't matter. I'm glad he made the right decision, for what's that's worth."

"It's worth something—" A commotion from outside cut Lisa's comment short. The sounds tumbled one atop the other, a man's yelp of pain, a horse's squeal, a series of solid thumps, the deep snarl of a dog.

Slocum reached the door in three strides, the Peacemaker in his hand, Lisa close behind him. Then he stopped abruptly and stared at the scene through billows of dust.

Coy lay in the street beside Slocum's horse, blood seeping from his right forearm, clasped in the jaws of the mongrel dog; then the spotted sorrel, ears backed and eyes wide, landed a solid kick on Coy's hip. The young cowboy yelped again in pain and fear. A few feet away, Coy's companion stood grinning.

"Get 'em off me!" Coy yelped over the dog's throaty growls, which were partly muffled by the arm in his jaws. "Somebody get 'em off!"

Slocum took his time holstering the handgun. The sorrel kicked again, the hoof hammering into Coy's thigh. Slocum finally called out, "Steady, Chief!" The horse, its left hoof raised to kick again, lowered the foot. The mongrel dog, Coy's arm still clamped in its jaws, shook its head. "Enough, boy," Slocum said. The dog loosed its grip and sat back on its haunches, still growling low in the back of its throat, its gaze steady on the downed man.

Slocum strode past Coy's saddlemate, who was now doubled over in full-blown laughter. Slocum stood over the writhing, moaning Coy. The cowboy's left hand clamped around his bloodied right forearm.

"You know, Coy," Slocum said as he pulled a cheroot from his pocket, "a man could get himself killed trying to steal another fellow's horse."

"Wasn't trying—to steal no horse," Coy stammered through teeth gritted in pain. "Was gonna—just cut through—saddle girth."

Slocum couldn't keep from grinning. "Coy, it looks like you're not having a very good day here."

"You can say that again, mister," Coy's companion said between chortles, tears streaming down his cheeks. "That palouse kicked the slats out of ol' Coy, all while that dog was chewin' on his arm."

"Chief's kind of a one-man horse," Slocum said casually as he scratched a match to life and fired his cigarillo. "He doesn't like strangers messing around with him."

Coy's friend dissolved into another round of hiccuping laughter. "Noticed that—right off," he finally managed to gasp. "That dog of yours ain't too friendly either. Why, I'd of paid money to see that wreck."

"Damn you, Jake," Coy gasped, still lying in the street, "you'd of stood there and let them two critters tear me to pieces." He moaned again. "I think I got a busted leg. And my arm's chawed half off—"

Slocum reached down, grabbed Coy's collar, hauled the dazed young man to his feet, and quickly checked him over.

"Nothing's broken and the dog bite's not that deep. You got out lucky again, son. If you were a cat, I'd say you used up at least three of your allotted nine lives in the last few minutes. I'd suggest you and your buddy ride out of town while you've still got six of them left."

Slocum waited as Coy's companion boosted him into the saddle, then said, "Might be a good idea to pour a little coal oil on that bite. I'm not sure, but I don't think the dog's got hydrophobia."

Coy's face went even whiter.

Lisa, Slocum, and the bartender stood and watched as the two cowboys rode off toward the southwest. "Well," the barkeep said after a moment, "there goes an older and wiser youngster. Next round's on the house, folks. Show like that's worth a drink in my place anytime."

Slocum stroked the sorrel's shoulder, then knelt to pat the dog on the scruff of the neck. His gaze settled on the "cafe" sign across the street.

"I'll be along in a minute," Slocum said. "I think this dog just earned himself a bonus." He scratched the cur's ears. "How about a nice raw steak, boy? My treat."

# 2

Slocum noted with interest that the shadowy figure in the corner hadn't moved when the others had gone outside to see what had happened to the kid named Coy.

Once again, a slight worm of recognition wriggled in his gut. Lisa didn't let it worry him long.

She stood at his side again, hip and thigh lightly touching his, and lifted her shot glass as Sam refilled Slocum's.

"Here's to Coy," she said with a wry smile, "who is going to have some very sore spots in the morning. I do believe he learned something today."

Slocum nodded. "Most likely. I've heard it said that a man carrying a mad bobcat by the tail is learning more about the procedure than the man who just gets told how to do it." He downed half the shot and sighed.

Lisa's smile faded. "This man you're looking for—well, it's none of my business, but maybe I can help. Or Sam. Between us, we know just about everybody in and around Chama." There was nothing in her tone that hinted she knew everybody because of her line of work. It was a simple statement of fact. Slocum accepted it as such.

"As far as I've been able to find out, he doesn't come through here often. Last time would have been maybe a year and a half ago." Slocum paused to finish off the dregs of his beer, which had lost its chill during the excitement, and grimaced. Cold coffee and warm beer weren't among his favorite drinks. Sam solved the problem by refilling Slocum's mug.

Slocum said, "The man I'm looking for is June Deschamp."

Lisa's sudden, sharp intake of breath, the surge of tension through her thigh and hip, caught Slocum by surprise. Shock, fear, and a touch of anger flickered in her brown eyes.

"It—it couldn't be—" Her voice was barely audible. "But the name—"

Slocum lifted an eyebrow. "You know him?"

The fear drained from Lisa's eyes. Her expression went cold and hard, full lips drawn into a hard, thin line, brows narrowed. A muscle twitched in the side of her neck.

His mention of Deschamp apparently had jarred more than the woman. At the corner of his vision, Slocum saw the dandy's head bob up. He stared at Slocum for a couple of heartbeats.

"If it's the same June Deschamp, I know the son of a bitch," Lisa said, her tone venomous. "Describe him."

"I've never faced him, but from the descriptions I've heard, I know what he looks like. Medium height, maybe five-foot-ten, going to paunch, pushing sixty," Slocum said. "Old scar on the left side of his face, from hat brim to jaw joint."

Sam, leaning against the bar across from Lisa, nodded. "That's him, all right. Him and his bunch damn near wrecked this place. Winter before last."

Lisa's breath quickened. "Do you know where he's from?"

Slocum nodded. "Arkansas originally. Not far from Pea Ridge."

Lisa barked a curse. "It's got to be him. It couldn't be anybody but him." She drew away from Slocum. "If you're a friend of that bastard, you can go to Hell for all I care."

Slocum said, "I probably will someday. But it's my intention to send June Deschamp there well before I shake hands with Old Scratch and Beelzebub. Deschamp owes me, Lisa. That's why I've come to Chama. To kill him."

"Then I hope to hell you do, Slocum." The bitter edge to Lisa's words would have cut an anvil in half at twenty yards. "I'd love nothing more than to hoist my skirt and piss on June Deschamp's grave. Right over his damned face."

The dandy in black, who also had stayed at his table during the commotion outside, abruptly stood and strode for the door. Silver inlaid Chihuahua spurs jingled as he walked. Slocum's inner warning bells jangled louder than the big spur rowels. He watched until the door closed behind the dandy, then turned to Sam. "Know the young man who just left?"

Sam shook his head. "Can't say as I do. He just rode in a

couple hours ago. Slocum, I don't normally stick my nose where it don't go. But if you're going after Deschamp, I can tell you he rides with a hell of a tough bunch.''

''Thanks, Sam, but I already know that,'' Slocum said. ''I've tracked him and his gang all the way from Idaho. He stole some horses from me. More than that, he butchered two friends of mine in the process. For no reason. They didn't even have a chance to put up a fight.''

Lisa put a hand on Slocum's forearm. Her fingers were chilled. ''Is he—do you think—Deschamp's in Chama now?''

''Not likely,'' Slocum said with a shrug. ''I figure I'm at least a day or two ahead of him. But he's headed this way. He's running short on whiskey and grub, looking for a place to sell stolen stock. Chama's the best place to do that for two hundred miles in any direction. He'll be here.''

A quiver ran through Lisa's shoulders. ''How do you know that?''

''I've tracked him nearly three months. I got to know pretty well how the bastard's mind works during that time.'' He tossed back the rest of his drink. ''Deschamp likes to send out a scout before he goes into a town. I have a feeling that kid who just left is on his way to tell Deschamp I'm here.''

Lisa glanced toward the empty table. ''He did leave in a hurry, come to think of it. Barely lowered the level on that bottle, and he paid for the whole thing.'' Her fingers tightened on his forearm. ''Slocum, what are you going to do?''

Slocum drained the last of his tepid beer. ''I'm going to wait. I'm going to let Deschamp come to me.''

''Jesus,'' Lisa said, her voice little more than a whisper, ''Slocum, there's so many of them—you could be killed. . . .'' Her voice trailed away.

''Every man dies, Lisa. Sooner or later. I quit worrying about that a long time ago. It's just a matter of putting it off until something more important comes along.''

''Like Deschamp?''

''Like Deschamp.'' Slocum's tone was casual, matter of fact. ''Maybe you'll have the chance to hoist your skirt over my grave too, Lisa,'' he said, ''but you have my solemn promise you'll get your chance to piss on what's left of June Deschamp.''

Lisa stared into Slocum's eyes for several heartbeats. ''You're a strange man, Slocum,'' she finally said.

"So I've been told. Another drink?"

Lisa nodded. "God, but I could use one. I'll get it." She strode to the table the dandy had left and returned with the abandoned bottle. "It's the most expensive brand we have. The best Tennessee sour mash this side of the Mississippi, and it's been paid for once. No need to let it go to waste."

She refilled her own and Slocum's glasses, then told Sam to bring Slocum another beer and put it on her account. She slid the whiskey bottle over in front of Slocum. "The rest is yours. I've reached my limit. At least for now."

Slocum re-corked the bourbon and handed her the bottle. "Save the rest for later, Lisa. We'll share it when this is over with."

She fell silent for a moment, gazing steadily into Slocum's eyes, then said, "What do you plan to do, Slocum? Just sit here and wait for a bunch of men to walk in the door and shoot you to pieces?"

"No, I don't. I'd prefer to live through this fight. I've picked the place. It's up to Deschamp to decide the time."

"Why not just shoot the bastard in the back?"

"That would be the smart thing to do. But I want Deschamp to know why he's going to die."

Lisa's brows narrowed. "You must hate that son of a bitch as much as I do, to take that big a risk."

"It goes beyond hate, Lisa. He took something from me that can never be returned."

"Like he did me." Lisa didn't elaborate. Slocum didn't push the point. Lisolette Barnes's private demons were her own matter. If she wanted to talk about them, he would listen. If she didn't, he wouldn't ask.

Lisa didn't speak again until Slocum had drained the last of his beer, but he felt the tension seep from her muscles during the silence. Whether it was the effect of the liquor or something else, Slocum couldn't tell, but he was relieved that she had begun to relax.

She had moved back to his side. The warmth through the thin cloth of her dress seemed to grow as she leaned against him. Slocum became aware of the tingle at his crotch. The faint fragrance of lilac water, the even fainter, slightly musky woman scent of her, caressed his nostrils.

After a time, she sighed; her lips parted in a smile that crinkled the crow's-feet wrinkles at the corners of gold-flecked eyes. "The bastard ruined my life, but I'm not going to let him take this day from me," she said.

Slocum raised an eyebrow in an unspoken question.

Her voice had gone low and husky again. "You did say Deschamp wouldn't be here until at least tomorrow?"

"That's how I've got it figured."

"Then we've got time, Slocum." It was a question as well as an invitation.

Slocum pondered the proposal. He was down to his last forty dollars and the emergency double eagle sewn into his boot top. He sighed. "I'm a little short on cash right now, Lisa."

"It doesn't matter. If you're going to kill Deschamp, no charge." Lisa downed the last sip of her drink and reached for the bourbon bottle. "I'll be in my room whenever you're ready."

The tingle in Slocum's groin grew. "I'll have to tend my horse first." He ran the side of his thumb over the scratchy stubble of his chin and winced. "And if you don't mind, grab a bath and shave. I'm packing a full eight hours of trail dust and whisker stubble."

"The barbershop's a block south of the stable," she said. "Take all the time you need. My room's through the curtain, last door on the right. I'll be waiting." She pressed her breast against his upper arm and said, "Skip the bay rum, Slocum. Your natural scent will be fine with me." She turned and strode toward the curtain.

Slocum watched until the cloth closed behind Lisa, then reached for his Winchester. As he strode toward the door, he noticed with a touch of surprise that the shadowy figure in the far corner was no longer there. Slocum mentally chided himself. No matter what a man had on his mind, he should always be aware of what was going on around him. And he hadn't seen the lean man leave the cantina.

The sleek black Tennessee gelding with the McClellan saddle was no longer at the hitch rail when Slocum stepped outside. The shadow man had likely picked up enough of the conversation to know a gunfight was brewing, and headed for safer pastures. A smart man, Slocum thought; probably smarter than I am.

The cur lay beneath the spotted horse's neck, gnawing at the bone left over from his reward steak. Slocum untied the sorrel and started for the stable, the gelding ambling at his side on loose rein. The brown dog trotted alongside in the gelding's shadow.

"Well, Chief," Slocum said to the palouse, "it looks like we've got a new partner." The horse's nostrils fluttered softly, as if to say that was fine with him.

Slocum rousted the hostler, a Mexican with a leathery face, stooped shoulders, and snow-white hair, from his siesta in the shade of the stable. Slocum looked over the livery. It would do; six box stalls lined the thatch-roof adobe shed. Two of the stalls were empty. The water trough in the corral was full, with no sign of the scum and slime that built up on untended troughs.

Three horses, a couple of cow ponies, and a big, strong and well-groomed chestnut with blaze face stood hipshot in a corner of the corral, tails battling summer flies.

Slocum paid the hostler thirty cents for a box stall, a bait of grain, and a couple of forks of prairie hay. He stripped the saddle from the palouse and rubbed down Chief as the Mexican filled the water bucket hanging in the stall. Chief already had his nose buried in the grain bin. The brown cur settled down to watch in a corner of the stall.

"Señor, I must tell you that I cannot promise that your saddle, maybe even your fine horse, might not be stolen during the night," the hostler said apologetically. "I have no one to stand watch in the dark hours, and Chama has many thieves about."

"I won't worry about it," Slocum said. He nodded toward the dog. "Just fetch a pan of water for the dog. He'll make sure everything's still here come daylight."

Slocum shouldered his saddle bags, picked up his rifle, and strode toward the barbershop, his alert gaze sweeping the street as he walked. The weight of the spare .44-40 Peacemaker he carried in the saddlebag was reassuring against his shoulder.

The sun was still a couple of hours above the western horizon when Slocum, freshly bathed, shaved, and his hair trimmed, tapped on Lisa's door.

"Who's there?" The heavy oak door muffled Lisa's voice.

"Slocum."

"Give me a minute," she called. "I'll be right there."

Slocum waited patiently until he heard the rasp of a bolt being drawn. The door swung open with a slight creak of iron hinges. Lisa flashed a smile. "Come in and make yourself at home. Sorry to keep you waiting. I wasn't expecting you for a few more minutes. Had to freshen up a bit.''

It was worth the wait, Slocum thought. He removed his hat as Lisa closed the door, slid the heavy bolt that served as a lock into place, and turned to face him. She had changed from the saloon-girl dress she'd worn earlier; she now wore a simple, pale rose housedress made of thin, almost transparent, cotton. She looked better than she had in her working costume.

Slocum suspected that she wore nothing beneath the thin cotton. The dark circles of pigment around the nipples that tipped her full breasts were clearly visible through the rose-colored material. The stirring in Slocum's crotch returned. He made no effort to take his gaze from her. The expression in her eyes and the smile on full lips told him she didn't mind his staring.

After a moment, she waved toward a padded chair beside a small table within arm's length of the bed. The bottle of Tennessee bourbon and two small glasses stood in the center of the bed, flanked by a cut-glass ashtray.

Lisa gestured toward a row of pegs hanging beside the door. ''Hang your hat, Slocum, and put your gunbelt wherever you feel most comfortable. Make yourself at home and pour us a couple of drinks while I adjust the curtains. I like a little light, to see what I'm doing—but not too much.'' She flashed a wicked grin and a lecherous wink; she did the whore's act well, Slocum thought.

Slocum unbuckled his gunbelt, hung it on the arm of a chair within arm's length of the bed, and reached for the bottle. He paused, the bottle forgotten beneath his hand, as Lisa strode to the single window. He soon realized that he had been right; Lisa wore nothing beneath the thin cotton dress.

Sunlight flowed through the partly opened window to silhouette her body. The backlight effect sharply outlined long, shapely, yet solidly muscular legs, and the swell of sturdy, firm hips; her waist, Slocum noted with appreciation, didn't pinch in abruptly—it flowed at a smooth angle from hip to rib cage. She reached up to make a final adjustment on the curtain valance, the silhouette of a startlingly full but firm breast in sharp outline for a moment.

The ache in Slocum's groin grew. He finally forced his attention back to the business of pouring a couple of fingers of bourbon in each of the two glasses. As he put the bottle down, he noticed, on the far side of the neatly made bed, a handgun on a night table.

The gun seemed out of place in a woman's room. It wasn't a typical lady's weapon like a derringer or little four-shot cloverleaf pocket pistol. Diffused sunlight glistened on the cylinder and backstrap of the big top-break Schofield Smith & Wesson with an eight-inch barrel. The weapon was a man-stopper, .45 caliber, and it threw a big chunk of lead downrange when you pulled the trigger. Slocum wondered if it was Lisa's revolver; the thing would be a handful for a woman.

Her soft footfalls pulled his attention from the revolver.

Lisa stopped before him, her gold-flecked brown eyes smoldering. Slocum noticed for the first time the row of buttons along the front of the cotton dress; from throat to the tip of breastbone and from mid-thigh down, the buttons were undone. She stood with her hip cocked, the smooth, firm flesh of her leg exposed well above the knee, the round swell of her breasts tantalizingly near his reach. The scent of lilac water and the faint, musky smell of woman caressed Slocum's nostrils. The swelling in his Levi's grew.

Lisa came into his arms and kissed him. At first, it was a whore's kiss—lips together, moist, yet distant and unconcerned. Then, to Slocum's surprise, she melted against him; her lips softened and parted. The kiss became hotter, more urgent, the tip of her tongue traced a tingly line against his.

Finally, she pulled back, breathing hard. Slocum noticed that her nipples had become erect.

"Damn, Slocum," she said huskily, "what the hell is it about you? I've never felt—felt what I did just then."

Slocum reached out, placed his right hand against her cheek, then felt her hand close over his. She pulled his hand down until his palm rested on the warm swell of her upper breast. She leaned back and moaned deep in her throat when Slocum ran his hand along the pliant mound of flesh and down to cup her breast in his palm. She pressed her lower body against his, leaning slightly to her right to let Slocum's hand fondle her breast.

Lisa whispered, "I don't know—what the hell's—happening to me? I never felt—" A short, quick gasp cut her words short as Slocum's fingers stroked slowly upward and brushed across her nipple. The nub of flesh was firm and erect beneath his touch. She shuddered as he took the nipple between thumb and forefinger, gently massaging.

"Jesus, Slocum." Her voice was soft, husky, even though it quavered a bit. She shifted her position, let her hand ease gently from his shoulder down his chest, his belly. Her palm came to rest against his crotch. The warmth from her hand, the slight back-and-forth movement against his shaft, brought him to a painfully full erection. He felt her left leg slip up between his. Her breath was quick and rapid against his neck.

"My God, Slocum," she muttered, "I don't understand this—my heart's pounding like crazy." Her fingers were urgently fumbling at the buttons of his shirt.

"I—feel like—a schoolgirl," she muttered breathlessly. She undid the last of his shirt buttons, his belt, and the top few buttons of his Levi's. She kissed him again, deep, wet, and urgent, her tongue probing, as she stroked his swollen shaft. Finally, trembling, she stepped back. "Get out of those boots and clothes, Slocum. Now," she said.

She unbuttoned her dress, stripped it away, and stretched out naked on the bed, propped on one elbow, as Slocum finished undressing. He stood for a moment staring at her, the large, perfectly shaped breasts uncovered, aureoles and erect nipples dark brown against her skin. A dense thatch of black hair covered her crotch for a handspan up toward her belly button.

"Come here, Slocum." Her whisper was deep, throaty.

He eased himself onto the bed, lying on his side, facing her, his heart pounding and chest heaving. He kissed her, long and deep, letting his hand drift over the fullness of her breast, linger at the nipple, then ease down her hip and upper leg. As his hand moved back up the inside of her thigh, she spread her legs, moaned softly, and pressed her pelvis against her hand.

Slocum's hand lingered at the lips of her damp, hot crotch, barely moving for a moment. She moaned softly. He parted the lips, found the swollen nub of flesh, and massaged it lightly. Lisa whimpered aloud. Her hand slid down to stroke his shaft. Slocum's scrotum tightened. He lowered his lips to the swollen nipple of her left breast and tongued the firm, erect flesh, while his finger worked gently and slowly around and over her clitoris.

She arched her back, gasped, cried out softly; her whole body tensed, then shuddered against him, her pelvis thrusting in spasms against his hand. Sweat slicked their bodies where the skin touched.

"Oh—oh, Christ," she finally muttered, breathless, as her spasms wound down. "I didn't—how did—" She gasped as his finger teased her clitoris again.

"Wait," she said. "Just a—moment."

Slocum reluctantly moved his hand from her crotch. She kissed the side of his neck, then his chest, her fingers still gripping his shaft. Slocum's heart pounded harder as her cheek slid down his belly; her thumb slid gently across the slit in the head of his engorged penis.

Seconds later, her lips slid over the head and partway down his shaft. Slocum moaned as her tongue slid over and around him, her head moving slightly as she took him into her mouth, then backed off to lick at the head. Slocum was about to lose it; he could feel the almost painful swelling of his shaft as the tension built in his testicles.

Lisa lifted her head. Tears welled in her lids. "Not yet, Slocum, not yet. This time, I want you inside me. And Christ, I never thought I'd say it, but I want—truly *want* to feel you in me." She rolled onto her back, all but dragging him with her. She spread her legs wider. Slocum lowered his head to again tongue her nipple. She moaned again, louder and more urgently. Her fingers slid to her crotch and guided him into her.

Slocum lay for a moment without moving, afraid her hot, wet tightness would push him over the edge too soon. He felt the muscles deep inside her tighten, then loosen, tighten again. She cupped his testicles in her palm ever so gently, then slid both her hands onto his buttocks and pulled him as deeply into her as she could.

After a long, luxurious moment, Slocum moved his hips, easing his swollen shaft almost out of her, then back in, slowly and deeply; he eased his hand between their pelvises, his index finger again toying with her clitoris. Lisa's breathing came in short, quick bursts as her hips moved, meeting his thrusts. She leaned her head back, mouth open, her lips making small mewing sounds as the tempo increased. Her mewing sounds grew louder, turned into deeper gasps. The explosions of her breath against his neck added to Slocum's growing sense of urgency. He knew he couldn't hold back much longer.

Lisa cried out aloud, short, guttural bursts, then a long, deep moan. Her pelvis arched hard against him; her thighs wrapped around the backs of his legs. The muscles deep inside her pulsed involuntarily as her entire body convulsed in spasms. Slocum gasped aloud, his free hand clutching the sheets, as he exploded in her. It seemed to Slocum that the deep, jarring throbs would never stop; just as the release began to ease, it returned with a renewed urgency. Slocum's heart hammered against his ribs.

After what seemed an eternity, Slocum felt himself wilting in her. He lingered for a moment, then, jaded and spent, rolled off her, not wanting his weight to cause her discomfort. She snuggled, sweat-drenched, against his side.

"My God, Slocum," she said, her voice quavering, "I've never had—a man I didn't have to fake it with. Can you—believe that it's the first time—for a whore?"

Slocum knew she was telling the truth. He had been with enough women to know when they were faking orgasms. And when they weren't. He reached out and traced a shaky finger along her cheek and jawline. "I believe you, Lisa," he said tenderly.

Lisa's breathing gradually returned to normal; the rapid rise and fall of her impressive breasts slowed. She turned her face to him, put a hand behind his head, and kissed him, gently, tenderly, without the urgent earlier need. After a moment, she pulled away. Her cheeks were moist with her tears and their sweat.

"I know what you're thinking, Slocum. Here's a whore who wants you to think it's the first time she's ever—"

Slocum put a finger against her lips. "Lisa, the term 'whore' doesn't fit you. There's a lot more to you than that." He eased his finger from her mouth.

"Thank you for saying that. It means a great deal to me." She sighed in contentment, her eyes sparkling. "God, I need a drink. And a smoke."

Slocum chuckled softly. "I'm afraid you'll have to get your own, Lisa. I don't think my knees work at the moment."

"Jesus, Slocum," she teased petulantly. "All this time I thought you were a gentleman."

"You didn't hear that from me."

She lay by his side a bit longer, her hand on his chest, then sighed. "What the hell. I'm not sure I can walk either, but I'll give it a try. I'm dying for a drink and a cigarette." She swung her legs over the edge of the bed and stood, then glanced over her shoulder at Slocum in surprise. "Good Lord, Slocum, but you do pack a load."

She strode on unsteady legs to the table holding the bottle, glasses, and ashtray, studied the situation for a moment, then dragged the whole thing to the side of the bed. She poured two drinks, handed one to Slocum, then pulled a sack of Bull Durham from a bureau drawer.

"Didn't know you smoked," Slocum muttered. He hadn't felt so relaxed in weeks.

"Girl's got to have some bad habits." She winked at him. "Besides drifters with black hair and green eyes, I mean. Slocum, you may not know it, but you're one hell of a man."

Slocum sipped at his drink and studied her anew as she expertly rolled and lit a cigarette. "You're not exactly hard to look at yourself, Lisa."

She handed the quirly to Slocum, rolled another for herself, and lit both smokes with a sulphur match. She inhaled deeply, let the smoke trickle from her lips, and downed half her drink before she sat back on the bed, halfway turned to face him, a smile toying at the corners of her mouth.

"Are you a tit man, Slocum?"

Slocum lifted an eyebrow. "Not before today," he said.

"I've always had nice tits. Or so I've been told."

"You weren't lied to. They're beyond nice, Lisa. The word magnificent comes to mind." Slocum paused for a sip of his drink and a drag on the cigarette. "And I'd add that the rest of you is the same. In case you hadn't noticed or no one has told you, Lisa, you are a beautiful woman."

A wistful expression flickered in her eyes. "Thank you, Slocum. I do believe that compliment is genuine, not like the lewd remarks I usually hear in this business." She stubbed out her smoke, finished her drink, and stretched out on the bed beside him. "Did you get a room at the hotel?"

Slocum shook his head. "Knew I was forgetting something."

She reached for his cigarette and glass. "Good. Because you're not going anywhere tonight. I've got a slab of cold roast beef, a loaf of bread, and cheese for supper later on—and I'm not through with you yet, fellow. Do you think you can make me feel that—that sensation—again? God, it was wonderful. . . ."

Slocum winked at her. "I'll do my best, ma'am," he said.

• • •

Slocum came awake with a start, his hand slapping against the butt of the holstered Colt beside the bed. He had no idea what time it was; the room was pitch black.

Beside him, Lisa sat up abruptly. "What is it?"

Slocum cocked the Colt. "Heard something outside—"

A tap on the door cut off his whisper.

"Slocum?" The voice from behind the heavy door was unfamiliar, slightly muffled by the heavy wood. "I'm leaving a pot of coffee and two cups out here. Figured you might need them. June Deschamp will be here before noon."

"Where'd you get your information, stranger?" Slocum asked as he cautiously headed for the door.

"Just take my word for it. I've got as much interest in seeing Deschamp stopped as you do. . . ." The voice began to trail off toward the end of his reply.

Slocum swung open the door, pistol ready. But the stranger was gone without a trace, except for the pot of coffee left in the doorway. As Slocum brought the tray into the room, he wondered what to make of the mysterious man's warning. Something in the voice, maybe the determination or maybe just the sheer hatred when he spoke Deschamp's name, made Slocum think it was on the up and up.

Slocum stowed the Peacemaker and reached for his pants. An image flashed through his mind as he dressed. The image of a small, bloody form lying naked and spread-eagled on the bearskin robe of a distant lodge. He glanced at the woman in the bed. The same thing could easily happen to her.

"Lisa," he said as he buckled on his pistol belt, "is there some place you can go for a few days? A friend's house, maybe?"

"Why?"

"If Deschamp gets past me, which is a distinct possibility, I'd like to go down knowing that you'll be safe. I've seen what Deschamp's gang can—will—do to a beautiful woman. It isn't pretty."

Lisa glanced at the Schofield lying on the table. "I can handle myself, Slocum. And that gun."

"I don't doubt that. You might kill Deschamp, Lisa, but there's too many of them for you to tackle alone."

"You're going to."

"Yes. But on my terms, on my field of battle. With all due

respect, Lisa, I think I may be better at that sort of thing than you. Think it over while I pour the coffee.''

Lisa nodded, reached for her housedress and slipped into it. ''I could go to the Montoya place, about a dozen miles out of town,'' she said. ''If you think it's necessary. And if you promise to come get me when it's over.''

''It's necessary. For my peace of mind, if no other reason.'' Slocum sipped at his coffee. ''And I'll come for you. If I'm able. If I don't show, beg, borrow, or steal a horse. And get the hell out of Chama.''

# 3

Slocum crouched behind the boulder fall in the faint gray light of false dawn and studied his chosen battlefield.

It would do. Even considering the odds of facing a dozen or so men who carried guns and could use them, he had a chance of getting out alive. Maybe not without taking a chunk or two of lead with him, but alive. He would be satisfied with that exchange. All he wanted was to get June Deschamp in his gunsights one time.

He saw no movement up the narrow valley. It was early yet; he had time for a smoke before Deschamp and his bunch rode in. He fished a cigarillo from his pocket and fired it with a lucifer held in cupped hands. The slight breeze was in his face, blowing from north to south, carrying the scent of Mexican tobacco back toward Chama. Unless Deschamp had slipped an advance scout behind him in the darkness, no one would smell the cigarillo.

The valley floor in front of him, where the Rio Chamita canyon pass, known as Cumbres pass, narrowed and made an abrupt bend to the west two miles out of Chama, was almost free of usable cover. Since few knew of the shortcut through the San Juan Mountains, and those that did rarely favored its rugged, painstaking trail, Slocum was reasonably sure that Deschamp's gang would pass this way.

There were a few boulders, a couple of narrow washes, and a fallen pine-tree trunk rotting at the edge of the stream. But for the most part, Slocum would have a clear field of fire. If Deschamp's gang came soon after sunrise, the sun would be in their eyes and at Slocum's back. It wasn't much of an edge, but it was better than no edge at all.

Slocum waited patiently, enjoying the rich, heavy flavor of the Mexican cheroot. His sorrel palouse was tied thirty yards away, deep in a pinyon grove up a brush-choked arroyo that branched off the main canyon. The horse would be in little danger of catching a stray slug. He didn't worry about Chief nickering a greeting to the horse scent that might drift in ahead of Deschamp's gang. The sorrel was well trained; Quill had seen to that. She could work wonders in training a war pony, though she had never fired a weapon or wielded a knife in battle.

The thought of Quill lying dead, raped and mutilated, of Joe Summerhawk scalped and gutted, in the smoldering remains of the Nez Percé village, fueled Slocum's carefully controlled rage. Blind fury had gotten many a man killed. But Slocum had learned on the bloody killing grounds of the Civil War that a man could turn anger and hate to his advantage. The familiar, relaxed calm that preceded battle settled comfortably around his shoulders.

The memory of Quill was not dimmed in his mind despite the night spent with Lisolette Barnes. They were different memories, different women. Quill; young, slight, gentle, slender, and supple, outwardly delicate. Lisa; older, taller, full-figured, and as lusty as Quill had been but in an earthier, sweatier way.

Slocum knew the difference. He had spent months with Quill. He knew almost nothing about Lisa, beyond the one night—and the hate she shared with him toward June Deschamp.

Lisa had hinted that Deschamp had ruined her life. Beyond that, Slocum knew nothing of why she despised the outlaw with such a passion. He hadn't pried, and she hadn't volunteered much information. She had said one thing that stuck in Slocum's mind this morning.

She had changed into men's clothing, tucked the remaining quarter of the Tennessee sour mash into her Gladstone bag, and turned to Slocum. "I'll save the rest of this, Slocum. If you're still alive when June Deschamp is dead, we'll share what's left."

"And if I don't, you'll drink a toast to my memory?"

"If you don't, I'll drink to your memory—somewhere well

away from Chama. I've been planning to leave this godforsaken place anyway.'' She tucked the big, ugly Schofield in her waistband and said, ''That miserable bastard is not going to get his hands on me again. If he does—if he gets past you and finds me—I'll put four bullets in his gut.''

''Why not five?''

''I'll save one for myself. Just in case his men get too close to me.'' Then she threw her arms around Slocum's neck and kissed him. Tears welled in her gold-flecked brown eyes as she stepped back. ''Damn you, Slocum, don't get yourself killed or I'll never forgive you!''

With that, she saddled up and rode away toward the southeast, astride the big chestnut Slocum had noticed in the livery corral, a handful of personal belongings tied in canvas sacks behind the cantle of her single-rig saddle.

Slocum was still a bit surprised at the burning intensity of the brief, parting kiss. The warm softness of her lips seemed to linger. Lisolette Barnes was a very complicated woman.

As he waited, Slocum wondered again who had come to Lisa's door in the night to warn him that Deschamp was on the way. Slocum hadn't recognized the voice. He hadn't heard footsteps as the man strode away on the creaky plank flooring. Whoever he was, he'd moved like a cat.

Slocum realized the false dawn had stepped aside for the new day, leaving the valley below in a growing wash of light. The first rays of the rising sun touched the tips of the tall pines on the west ridge of the valley.

He forced thoughts of Lisa and the unknown night visitor from his mind. There was more serious business waiting.

And the approaching horsemen who had just rounded the bend into the valley told him it wouldn't be a long wait.

Slocum surveyed his position one last time and nodded to himself. He slipped his Colt from its holster and spun the cylinder. Satisfied that the weapon was fully loaded, he checked the spare handgun and tucked it back into his waistband. His rifle lay beside him in the rockfall. Slocum decided to leave the long gun where it lay, at least for now. Handguns were easier to handle in a close-range shootout.

June Deschamp yanked his dappled gray to an abrupt stop and stared down the Rio Chamita valley, his right hand on the scarred stock of the .45-60 Kennedy lever-action rifle sheathed beneath his leg.

The lean young man on the sweat-streaked bay gelding reined in alongside Deschamp. "What's the matter, June?"

Deschamp didn't reply for a moment. His gaze swept the canyon floor, his left eye pulled narrower than the right by the heavy ridge of scar tissue that ran from hairline to jawbone. He saw nothing out of the ordinary. But he couldn't shake the crawly feeling in his gut.

"I don't like the looks of this, Bud," Deschamp finally said. "That jasper you heard runnin' his mouth in the saloon could be anywhere down there."

The rider cast a sharp glance at Deschamp, his lips drawn into a line, then sniffed in disgust. "Slocum? Hell, I wouldn't worry about him."

"Dammit, Bud, you ought to," Deschamp snapped. "When a man says he's gunnin' for you, you better worry. I've heard about this Slocum. And if half what I hear is true, he's a pure scorpion with a handgun or rifle."

The lean man shrugged. "He didn't look so waspy to me. Besides, there's just one of him. There's a dozen of us." The lean young rider palmed his Colt, spun the cylinder, drew an imaginary bead on an unseen enemy, said, "Pow! Just like that," and holstered the handgun.

Deschamp glared at the young man in open disgust. "Jesus Christ, Bud, quit playin' with that damn pistol. This ain't no boy's game, and you ain't no gunhawk."

Bud's lower lip swelled in a sullen pout at the scolding. "I did all right on that Indian, didn't I? Four shots you could have covered with a dollar."

"And the Injun didn't have a gun, was a hundred years old, and had his back turned." Deschamp shifted the chew in his right cheek and spat. He twisted in the saddle. The first of the stolen horses came into view around the sharp bend of the river. "Go tell the boys to hold them horses a spell, and you stay with 'em. Send Grant, Turk, Bones, Orv, and Tully up here. We're gonna scout out this canyon."

"Aw, June," Bud said in a near-whine, "you gotta let me go with you. You need the best guns you got."

"Which is why I'm sendin' you back to herd ponies, Bud."

"June, I rode half the night to tell you about this Slocum."

Bud's eyes glittered. "The man who takes Slocum earns a big reputation. I got a right—"

"Bud, I ain't tellin' you again," Deschamp snapped. "Now, git! Do what I say or I'll send you back to your ma in New Orleans before you can scat a cat."

The young gunman glared into Deschamp's uneven eyes. "Dammit, June, if I'd known you were going to do this to me, I'd have thrown down on Slocum in the cantina."

"And got yourself killed," Deschamp snapped. "Now get your butt back there with the horses and stay out of the way."

Bud's cheeks darkened in anger. "One of these days, June, I'm going to do things *my* way." He reined his horse back toward the upper end of the valley.

Deschamp waited and fretted, yanking at the reins when the gaunt-flanked gray gelding lowered its head to nuzzle the clear, cold water of the Rio Chamita, until the five men he'd sent for rode up.

"What is it, Boss?" the lead rider asked.

"Got a feelin', Grant. That there's somethin' up ahead." Deschamp pulled the Kennedy rifle and levered a round into the chamber.

The man called Grant shifted the stub of cigar to the corner of his mouth, nodded, and swung the long-barreled, 10-gauge shotgun from the sling over his back. "Let's go check it out."

Deschamp nodded toward a tall, consumptive-looking man whose eyes didn't match; one was blue, the other brown. "Tully, take the left flank." The thin man nodded and pulled his Winchester. Deschamp turned to a big rider who had no visible neck. "Turk, you got the right. Grant, you and that smoothbore cannon stick close to me. The rest of you fan out either side of Grant and me. Stay at least ten yards apart. You see one damn thing move out there, cut loose on it."

Saddle leather creaked and horses snorted as the men moved into position. Deschamp waited, the brass butt plate of the Kennedy resting on his right thigh, muzzle pointed skyward.

"All right, Slocum, or whoever you are—if you're out there, get ready to howdy all your buddies in Hell." The bluster didn't calm the yips in Deschamp's gut. He gouged spurs into the gray's ribs. The skirmish line moved forward at a slow trot.

Slocum muttered a soft curse as the line of horsemen neared the rockfall.

Deschamp might be a vicious bastard, Slocum thought, but he wasn't stupid. And he had the survival instincts of a coyote. Somehow, he had sensed the trap. The odds had shifted.

Slocum knew he could take two or three, possibly four, gun-hawks down—with a little luck. And if he didn't catch lead in the wrong place. But going up against six hard men fanned out in a skirmish line was bucking a stacked deck. A smart man would cut and run when he knew he was hopelessly outgunned. But the calm, black rage in his gut overpowered common sense.

At least, he thought as he thumbed back the hammer of the Peacemaker, no matter how this turned out, he had picked the right field of battle. Out here, far from Chama, no innocent bystander would be hit by a stray slug. It was Slocum's fight. He couldn't risk a woman or child being killed by accident.

The growing light washed away the last bit of Slocum's war-iness at facing six outlaws alone. Even at a hundred yards, he could make out the limp, dark objects hanging from the near side of Deschamp's saddle strings. Scalps. The realization that one of them could be Quill's fueled Slocum's hurt and fury.

The killers closed steadily, Deschamp in the middle, flanked by three men, one carrying a big shotgun across the crook of an elbow. A lean, hunched rider with rifle at the ready rode flank to Slocum's left on the far bank of the Chamita; a man whose sheer bulk made the tall sorrel he rode look like a starved mustang rode near the canyon wall to his right. The big man also carried a rifle, one with the distinct silhouette of a .45-70 Springfield. Of the two men who rode with Deschamp, one held a handgun, the other a rifle.

Deschamp had his troops deployed in a classic skirmish line, spaced apart so that no two riders could be hit by the same burst of gunfire.

Slocum picked his targets. Deschamp would be the first, the man holding the shotgun next; a scattergun was bad news in a close-quarter fight. Then the man at Deschamp's left who held the revolver. A man fighting from horseback with a handgun had the edge on a rifleman; it took two hands to handle a long gun with any accuracy.

Slocum didn't plan past those three. He would worry about the others as the fight unfolded.

Deschamp and the two men with him were at fifty yards now, just about Slocum's ideal handgun range and a bit beyond the abilities of most pistoleers—especially if they were having to control a spooked horse and aim at the same time.

Slocum drew a slow, deep breath, and stood. "Deschamp!"

The stocky outlaw visibly started at the call, then yanked hard on the reins. He stared for a heartbeat at Slocum.

"Who the hell are you?" Deschamp called.

"Name's Slocum. I'm here to collect a pair of Indian scalps from you! And add yours to them! You've butchered your last Nez Percé girl, you bastard!"

Deschamp barked a curse and tried to level the Kennedy. The rifle barrel barely moved before Slocum's slug hammered into Deschamp's upper chest. The scarred man yelped, twisted, almost dropped the Kennedy, then sagged forward over his saddlehorn.

Slocum cocked the Peacemaker at the height of the weapon's recoil and let it fall into line on the shotgunner. Slocum was looking into the twin black holes of the smoothbore when he let his thumb slip from the Peacemaker's hammer. An instant after the weapon bucked against his palm, he heard the satisfying whack of lead against flesh. The soft-lead slug caught the shotgunner in the bridge of the nose; the man's head snapped back and he tumbled over the rump of his horse, the shotgun blasting a double load of buck toward the sky.

Slocum felt a tug at his sleeve, then heard the report of a handgun. He swung his Colt toward the other man at Deschamp's side, waited half a heartbeat to line the sights, and stroked the trigger.

The rider's breath left him in a burst as Slocum's slug took him just above the belt buckle. The horseman dropped his pistol, then reined his spooked, wild-eyed horse around and spurred back the way he had come. Slocum barked a curse; through the dust of haze and powder smoke, he saw Deschamp hunched over, riding hard, driving steel to the gray, more than a hundred yards north up the canyon.

Slocum thumbed the Colt, aimed at Deschamp's back, fired, grimaced in disgust. A clean miss—

Lead screamed past Slocum's left ear and spanged from a rock on the canyon wall behind him. Slocum twisted toward the west canyon wall from where the shot had come, but saw only the gunsmoke drifting from a juniper clump. He slapped a hurried shot toward the smoke, dropped back behind the cover of the rockfall, holstered the empty Colt, and picked up his rifle.

Stone chips showered down on Slocum as the rifleman's slug nicked the top of the rock above his head. Slocum glanced to his right, and caught a quick glimpse as the big man with the Springfield darted into a tangle of pines and rocks on the west canyon wall.

Slocum's heart sank. He knew his luck had run out. Two riflemen would have him flanked, caught in a cross fire, within minutes. At least, he promised himself, those two would know they had been in a scrap before they took him down—he flinched as a heavy rifle slug screamed past his right shoulder and hammered into the boulder. The muzzle blast of the Springfield echoed down the valley.

Another slug kicked sand near his left boot heel. Slocum slapped two quick rifle shots toward the west canyon wall, knowing he wouldn't hit anything with unaimed fire but hoping to give the man something to think about. The gunman didn't think about it long; two, then three, slugs spanged from the rockfall.

Slocum ducked low behind the boulders and thumbed cartridges into the loading port of his Winchester. He had one chance. That was to take out the sharpshooter on the west canyon wall, then break for cover while the big man with the Springfield was reloading on the bluff above to his right. With luck and one clear shot, he might make it—

A heavy slug hammered into the receiver of Slocum's rifle and ripped the weapon from his grasp, the shock numbing Slocum's hands. He tried to pull the spare Colt from beneath his belt; the fingers of his stiff hands refused to close on the revolver grips. A shadow fell on the rocks above him.

Slocum twisted around, trying to will his hands to close on the Colt—and found himself staring at certain death.

The big man with the Springfield stood atop the canyon wall, casually thumbing a cartridge into the chamber of the trapdoor single-shot. Slocum's palm was on the grips of his spare Colt, but his fingers wouldn't close. He braced himself for the impact of lead as the Springfield's muzzle swung toward him.

The big man suddenly lurched to the side. The Springfield spun from his grasp. An instant later Slocum heard the distinct, meaty whack of lead against flesh; a heartbeat later, the sharp, heavy blast of distant big-bore rifle slammed against his ears. He became aware that the gunner on the west side had stopped firing. He shook his numbed hands, trying to get some feeling back in the fingers, squirmed back behind the rocks, and chanced a glance at the west canyon wall.

The lean man who had thrown lead at Slocum unexpectedly broke from cover and ran. He made half-a-dozen steps before something picked him bodily from his feet, sent him sprawling face-first down the rocky slope of the canyon wall, and the thunderous blast of the unseen rifle seemed to shake the ground beneath Slocum.

The firing stopped. Slocum lay confused for a moment, unsure what had happened. He glanced at his fallen rifle. The Winchester's action was twisted and bent. A bright smear marked the spot on the receiver where the heavy bullet from above had slammed into the rifle. Slocum's fingers began to tingle, then ache. After a time, he recovered enough feeling to pull the Colt and cock the heavy hammer. The muzzle wavered as Slocum crouched.

"Slocum!" The call was distant, barely discernible over the ringing in Slocum's ears, the voice familiar—the voice that had been outside Lisa's door this morning. "Hold your fire! I'm coming in!"

Time seemed to drag as Slocum waited. Strength flowed back into his fingers until he was able to hold the Colt steady in one hand. Finally, a horseman came into view from the shadows at the base of the canyon bend to the south.

The man looked familiar, but somehow strange; Slocum finally realized that the rider's shape was somewhat distorted by the long double shape that rested against his shoulder.

"Put the handgun away, Slocum," the man called as he neared. "It's over."

Slocum lowered the weapon, but made no move to ease the hammer. Not until he knew for sure who was riding toward him. The horseman rode easily, his back straight and erect in the old McClellan saddle. He reined in a few feet from Slocum, still mounted, and nodded. Slocum recognized the man now, the shadowy figure from the back table in the cantina.

"You all right, Slocum? Were you hit?"

Slocum stood stiffly, lowered the hammer of the Peacemaker, tucked it back into his waistband, and shook his head.

"No," he said. "Slug wrecked my Winchester. I thought for sure I was a dead man. Were you the one who laid out those two outlaws?" At the man's nod, Slocum touched bruised fingers to his hat brim. "Then I'm in your debt, mister."

The man in the McClellan shrugged. "My pleasure. I wish I had gotten into position earlier, though. You had a close call here, Captain."

"Cap—" Slocum's voice caught in his throat. He studied the horseman, final recognition just out of his reach. But he knew he had seen the man somewhere, before the cantina.

The horseman was clean shaven, of medium height, with a lean build, his face framed by a shock of brown hair that fell in waves from beneath his narrow-brimmed hat to below the collar of his dark blue shirt. A streak of white hair marked what could have been a scar above his left ear. The little finger of his right hand was missing. The deformed hand rested on the receiver of a rifle the likes of which Slocum had seen only once. The heavy octagon barrel had a bore that looked to be a half-inch wide, and running almost the length of the barrel was a brass telescopic sight.

"You have me at a disadvantage, mister," Slocum said. "You seem familiar, but I don't believe we've met."

"We've met, Captain. At Little Round Top, then at the hill's big brother." The horseman smiled, displaying a full set of white teeth. "We spent most of two days taking potshots at each other. I think you came out in better shape than I did. Mind if I step down?"

Slocum shook his head. The rider slipped the long, scoped rifle into its saddle boot and dismounted, light on his feet. He strode to Slocum and extended the damaged right hand.

"Lieutenant Dan Waggoner, Captain. Originally First Maine Volunteers, later assigned to Berdan's Sharpshooters. It's a pleasure to finally meet you at less than extended rifle range."

Final recognition dawned on Slocum as he took the man's hand. "You were the sniper I played tag with on the Round Tops at Gettysburg?"

"One and the same, sir." Waggoner lifted a brow. "My compliments. You're one hell of a rifle shot, Captain. I thought I was superior to Rebel sharpshooters until those couple of days. Are you sure you're all right?"

"A little bruised is all—hands and ribs, where the rifle hit me." Slocum picked up the wrecked Winchester. "Shame. I was fond of that weapon. But it saved my life again, catching a slug that would have been in my ribs otherwise. I can always replace a rifle. Might be harder to get new lungs."

"Forty-five-seventy slug does pack a wallop at that." Waggoner patted the stock of the long rifle beside his knee. "Not as much as this one, but enough. Well, Captain, let's see what we've got here."

Waggoner scrambled up the slope, Slocum a step behind, and stared down at the body of the big man with no neck. Beneath the dead man's right armpit was a bloody hole almost the size of Slocum's fist.

"This one's Turk Devaney," Waggoner said calmly. "There's a hundred-dollar reward on him. The thin one across the river goes by the name of Bones Turlock. That's another fifty dollars." He nodded toward the bodies in the valley below. "The fellow with the shotgun and your bullet hole between his eyes was Grant. He's worth an even one hundred dollars. The one with your slug in his gut who took off after Deschamp is called Orv Hollowell."

Slocum lifted an eyebrow. "You know these men rather well, Lieutenant Waggoner."

"I should." Waggoner's eyes narrowed. "I've been hunting them off and on since two years after Appomattox." He didn't elaborate. Slocum didn't push. If Dan Waggoner wanted him to know the details, he'd tell him.

"We've accounted for four. Six of them rode in, including Deschamps."

"The one called Tully—tall, consumptive fellow, one blue eye and one brown—escaped along with Deschamp and Orv. I don't think Tully was hit, but I can't say for sure."

Slocum took a deep breath; the mountain air seemed to cut some of the smell of burned powder, blood, and dust from his nostrils. One thing about damn near getting killed, Slocum thought; it made the air smell a lot sweeter and feel a lot cleaner. Slocum didn't know what it was like to be dead. He hoped it would be a long time before he would find out.

"After all this, Deschamp still got away," Slocum said in disgust. "And he was the one man I really wanted." Slocum picked up the .45-70 from beside the dead man. The weapon was old, the stock scarred, but it appeared to be in good shape. It was worth keeping until he could replace his .44-40 Winchester.

Waggoner pulled a sack of Bull Durham from his shirt pocket, rolled a smoke, and held out the tobacco. Slocum took it with a nod of thanks and rolled his own quirly.

Waggoner said after a moment, "You got a slug into Deschamp. If he dies, it will be a long and painful death. That might not be so bad. But I have to be honest with you, Captain. I'm somewhat relieved you didn't kill him outright. There's still a chance to take him alive."

"Alive?"

"I'd like to ask him a few questions before I kill him. Or in this case, we could flip a coin to see which of us gets to put a slug between his eyes." Waggoner's tone was soft, matter-of-fact. "We can discuss that later. We'll pick up the bounty outlaws here on the way back. For now, let's fetch your horse and see how far we can track what's left of this bunch."

"Suits me," Slocum said. "They must have left the remuda somewhere. Some of those stolen horses belong to me. I'd like to get them back."

Waggoner nodded. "They left the horses with a rear guard a mile or so north up the valley. We won't have any trouble finding their tracks, Captain." He cut a quick glance at Slocum. "Sure you're up to riding?"

Slocum took a deep drag of the rich tobacco and managed a half smile. "I never felt more like riding in my life, Lieutenant. Let's go."

The sun had past its midway point and started down the western sky when Slocum reined his spotted sorrel to a stop at the edge of the mountain range and studied the dry, broken landscape below.

At his side, Waggoner rolled a cigarette, his gaze also sweeping the barrancas and hardpan swatches of the badlands to the east.

"Tough country out there," Waggoner said after a moment. "Badlands, rock beds, shale slides, lava flows. Thirty, forty miles to the nearest decent water. It would be all but impossible to track them through that, with no supplies or water to see us through."

Slocum glanced over his shoulder. Thunderclouds piled high above the western mountains. Dark, heavy cloud banks boiled and flickered, shot through by lightning bolts. The breeze had shifted. It carried the faint, fresh scent of rain.

"Waste of time to even try," Slocum said. "Those storms are headed this way. If it rains the way I suspect it's going to, the trail be washed out by sundown."

Waggoner nodded. "That's how I see it, Captain. We might

as well turn back. By the time we pick up the trash along the Rio Chamita and make it back to Chama, we're likely to get wet.''

Slocum sighed, reluctant to give up the chase, but knowing it would be futile without grub and fresh water. What was left of Deschamp's gang had too big a lead on them. The outlaws had driven the stolen horses fast and hard for miles after the shootout at the river.

"Besides," Waggoner said as he stubbed the butt of his smoke on the McClellan saddle, "I know where they're headed. It won't be hard to cut their tracks later.''

Slocum cut a quick glance at the former officer. Waggoner's expression hadn't changed throughout the long ride—calm, cool, and collected, a man who knew what he was doing. Slocum didn't ask how Waggoner knew where Deschamp's gang was bound. The man would talk when he was ready. If he wanted to.

Slocum reined Chief around. Waggoner kneed the sleek black Tennessee racer into position at Slocum's left stirrup. Slocum noted that Waggoner didn't wear a gunbelt like most Westerners. Instead, a pommel holster, with a flap to keep dust and rain out military-style, rode on the left side of his McClellan saddle. The size and bulk of the holster told Slocum it held a large handgun. It was a true left-hand holster, not a right-hand cross-draw, which most ex-cavalrymen wore.

The two rode in silence for a mile before Slocum spoke.

"Lieutenant, you pulled my bacon out of the fire a couple of times in less than a day. How did you know Deschamp was coming?''

Waggoner shrugged. "I followed the young man from the cantina—the one with all the silver conchas. He took me straight to Deschamp's camp. I slipped in close enough to listen to their plans. Despite the pounding my ears took in the war, Captain, I still have superb hearing." He sighed. "Sometimes acute hearing can be a curse. And I owe you an apology for that. I wasn't deliberately eavesdropping on you and Miss Barnes, but I overheard most of the conversation. That's how I knew where to find you after I got back from Deschamp's camp.''

Slocum twisted in the saddle to study the darkening clouds. The flicker of lightning was almost constant now, quick flashes of eerie light illuminating the turbulence within the ever-changing cloud mountains.

"I hope Lisa doesn't get caught out in this storm," Slocum said worriedly. "It's going to be a bad one."

Waggoner said, "I followed her after she left Chama early this morning. That's why I was a bit late getting into position to lend a hand, for which I apologize. But I was concerned that she might accidentally ride into some of Deschamp's men. She turned south a mile out of town, heading toward the Montoya ranch. She should have reached there long ago."

Slocum sighed in relief. "That's good to know, Lieutenant."

A slight smile tugged at Waggoner's lips. "I'm afraid you may have lost a friend, though, Captain."

"A friend?"

"Your dog went with her."

Slocum grinned. "Loyalty doesn't count for anything among males when it comes to women, I suppose." He didn't admit that he was pleased to hear the news. The dog would be some protection for Lisa if anything happened.

The best news of all, Slocum thought, was that Lisa hadn't gone far from Chama.

# 4

Slocum pushed back his plate, reached for a cigarillo, and smiled as Lisolette Barnes attacked the last two bites of apple pie, the specialty of the house in the small but clean Chama Cafe.

He hadn't minded in the least riding through the last gasps of the overnight thunderstorm to fetch her and the brown cur dog back from the Montoya ranch yesterday. She had been somewhat relieved and glad to see him. So glad, in fact, that Slocum hadn't slept much in the last few hours. He didn't mind that either.

Lisa leaned back, sighed, patted her belly, and said, "God. I feel like I'm pregnant."

Slocum lifted an eyebrow. "Hazard of the profession?"

"Hazard of eating too damn much supper," she said. She reached into the handbag beside her chair, pulled out a sack of Bull Durham, and rolled a quirly. Slocum lit it for her and ignored the frown of disapproval the middle-aged blond waitress cast at Lisa as she refilled their coffee mugs.

Lisa waited until the woman went back behind the counter, then said, "Tish disapproves of women smoking. Says it isn't ladylike. Does it bother you that I enjoy a smoke?"

"Not in the least," Slocum said honestly.

"Good. A girl's got to have *some* bad habits." Lisa dragged at the hand-roll and let the smoke trickle from her nostrils. "Strange thing about Tish. She doesn't seem the least bit bothered by the fact that I am—or was—the town whore, but she gets upset when I light a cigarette."

Slocum half smiled. "I gave up trying to follow female logic years ago—wait a minute. Did you say 'was'?"

"I did. I told you I was planning to leave Chama. The other half of the story is that I've decided to quit the business. I have a little money saved. Not much, but enough to get a fresh start somewhere. Maybe find a job. I'm told I'm a fair cook. And regardless of what you may think about the way my room looks, I *can* clean houses." She leveled a lewd wink at him. "When I don't have anything better to do, that is."

"You should be able to do better than cook or maid work, Lisa. Both are honorable and necessary professions," Slocum said, "but I can picture you doing something with better pay and working conditions. Bank clerk, maybe. An office job with a railroad or shipping company. Or a schoolteacher."

A hint of sadness came to Lisa's eyes. "Not likely, Slocum. I can't work in those professions." She dropped her gaze. "I never learned to read and write."

Slocum sat in surprised silence for a moment; come to think of it, he hadn't seen a book or newspaper in Lisa's room. "I'm sorry. It never even dawned on me that would be a problem."

She sighed wistfully. "It's a hard world for an illiterate person, Slocum. Especially a woman."

He lifted an eyebrow. "It's never too late to learn."

Hope flickered faintly in her gold-flecked brown eyes. "You think so, Slocum? That I'm not too old and too dumb?"

"No. You're not too old, and you're certainly not dumb, Lisa. In fact, I would say you're one of the most intelligent women I've met." He paused to drag at his smoke. "You have a quick mind and a lot of common sense. A few weeks with a good teacher is all you need."

"Will you teach me?"

The unspoken implication of the question gave Slocum a turn. It implied a longer relationship than he was prepared to handle. He enjoyed Lisa's company, even out of bed. She was one of the few women he had ever really felt comfortable being around. The latest, before Lisa, had been Quill. And that was the problem. Unfinished business.

He stalled a moment by sipping at his coffee. "Lisa, I don't know how long I'll be around," he said.

"None of us know that. It was unfair of me to ask." For the first time since Slocum had met her, Lisa's voice seemed soft and frail, the expression in her eyes full of self-doubt. "It's just that—well, it's been a dream of mine for a long time. Learning to read and write, I mean. And getting a real job, where I didn't have to spread my legs to make money. I just never had the courage to mention it to anyone before." She sighed heavily. "I've been faking my way through life, Slocum, in bed and in reality. I'm tired of faking."

Slocum drew a deep breath. She had given him a way out. He needn't make any long-term promises. "I understand, Lisa. Maybe away from Chama, you can find a teacher, a tutor. I don't believe I'm capable of teaching anyone to read and write. It's a scary thought."

A wry smile lifted Lisa's lips, deepening the crow's-feet wrinkles at the corners of her eyes. "I didn't think you were scared of anything, Slocum."

"Then I had you fooled. Everyone's afraid of something. Anyone who says they aren't is, in your own words, faking it." He tapped the ash from his cigarillo into the glass tray between them. "We all have private demons, Lisa. It takes a strong person to face those demons and make them back down."

"And you, Slocum? May I ask what your private demons are?"

Slocum smiled. "You may ask. That doesn't mean I'm going to tell you. Then they wouldn't be private."

She chuckled and shook her head. "You are a puzzlement, Slocum. In many ways." Lisa took a final drag from her cigarette and puffed out a perfect smoke ring. It settled above the crown of Slocum's hat. "Like a halo," she said, pleased with her effort.

Slocum glanced at the smoke ring, which was already beginning to break apart. "That's the wrong place for any halo," he said. "Even a lopsided and tarnished one."

"Everybody's entitled to an opinion. You keep yours, I'll keep mine. Lord, I'm stuffed. I don't always eat like a field hand. I do have *some* feminine traits." She stubbed out her cigarette. "Let's get onto something less embarrassing than baring our souls and airing our shortcomings. Like for instance, we need to give that dog a name. 'Boy' just doesn't seem personal enough."

Slocum glanced toward the open door. The brown cur waited on the board walkway outside, gnawing on the remnants of yet another raw steak. Slocum had to admit he was relieved that

Lisa had turned the conversation to a more comfortable topic. "How about T-Bone? At the rate that dog puts them away, I'll be going broke keeping him fed."

Lisa grinned. "T-Bone it is, then. Wonder how long it'll take him to discover his name's not Boy anymore?"

"About one more steak's worth," Slocum said. He fished in his pocket and dropped a quarter on the table as a tip. He knew it was overly generous, but the meal and service had been more than adequate—and maybe it would help ease Tish's huffiness about women smoking in her place of business.

Strange thing about women, Slocum mused; Tish had no qualms about Lisa's being a prostitute, but disapproved of her smoking in public. He hadn't lied to Lisa. He had never been able to understand the workings of the female mind. Women were strange creatures. And she thought *he* was a puzzlement. It was one of those things that made the differences between men and women endlessly interesting. And, at times, confusing.

Lisa Barnes was one of the more interesting women.

The way she was dressed today, a stranger would take her for anything but an illiterate prostitute. She looked like a schoolteacher. A well-endowed one who smoked in public, maybe, but still a schoolmarm. Lisa wore a rather prim, high-necked brown dress, complete with petticoats and lace-up brown leather shoes. Even her handbag was somewhat staid, except for what it contained. An impressively big, ugly Schofield .45. He made a mental note to ask her why she carried such a hand cannon. And kept it within reach of her bed.

They finished their coffee in silence. Lisa brushed a wayward crumb from her lap and said, "Ready, Slocum?"

He was. He paid the check, glanced both ways up the street through the open door to make sure nobody was waiting with a drawn weapon, then stepped aside to let Lisa go out first. The brown cur yawned, stretched, and tagged along at Lisa's heels as they started across the street.

Less than twelve hours after the rain stopped, there were few remaining puddles and less mud on the street, Slocum noted. The soil in Chama soaked up rain like a drunk soaked up cheap whiskey.

"My place or yours?" Lisa asked, her hand tucked under Slocum's arm, fingers resting just below his elbow. Her hand was warm against his skin.

"How about . . ." Slocum stopped in mid-sentence, staring

up the street. A lean man riding a leggy black and leading two other mounts had rounded the corner from the Santa Fe Road.

"What is it?" Lisa asked.

Slocum nodded toward the horseman. "Dan Waggoner's back."

She turned to look, then nodded. "I should run out there and hug his neck. You might not be here if it weren't for him."

Waggoner reined in before Slocum. "Afternoon, Captain, Miss Barnes." He nodded to Lisa and lifted fingertips to his hat brim.

Slocum nodded. "Afternoon. Didn't expect you back so soon, Lieutenant."

"The business in Santa Fe was concluded by late yesterday. I decided to ride straight back the night through."

Waggoner looked like a man who had logged many an hour in the saddle without sleep, Slocum thought. His eyes were bloodshot, his shoulders sagged, and dark stubble shadowed the angular cheeks and jaws. Slocum figured Dan had earned the right to look a tad shopworn. If Waggoner had followed the saloon dandy to Deschamp's camp, then back to Chama, then to Santa Fe and again back to Chama, he had gone at least forty-eight hours without sleep.

Waggoner glanced from Lisa to Slocum. "I wouldn't presume to interrupt any plans you two have, Captain, but there are some things I would like to discuss with you, if you don't mind. In private. It may take some time. Would that be a problem?"

Lisa smiled up at Slocum and squeezed his arm. "Go ahead, Slocum. You men get your talking done. You know where to find me when you're finished." She strode to the cantina door, then knelt to pat T-Bone and mutter something. The dog obediently plopped down beside the door as Lisa turned to wave. She went inside.

"Sorry to intrude, Captain."

"No problem, Lieutenant. I'll give you a hand with the horses."

Waggoner handed over the lead rope and swung from the saddle. "I would appreciate that. I'm ashamed to admit I may have abused my mount a bit more than I had intended in the last couple of days." He rubbed a hand along the black's neck. "Midnight's tough and well conditioned, but he was stumbling from time to time the last few miles." He started for the livery, the black walking alongside on loose rein, its head even with Waggoner's shoulder. Slocum had to give a slight tug on the lead rope to get the two extra horses moving.

"How did it go in Santa Fe?"

"Quite well. There was no trouble collecting the bounty. The Santa Fe marshal recognized the dead men immediately. A couple of hours later, the rewards were paid. I sold the dead men's surplus weapons, saddles, and all but two of the best horses. We might need them for pack animals or extra saddle mounts."

There he goes with the "we" business again, Slocum thought.

The white-haired Mexican hostler swung open the livery gate. Slocum led the extra mounts to the water trough and studied them with a practiced eye as they drank. One was a heavily muscled and short-coupled blue roan, a powerful animal built for quick bursts of speed. The other was a wiry line-backed dun with the bony, rawhide look of a mustang about him. Slocum figured the tough little gelding had a lot of bottom—the endurance to go a long way on short feed and scant water. It was obvious from the outlaw mounts he'd kept and the black Waggoner rode that the man knew horseflesh.

The hostler offered his help, which Waggoner dismissed with a wave of the hand. "I prefer to see after my own animals."

All the box stalls were full, so Slocum fed the roan and dun at a long trough beside the rail fence. A couple of other horses in the corral decided to horn in the grain, but abandoned the idea in a hurry after the little mustang dun peeled part of an intruder's shoulder hide with one quick slash of bared teeth. The pecking order was sorted out within seconds.

Slocum stopped at the open door of the box stall as Waggoner finished rubbing down the Tennessee black. Dan unstrapped the oversized pommel holster and the long doeskin rifle cover before stowing the scarred McClellan saddle in the tack room.

"Ready, Captain?" At Slocum's nod, Waggoner added, "I'd prefer we talk in my room, if that's satisfactory. I'm afraid I don't have any liquor to offer. I never was much of a drinker. We could stop and pick up a bottle, if you like."

"No need. I've got a quart of decent bourbon waiting for later." Chama was showing a bit more life, Slocum thought as the two men strode to the Murphy Hotel, where Waggoner rented a room. Several horses were now hitched before drinking establishments and restaurants, a buggy and a buckboard shared available space before the general store, and a heavy Studebaker freight wagon creaked past in a cloud of cusswords. The teamster did a passing fair job on the fine points of creative cursing, Slocum thought.

Inside Waggoner's small but functional room, Dan slipped a big First Model Colt Dragoon percussion revolver from the pommel holster and placed it on the table near the bed.

Waggoner's room was in semi-darkness, the curtains pulled over the single window. Waggoner scratched a match and lit a small oil lamp on the table.

"Have a seat, Captain," Waggoner said, gesturing toward one of two wooden chairs at the table. He pulled the Bull Durham sack from his shirt pocket, rolled a cigarette, handed the makings to Slocum, and sank wearily into the other chair.

"Okay with you if we drop the military titles?" Slocum asked. "I never was comfortable with them anyway."

"Fine with me. It's a bit of painful reminder of what might have been anyway. Call me Dan." He extended his right hand, the one with the missing finger. Slocum took it; Waggoner's grip was firm, with a hint of strength that belied his slender build.

Slocum studied Waggoner as he rolled himself a cigarette, then paused as he twisted the ends of the quirly. "You haven't changed all that much since Gettysburg, Dan. The first time I saw you was at Little Round Top."

Waggoner half smiled. "And then Big Round Top. We stalked each other for two days. It was one of the more interesting duels of the whole war." He held up his damaged hand. "You nailed me twice, Slocum. Once in the hand, the other a crease alongside the head."

Slocum nodded. "It was interesting at that. Almost too interesting. I have to say I've never gone up against a tougher man or a better shot."

"Two sharpshooters, one in blue, the other in gray. That hunt turned into a legend of sorts in Union camps." Waggoner sighed. "But that was a long time ago. No lingering hard feelings?"

"None on my part. We were just two men doing a job." Slocum paused to light his cigarette. "It was one I didn't particularly like."

"Nor I," Waggoner said, "except for the challenge involved. Long-range shooting at total strangers just because someone higher up wanted them killed was a messy part of the war.''

"The whole damn war was messy, Dan."

Waggoner sighed again. "It was. But enough of that for now. Leave it to the history books." He drained his whiskey, reached into his back pocket, and brought out a thick leather wallet. He thumbed it open, produced a sheath of bills, and separated them into two piles. He placed one of the stacks before Slocum.

"What's this?"

"Your share of the reward money on Deschamp's men. Plus what their horses and equipment brought, and the cash they were carrying at the time."

"I didn't expect any money, Dan."

Waggoner smiled; the grin took ten years off his face. "Never turn down cash, Slocum. Dan Waggoner's Second Rule of Survival."

"What's the first rule?"

"Don't get killed." Waggoner refilled his glass. "You earned it, Slocum. In addition to the reward money, the dead men had another sixty between them. Their horses and equipment brought another hundred twenty. That makes five hundred thirty, your half of which is two-sixty-five."

Slocum stared at the stack for a moment. It was a lot of money. Especially since he was down to his last two double eagles. "I don't know, Dan. I like money as well as the next man, but money wasn't what I was after."

"Nor I." Waggoner stubbed out his cigarette and rolled another. "Like you, I want Deschamp. But perhaps for a different reason." He lit the new quirly and let the smoke drift toward the ceiling. "I'm no bounty hunter, but I'm not above cashing in a wanted man to fund a worthwhile expedition. And Slocum, this is penny-ante stuff. Deschamp is the big money."

"Just out of curiosity, how much is the reward on him now?"

"I'm not talking about a pittance of a reward on a man's head, Slocum." Waggoner paused for emphasis. "I'm talking about nine thousand dollars. Shared equally."

Slocum's brows went up. "What?"

"It's a long story."

"That much money buys a lot of time. You have my undivided attention."

"Then I take it you would be amenable to working with me in tracking down Deschamp?"

For a moment, Slocum didn't reply. Then he sighed. "I'll lay it straight out for you, Dan. I prefer to work alone. The more cooks tending the skillet, the more often the bacon gets burned."

"I agree. Under normal circumstances, I wouldn't even have broached the subject. I like to stomp my own rattlers, as do you. But we both want Deschamp, for different reasons. The money is a secondary objective, but to me, the most important."

Slocum lifted an eyebrow.

Waggoner noted the unasked question in Slocum's eyes. "First things first. I know why you want Deschamp dead. I want him because he ruined my military career. A bit of background?"

"If you think it makes a difference," Slocum said.

"I'll try to keep it as brief as possible. Before the war ended, I had a battlefield promotion to brevet major." A muscle in Waggoner's temple twitched; the expression in his eyes was somehow wistful and angry at the same time. "I had a handful of citations, a couple of medals. Enthusiastic evaluations and commendations from my superior officers. I thought I was set for life in the army. I was an ambitious young man, Slocum. I could see no reason why a brigadier general's rank was beyond my reach." Waggoner snuffed out his half-smoked cigarette.

"And something happened?"

"June Deschamp happened. After the war ended and while I was recovering from wounds sustained at Five Forks, I was assigned to first one post and then another. Desk jobs. I wanted to be back in the field. Eventually, I wound up in Colonel Mackenzie's 4th Cavalry Regiment as an adjutant."

Waggoner leaned back in his chair, his shoulders slumped. "One of my duties was to oversee security escorts of monetary shipments that passed through Fort Richardson. Army payrolls, supply payments bound to the reservations in the Indian Nations, and the like." He sighed. "I'll get straight to the point here, Slocum, and skip some rather painful personal details. Just when it seemed I was on my way up the chain of command, with a promotion to lieutenant colonel within my grasp, a certain sergeant in the quartermaster corps engineered the ambush of a cavalry patrol escorting a paymaster."

"Deschamp?"

"Yes. He put together a band of deserters, renegades, and just plain outlaws. They killed the escort party to the last man and made off with ten thousand in army money."

"And you were blamed for it," Slocum said.

"Ranald S. Mackenzie was not a stable man, Slocum. He went berserk. The fact that I was confined to the post hospital at the time with dysentery—a somewhat more common but much less glamorous malady than a battle wound—meant nothing to him. He laid the fault at my feet. Shortly thereafter, I was summarily reduced in rank to lieutenant and 'encouraged' to resign my commission. I've been tracking Deschamp ever since."

Slocum leaned back in his chair. "So you're looking for the bastard who ruined your career. How does that tie into the money?"

"Deschamp didn't get to spend that much of it, Slocum. As best I can figure, he was able to keep perhaps a thousand. I got out of that hospital bed and led a patrol of our best men, including a fine Lipan tracker, on Deschamp's trail within hours of the time we found out about the massacre of the escort detail. We kept the pressure on them. Deschamp got away, but he buried the money along the way."

Slocum frowned. "And you don't know where?"

"Not precisely. We wounded and captured one of his men in a skirmish at Yellow House on the Staked Plains. The man was gutshot and delirious. He told us only that most of the money had been buried at a red bluff overlooking the Pease River. He couldn't remember the precise spot."

Waggoner paused for a moment, then sighed. "That money is still there, Slocum. Help me find it, and half is yours. But to find it, we have to take Deschamp alive. None of the men riding with him now know where it is. The others, the ones who actually participated in the ambush, are dead. I got three of them. None lived long enough to talk. Deschamp knew someone was on his tail. So he killed the others himself, to keep the location of the cache secret."

Slocum sat for a moment, thinking, then looked into Waggoner's bloodshot eyes. He saw no expression there, just the calm resignation of a man patiently waiting an answer.

Slocum finally said, "Before I say one way or another, I'd like to know a couple of things, Dan. First of all, why me?

Why not just keep on the trail yourself until you catch up with Deschamp?''

Waggoner leaned forward, his elbows on the table. ''Several reasons. We both want Deschamp. Working alone, either of us would be outgunned and outnumbered. True, we cut into Deschamp's forces in the canyon fight, but he still has half-a-dozen men at least. He believes in numbers; he will recruit more. Between us, we know the man's habits. What kind of whiskey he drinks, the kind of women he prefers.''

The comment about women sent a knife blade through Slocum's gut. The blade was what Deschamp and his gang had done to Quill. Slocum's jaw muscles clenched.

''I've seen you work a handgun and rifle, Slocum. Twice. I've never seen a man better at the trade. Each of us are fine riflemen. I can't match you in the side-arm department; I'm a long-gun man myself. I don't handle a revolver as well as a rifle. We're both first-rate trackers, or we wouldn't have been this long on Deschamp's trail separately. In short, the two of us working together would have a much improved chance of catching him—and living through it.''

Slocum's brow knit in thought. Waggoner had a point. Several of them. ''A two-horse hitch can pull a heavier wagon, true enough,'' he said. ''But I have a feeling there's another reason you want me along on the hunt.''

''There is,'' Waggoner said calmly. ''If we go our separate ways and you find him first, I strongly suspect you will kill Deschamp on sight. That would deprive me of my justice. And a substantial amount of money for us both. If you haven't already killed him, that is. You did get a slug into him.''

Slocum nodded in agreement. The memory of Joe Summerhawk and Quill was still too fresh in his mind. The intensity of his hate could override common sense once he set eyes and a gunsight on Deschamp again. With Waggoner to remind him, he would be less likely to make that choice.

''One more question, Dan. Can you work with a Rebel? A man who tried to kill you?''

''Can you work with a Yank who tried to kill you?''

Slocum sighed. ''Like you said, that was a long time ago. The war's over.'' He stood, leaned across the table, and offered a hand. ''When do we leave?''

Waggoner took his hand. ''Tomorrow's soon enough. I plan to turn in shortly and sleep until dawn. And you have a most attractive woman waiting for you, Slocum. I've kept you too long as it is."

"Tomorrow morning, then," Slocum said. He started for the door. He paused as Waggoner spoke.

"You forgot something."

Slocum turned. The cash Waggoner had counted out still lay on the table beside Slocum's glass. "Keep it for now, Dan. If we're going to be partners, take half the expense of supplies from my share. We'll settle up later."

"Fair enough." Waggoner was already reaching for the top button of his shirt. "Sleep well, Slocum."

Slocum glanced into the hallway, saw no threat, and closed the door behind him. As he strode toward the cantina where Lisa waited, Slocum realized with a bit of a start that for the first time in his life, he hoped a man he had shot in hate didn't die.

June Deschamp deserved a much slower death than that.

All they had to do was find him. In some of the wildest, most rugged country in the West. And live through the finding.

# 5

June Deschamp winced in pain as he lifted the crusted rag from his upper chest. The wound showed no sign of festering, but it still hurt like hell.

The wind whipping the camp on the east side of the badlands swirled campfire ash and dust over the man who lay moaning on the bedroll across from Deschamp. The constant groaning grated on Deschamp's nerves. He was surprised that Orv had lasted this long.

The thin man's guts had been torn to shreds by a slug from the gun of the man called Slocum. Deschamp hurt, but his pain was a bee sting compared to what Orv had gone through the last couple of days. Orv moaned again and lifted his ash-white face toward Deschamp. The whites of Orv's eyes showed the yellowish tinge June had seen in gutshot men's eyes a few hours before they died. It was a hell of a nasty way to go.

"June—for God's sake—get me—doctor." Orv's normally deep voice was thin and weak, the words forced through teeth clinched in agony.

Deschamp ignored the thin man's plea. The nearest doctor was half a hundred miles away, and the best surgeon in the world couldn't help Orv. Nobody could put that mess back together again. Deschamp glanced up at the crunch of footsteps on the grayish-black volcanic sand of the campsite.

Bud knelt beside Deschamp, his dapper black outfit stained by dust and sweat. The young dandy peered at June's shoulder wound. "Looks like it's coming along," Bud said. "You got mighty lucky, June," he said.

53

Deschamp couldn't argue that point. Slocum's slug would have drilled him through the heart if it hadn't hit the medicine bag in his shirt pocket. The damned old Indian up on the Lapwai, whose scalp hung from his saddlehorn now, had saved his life. The medicine bag held a collection of shiny stones, bone fragments, some feathers, and two silver dollars. Slocum's slug had hit one of the dollars; the coin had stopped the slug. Bent and twisted by the impact, the silver dollar had driven an inch into Deschamp's flesh. It hurt like the fires of hell, but he wouldn't die.

"Luckier than Orv," Deschamp said, not caring whether the thin man heard the conversation or not. "He ain't got a prayer."

"He's slowing us down, June. We can't waste water on a gutshot man. We're down to two canteens as it is."

"Don't matter. Orv'll die soon."

Bud stood, pulled his handgun, and shot Orv through the head. The young man grinned as he holstered the weapon. "Reckon you were right about that, June. He died quicker than anybody expected."

Deschamp snorted in disgust. "You are one hell of a gunhawk, Bud. When it comes to backshootin' old Injuns and killin' gutshot men, you're top-drawer bad. Reckon you're mighty pleased with yourself about now."

The young man bristled. "Dammit, June, if you'd let me go with you in the first place, I'd have nailed that Slocum dead center and wouldn't nobody else have got hurt. And everybody would know who I am."

"Bud," Deschamp snapped, "Slocum would have shot your balls off one at a time. Now, *that* sonofabitch is a gunhawk. Best I ever seen."

"Hell, I can take him easy. I'm faster than he is. Faster than anybody."

Deschamp lifted an eyebrow. "Fast don't make a shooter, Bud. If I were you, I wouldn't bet that fancy silver-studded saddle on it." He raised his right hand to cut off the young man's protest. "You'll get a chance to find out. That Slocum bastard shot me. He's gonna pay for that. You can have first crack at him if you're that determined to get yourself killed."

"I'll hold you to that, June," Bud said. "The man who brings down Slocum earns a reputation. That'll be me."

Deschamp ignored the comment. He glanced at a stocky man

mending a bridle at the edge of the camp. "Curly, saddle up and drag Orv off a ways. Don't like havin' dead men layin' around camp."

Curly nodded without speaking and went to fetch a horse.

Deschamp glowered at Bud. "Some shooter you're turnin' out to be. Pretty plain you don't know the first thing about gunfightin'."

Bud's face colored beneath the light stubble on his cheeks. "What are you talking about, June?"

"You didn't reload after you shot Orv." Deschamp snorted in disgust. "Get yourself in a bind, the hammer falls on a spent cartridge or you come up one round short, and you're a dead man for sure."

Bud sheepishly pulled the Colt, worked the ejector rod to kick out the spent cartridge, and thumbed in a fresh round. "Guess I wasn't thinking there for a minute, June."

"That's the problem with you, Bud. You don't think. It's gonna get you dead." Deschamp tossed aside the blood-soiled bandage. He fumbled in a saddlebag for a clean bandanna and pressed it against the jagged hole in his chest. "Go check on them ponies, Bud. Do somethin' useful for a change."

"I just did. They're sore-footed and gaunt in the flanks. Even those tough spotted-butt Indian horses are showing some rib. If we don't find grass and water soon, we'll lose most of them."

"Dammit, I know that," Deschamp barked. "Noon tomorrow, we'll be out of these gawdawful badlands and hit the Canadian River breaks. There'll be grass and water there. Take the first leg on nighthawkin' at sundown, Bud."

"Aw, June! I had that last night, and the night before! How come Curly or somebody else can't do it? I gotta get some rest."

Deschamp's neck reddened. "You'll do what I tell you. And for Christ's sake, stay awake. Them horses scatter lookin' for water, I'll have your balls for breakfast. Now, git!"

He watched the young man stride away. Nephew or not, Bud was going to push him too far one of these days. If Slocum didn't kill him first.

Deschamp winced at a fresh stab of pain, pulled a pint flask from his saddlebag, and downed two swallows of whiskey. The stuff scorched his throat, but it would ease the hurt. He gingerly leaned back against his bedroll and wondered about the man named Slocum.

Deschamp had no idea why the gunman was after him. Slocum rode a spotted-butt horse, Bud said, so maybe it had something to do with the Indians up on the Lapwai. Didn't make sense, though, a white man getting that mad over a few scruffy redskins. The girl hadn't been scruffy, though, he thought. She'd fought like a panther, but she'd been worth it.

The memory of those few minutes with the girl, before he'd turned her over to the boys, combined with the whiskey to warm Deschamp's gut and ease the pain. Fine looker for a squaw she had been. Until the boys got done with her and halfway skinned her out. Deschamp still found himself fingering the long, black scalplock from time to time. Just doing that still gave him a hard-on. Should have kept the squaw around a while, he thought. Would have been a good way to pass the nights. He forced the thoughts of the girl from his mind. He had other troubles to think on.

The first was the horses. Much as he hated to admit it, Bud was right. If they didn't find water and grass soon, they'd lose most of the remuda. And that meant they'd lose several hundred dollars. Money he needed to get back to the red bluff on the Pease. Once he had that army money back, it wouldn't cost much sweat to get rid of the rest of the boys. June Deschamp could be a big man in Mexico, maybe even Brazil, with that much money.

He tried to build the vision in his mind of easy living, good whiskey, young dark women with brown eyes and big tits. The vision wouldn't come.

A black-haired man who was a heller with a handgun kept getting in the way. And Jules would have sworn he'd heard a big-bore, long-range rifle—a buffalo gun or some such—along toward the back end of the shootout on the Chamita. Some of the other boys had heard it too, and it was from way off. That meant there had to have been a second man, a long-gun expert, backing Slocum's play.

It didn't fit.

From what he'd heard about Slocum, the man was a loner. He tried not to think too much about the other stories he'd picked up around wild country campfires and town saloons. If half the yarns were true, and this Slocum was after him . . .

It was enough to give any thinking man the knee-bone weebles. Deschamp reached for the flask again. It was almost empty, but he needed it now.

There was one outside chance. Bud thought he was a real wosshopper with a handgun. Maybe he'd get lucky and bring Slocum down. Even if he didn't, Slocum would get rid of one problem for him. Bud. It would save him the trouble later on. Nephew or not, he didn't like the cocky little son of a bitch.

The longer June thought on it, the more he liked the idea. Slocum had to be taken down. And he might as well get that tended to first, while he still had the men to get the job done.

Deschamp knew Slocum would be on his trail as long as those scalplocks were tied to his saddle—a fresh twinge of pain bit Deschamp's shoulder. "Let the son of a bitch come," he muttered aloud. "Catchin' us will be the last thing he ever does. . . ."

Slocum leaned back against the headboard, sated and relaxed, hands cupped behind his head, and watched as Lisa washed up. She could get a man's blood pumping with just a washrag, Slocum thought.

Lisa stood facing him, one foot hiked up on the seat of a chair, the wet cloth stroking her upper thighs and the dense black triangle of hair at her crotch. Her breasts jiggled slightly, diffused sunlight from the window dancing on wet skin and dark, erect nipples.

She glanced up, saw Slocum watching, smiled, and shook her head. "Get that look out of your eye, cowboy. You've had all you're going to get for a couple of hours at least. I'm hungry." She squeezed the excess water from the cloth, draped it on a peg beside the basin, and reached for a towel. "You're going to have to feed me first."

Slocum's gut rumbled. "Now that you mention it, I've got a hungry on, myself."

She dampened a clean rag and tossed it onto his belly; the shock of the cool wetness made him gasp. "Clean yourself up, Slocum. I'd do it for you, but I don't want to get sidetracked again before supper." She arched her back, nipples pointed at a spot somewhere above Slocum's head, stretched, and flashed a wicked grin. "In case I haven't mentioned it, fellow, you're good. Damn good. I didn't think I could ever again—since . . ." The grin faded and her expression turned somber as her voice trailed away.

Slocum busied himself cleaning up. Whatever had happened to Lisa, he would know when, or if, she decided to tell him.

"How'd the meeting with Waggoner go?" Lisa asked as she started dressing.

Slocum filled her in, leaving out the personal stuff, as he finished washing and dressed. He hesitated for a moment at the end of the story, for some reason unwilling to add the last sentence. Finally, he said, "Dan and I will be leaving tomorrow morning."

He had halfway expected Lisa to show some sort of reaction. Anger, perhaps, or disappointment. She merely nodded.

"I'm going with you," she said.

Slocum paused in the act of buckling his gunbelt. "Lisa, you can't. Where we're going is no place for a lady."

"I'm a woman, Slocum. I've never been accused of being a lady. And you aren't leaving Chama without me."

"Lisa—"

She turned to face him, hands on hips. "There is one way, and one way only, that I'll not be riding with you, Slocum. That is for you to expressly forbid it. And then, I'll follow you from a distance." Her hands dropped away from her hips, the defiant pose abandoned. "I told you I'm leaving Chama, Slocum. With you or trailing you, I'm leaving."

Slocum buckled the cartridge belt, settled the leather about his hips, strode to her, and put his hands on her shoulders. "Lisa, you have to understand. There'll be shooting, people getting killed. We're going after some dangerous men—"

"And one of them is June Deschamp," she interrupted. Hate flickered in her gold-flecked eyes. "That's why I'm going. I want to handle that—that *bastard*—myself." Her tone went hard and cold. "For years, Slocum, I've lived for the day when I can show that son of a bitch his own balls, stick his own prick in his mouth—and then gut him like a fatted calf. I want him to suffer the way he made me suffer."

She glanced toward the Schofield on the table. "If you're worried about my getting in the way or slowing you down, Slocum, I can hold up my end. I can handle that Schofield, and I hit what I aim at." The tension drained from her shoulders. "After it's over and Deschamp is dead, if you want to dump me someplace, then I won't argue."

Slocum stared into her face for a moment, saw the set of jaw and the expression in her eyes, and sighed. "If there's no way to talk you out of it short of tying you up here in your room, then I'll ask Dan about it. I just don't want to see you hurt, Lisa.''

Her expression softened. ''I'll take the chance, Slocum. It's that important to me. Now, let's go eat. I'm so hungry I could eat a wolf. Hair and all. Then you can ply me with booze and try to talk your way between my legs.'' She grinned lecherously, surprising Slocum with the quicksilver way she switched from hate and anger to pure feminine lust.

Lisolette Barnes, Slocum thought, was more of a puzzlement than most women. ''Maybe by then,'' he said with a grin, ''I'll have my weapon reloaded.'' He took her arm. ''Let's go.''

The sun had slid below the western horizon when Slocum led Lisa from the cafe. He paused outside the door to light her cigarette and fish a fresh cigarillo from his pocket. The brown cur, T-Bone, sat by Lisa's foot, waiting for a head-pat.

Chama was crowded, and getting more so. Horsemen jock-eyed with pedestrians, buggies, and buckboards for space on the main street. There was no room at the hitch rails before the town's three saloons, and more cowboys were riding into town by the moment. Lantern light spilled from open doors and windows, painting a faint yellow-gold wash along the street. Three doors down at the Silver Eagle Saloon, the notes of a banjo and piano mingled with whoops of celebration and the underlying murmur of voices.

''Busy night,'' Slocum said.

''Saturday and payday.'' Lisa took a deep drag from her cigarette and smiled. ''A good whore could make a lot of money tonight. Too bad I've retired from the business.''

''Think all these randy young cowboys know that?''

''If they don't, they'll find out soon enough. Now, about that drink?''

''Lead the way, scout. Pick your watering hole.''

''How about Sam's place? It won't be as crowded as the others. No cardplayers cluttering up the place. Sam doesn't hold with gambling,'' Lisa said with a wry smile. ''The fact that he won the place playing faro is beside the point.''

''Sam's it is, then. If you don't think too many of your customers will show up to bother you.''

''Former customers,'' Lisa corrected. ''And they won't bother me more than one time.''

Halfway across the street, they paused to let a spring wagon pulled by a matched pair of high-stepping sorrels pass, fine rooster tails of sand kicking up beneath the iron rims. Lisa nodded a greeting to the man in the business suit and bowler hat in the driver's seat. He touched his fingers to his hat brim in greeting.

"That's Otis Callahan," Lisa said to Slocum. "Biggest cattle buyer between Fort Worth and San Fran—"

"Slocum!"

The shout from down the street to his right brought Slocum around; he instinctively stepped in front of Lisa. At his side, T-Bone bristled and snarled, fangs bared. The lean young cowboy stood thirty feet away, his hand resting on the grips of the .38 holstered at his right hip, favoring the leg Chief had kicked.

For a moment, Slocum stood and glared at the cowboy without speaking. At the corners of his vision, Slocum saw pedestrians along both sides of the street scramble for cover. The residents and visitors of Chama knew enough to sense a gunfight about to happen and get out of the way.

The cur took a step forward and crouched, muscles tensed.

"Stay, T-Bone," Slocum said softly. The mongrel stopped, the hair on its neck raised. Slocum raised his voice. "What do you want, Coy?"

"Your pelt first, Slocum! Then the damn dog's! After that, I'm going to screw the tits off your whore. When I'm done with her, I'm going to take that spotted-ass horse of yours and ride the kicking son of a bitch to death!"

"Don't be a fool, Coy," Slocum said casually. "There's no need for this." He reached back with his left hand and nudged Lisa's shoulder. Softly, he said, "Stand aside, Lisa. I don't want you in the line of fire if I can't talk him out of this." He sensed, rather than saw, Lisa move a couple of paces away, as he took the cigarillo from his mouth and tossed it away.

"Let it go, Coy. What happened to you isn't worth getting killed over." As he spoke, Slocum flexed his knees slightly, shifting his weight over the balls of his feet. Coy had an edge of sorts; he already had his hand on his gun. And he was an amateur. It showed in the way he stood—and in the fact he hadn't already drilled Slocum from ambush. An amateur could be more dangerous than a professional. They were unpredictable.

"The hell you say, Slocum!" Coy's voice was high-pitched,

tight with rage. "I hear you're a pure heller with that handgun! I say that's a pile of shit."

Slocum couldn't see the cowboy's eyes in the half-light. He concentrated instead on Coy's right shoulder. The kid was tense, tight; before he could pull iron, that shoulder would twitch. Slocum's own muscles were relaxed in the familiar calm, almost a peaceful feeling, that came over him when he sensed a shootout was inevitable.

"Say what you want, Coy. I have no quarrel with you." Slocum became aware of a tense silence along the street. Even the out-of-tune banjo and tinny piano had stopped. "We don't want anybody hit by a wild shot. Happens a lot at night. Bad light makes for bad shooting."

"You scared of me, Slocum? You yellow?"

"Any man with brains is cautious about another fellow carrying a gun," Slocum said. "You might want to study on that for a while, Coy. Could mean the difference in whether you live or not."

Lisa said, "Coy—"

"Shut up, whore!"

"Listen to me, Coy, please. I know what's eating you. I meant no insult when I turned you down the other day—"

"I said shut up, dammit!" Coy snapped. "I'll take care of you later! All right, Slocum! Get ready to knock on the gates of Hell!"

Coy's shoulder twitched. Slocum's right hand whipped across his body to the grips of the Peacemaker.

Coy's handgun was still half in the leather when Slocum's first shot hammered into his chest. The young cowboy staggered back a half step under the impact. Slocum took his time, half a heartbeat, as he thumbed the hammer and lined the sights. The next soft-lead .44-40 slug snapped Coy's head back, sent his hat spinning, knocked his feet from beneath him. He fell heavily onto his back, boots cribbing at the dirt in reflex. Slocum knew the kid was dead before he hit the ground.

"Stay here, Lisa," Slocum said. "This isn't going to be a pretty sight. Keep the dog with you."

Slocum strode to Coy's side. Blood seeped over the bullet hole to Coy's heart, but the pump no longer worked since .44 slugs stopped such things. But Slocum had seen men shot through the heart and still get off several shots. A slug in the forehead discouraged that. It also made a hell of a mess on the backside. Brain matter, blood, and bits of bone and flesh fanned out in a spray pattern behind Coy's body.

Slocum knelt, pulled the half-drawn revolver free of Coy's holster, and tucked it into his waistband. He ejected the spent cartridges from the Colt's cylinder and reloaded.

The whole thing had lasted only a few seconds.

Slocum knew he should feel no particular remorse. He had given the kid plenty of chances to rethink his insanity. Still, killing a stranger went against the grain. That Coy had given him no choice didn't ease the heavy feeling in his gut. It had been a senseless waste of a young life.

"Dammit, Coy," Slocum muttered softly, "why didn't you listen to reason? There was no need for this."

"Jesus H. Christ," an awed voice said from an open window nearby, "I never saw anybody that fast in my life. . . ." The voice was drowned under growing murmurs as men streamed onto the street.

"It was my fault, Slocum. If I hadn't insulted him—Lord, he was just a baby," Lisa said at his side.

Slocum turned to her, irritation warming his gut; he had told Lisa to stay back, trying to save her from having to look at the mess that seconds ago had been a living, breathing young cowboy named Coy. His aggravation faded. Lisa's eyes reflected a sadness, a sense of loss. Her face paled. She shuddered. "My God, I could have gotten you killed."

Slocum glanced at her opened handbag and the Schofield revolver in her hand. "You can put that away now, Lisa," he said. "It's over. Don't blame yourself. Coy made a mistake, that's all. He let his pride get him killed."

Lisa looked at the big six-gun in her hand as if seeing it for the first time, then slowly lowered the hammer and put the weapon back in her bag.

"Lisa," Slocum asked, "would you have used that gun?"

"Yes. If it had been necessary. If he had gotten a bullet into you, I would have."

Slocum nodded. Somehow, he found comfort in her words.

T-Bone sniffed at Coy's boots, then settled back on his haunches at Lisa's side.

Slocum sighed. "I guess now there'll have to be a coroner's jury and an inquest."

"Not in Chama, mister," a bowlegged, weathered man in rough range clothing said, kneeling beside the body. "Half the town seen it. Wasn't your fault the kid was plumb et up with the dumb-ass.'' He spat a stream of tobacco juice across Coy's carcass. "There's a couple Walkin' T hands down in the Mex end of town.''

Slocum's eyes narrowed. "Think they'll take offense that one of their own got killed?''

"Nah. Everybody knew Coy was a hothead. Wasn't much better a cowboy than he was a gunhawk either. He won't be missed all that much.'' The weathered cowpuncher stood. "We'll get word to 'em they've got a dead 'un. They don't want 'im, we'll plant 'im in the paupers' boneyard outside town. Don't fret none on it.'' He turned to two men in the front ranks of the crowd. "Emmitt, Zeke, how about draggin' this kid out of the street into that alley. No need anybody havin' to gee-haw around him.''

It seemed to Slocum that within minutes, things were back to normal in Chama. The banjo picker and piano player were still out of tune, the card games were back to full bore, and people were laughing or cursing depending on the roll of dice. A man had died in a shootout and nobody seemed to give a damn.

Chama, he thought as he poured a couple of fingers of Old Overholt into Lisa's glass at a corner table in Sam's cantina, was a tough town. He told her as much.

"I know,'' Lisa said. "That's just one of the reasons I'll be glad to get away from here.'' She lifted her drink and swallowed half the contents. Her full lips tightened, a frown line between her eyes. "That—and June Deschamp. I'll tell you about him some day, Slocum, if you're interested. Not now, though.''

Slocum downed part of his drink and reached for a fresh cigarillo. "I'm interested in everything about you, Lisa. When you feel it's time to talk, I'll listen.''

She shrugged the frown away, pulled the makings from her handbag, and rolled herself a smoke. "When do we leave? I don't have much packing to do, just toss a few things together.''

"We'll move out soon after daylight.'' Slocum lit her cigarette and his own smoke.

"I'll be ready.''

"Just let me get *some* sleep.''

The pained expression faded from Lisa's eyes, replaced by

a spark of mischief. "You always take a girl for granted, Slocum?"

He chuckled. "Never. Well, once in a while I might take a chance on breaking that rule."

"Don't get in the habit of it, but I'll let you get away with it this once." The twinkle in her eye gave lie to the mock scolding. "We've got plenty of time before daylight." She puffed out a smoke ring and put a hand on Slocum's forearm. Her breathing deepened. "I've still got a lot of catching up to do, mister, so I won't promise you'll get much sleep tonight."

"Shootings always make you horny?"

"No. You do."

Slocum flashed a quick grin, topped off both glasses, and leaned back in his chair. His smile faded. "Lisa, I haven't mentioned anything to Dan about your going along with us. He may object."

"If he does?"

Slocum half smiled. "We'll try to talk him into it."

"I could show him my tits."

"Uh-uh. We just want to convince the man, not blind him."

"I have this sudden urge to show them to *somebody*."

"I'll bring the bottle."

# 6

Slocum reined in atop the heavily timbered ridge overlooking Castilla Creek and studied the banks of the winding stream below.

It had been five years or so since he had last camped at the secluded site in the high country north of Taos, but nothing seemed to have changed.

Time had skipped the narrow valley, which was little more than a wide spot between the banks of the sparkling stream. To Slocum, it was as if he had left the place only yesterday.

Tall pines and an occasional aspen grove fluttered in the breeze over the ripples of the small, swift-flowing stream. Within a month, Castilla Creek would be awash in red, gold, and green as autumn came to the high country, a brief but special time that brought stillness and a measure of peace to Slocum's heart. He found himself wishing the Time of the Turning Leaves had already arrived, yet dreading it at the same time. It also would remind him of last autumn. And the Nez Percé girl named Quill . . .

A mule deer doe and her yearling fawn grazed in the rich green grass at the edge of the creek, the doe lifting her head frequently to watch, listen, and sniff the cool mountain air. She was right in staying alert, Slocum thought. This was big cat country, and half-grown deer were high on a cougar's list of delicacies.

Slocum glanced up at a shrill *scree* from above. Against a deep blue sky, a red-tailed hawk soared effortlessly on the rising air currents. The bird was near enough that Slocum could see its head turn from side to side as it sought prey along the banks of the creek.

Slocum relaxed in the saddle, savoring the feel of the high country, satisfied that no danger—at least from humans—lurked below. Chief snorted softly, barely ruffling his nostrils. Slocum wondered if the spotted sorrel palouse felt as much at home here as his rider did.

After a moment, he turned in the saddle to study the twisting trail up the mountainside. Through the timber, he caught glimpses of Lisa on her big, powerful bay, Duke, the two pack horses trailing on slack lead behind her, T-Bone ambling along in Duke's shadow. Waggoner, astride his tall black Tennessee-bred racer, brought up the rear, the long rifle in its doeskin cover cradled in an elbow. The riders were scarcely fifty yards away as the crow flies, but the trail they followed covered a quarter of a mile before it twisted its way to the crest of the mountain.

Slocum dismounted and stood beside Chief, his arm draped across the saddle seat, as he waited for Lisa and Dan. He idly wondered how Lisa's rump and knees were holding up to the long ride. She rode well, astride the full-swell, deep-cantle stockman's saddle, her weight balanced over the stirrups, helping Duke up one mountainside and down another. If she was tired, it didn't show in the way she handled the horse. And she had never complained during the last two days and more than a hundred miles of riding through country that was more up and down than it was east and west.

Waggoner rode less casually than Lisa, his back straight and head erect in the military posture, but with a softer touch on the reins than most men accustomed to frequently ornery cavalry remount horses. The black gelding looked a bit winded, but that was to be expected with the thin air up this high.

Slocum's mountain-bred palouse had hardly broken a sweat during the steep, steady climb to the pass overlooking Castilla Creek.

Waggoner had surprised Slocum a bit. He hadn't raised even the slightest hint of a fuss about Lisa riding with them. He'd accepted as fact her statement that if she couldn't accompany them, she would follow them anyway. He had, in fact, almost insisted on her coming along; the rough northern New Mexico country, which was riddled with outlaw bands and renegade thieves, was definitely no place for a lady traveling alone, he'd said. A wry grin touched Slocum's lips. Lisa hadn't even had to show Waggoner her tits.

Lisa topped the ridge and reined in beside Slocum, her eyes wide as she studied the vista below. She didn't speak for several moments, then said in a soft voice, "My God, it's beautiful. So peaceful-looking . . ."

Slocum nodded silently, unwilling to disturb her absorption in the scenery, and secretly pleased that the place affected her much as it did him. While she stared at the vista below, Slocum studied her. It was a more than pleasant way to pass time.

Lisa's naturally dark skin seemed unaffected by the sunshine intensified by the thin high country air. Slocum wondered how she could look as fresh and female in trail garb and astride a big bay horse as she did in a dress.

Her natural common sense showed in the trail clothes she had selected. She wore simple but sturdy men's garments. The gray twill pants bunched a bit at the waist, cinched in by a sturdy leather belt and simple D-ring buckle. A blue cotton shirt, loose-fitting except where the cloth strained against her full breasts, molded itself to her body with the breeze. The dark hair that spilled from beneath her flat-brimmed Plainsman hat rippled in the wind. Her trousers were tucked into the top of supple cavalry-style riding boots that rose above the swell of her calves.

Her femininity even survived the somewhat jarring note of the Schofield .45 strapped around her waist in the new leather holster Slocum had bought for her. The confiscated Springfield .45-70 single-shot trapdoor rifle was in the saddle boot beneath her right leg.

Lisa finally broke the silence. "Lord, I could live here. How did you find this place, Slocum?"

"A Chiricahua Apache I rode with for a few months on the trail of a couple of bad hombres led me to it," Slocum said.

"What happened to him?"

Slocum sighed. "We found the bad hombres. They got a couple of slugs into him. He wanted to die here. It was a sacred spot to his band. I brought him back, even though he should have died three days before we reached the place. I buried him nearby."

Lisa sighed. "It's a pleasant resting place for a soul."

Waggoner's arrival brought an end to the conversation. The lean man studied the narrow valley and the mountains on either side, as if he were evaluating the military strengths and weaknesses of the place.

"We'll camp here tonight, Dan," Slocum said after a moment. "It has good grass, pure water, and I'd lay odds not half-a-dozen white men have been here since Kit Carson's time."

Waggoner nodded. "It appears to be an excellent campsite." Slocum saw Waggoner's gaze return to the doe and yearling fawn, his hand on the deerhide sleeve of the rifle. Slocum shook his head. "I promised Escopeta, the Apache who showed me this place, that there would be no game animals shot here, Dan."

"What? Oh. The deer." Waggoner's hand dropped away from the rifle sheath, his face flushed a bit. "I wasn't even thinking of that, Slocum. Just admiring the grace and beauty of the animal." He sighed. "I must admit that, for a few seconds, I had this eerie sensation of being home, in the backwoods of Maine. There are trees and creeks there too, and deer. And memories of hunts on crisp autumn mornings."

Lisa said, "That must have been a wonderful time for you."

"It was. Camping out with my brothers, I mean. Not the killing. I left that to them. I took a great deal of teasing over my unwillingness to make a kill."

Lisa raised an eyebrow. "You never shot a deer?"

"No, Miss Barnes. Only men." Waggoner shifted his weight in the saddle and glanced at the westering sun. "We'd best get on with setting up camp. If you'll be so kind as to lead the way down, Slocum?"

Slocum cast a final glance toward the southwest, where the blue-hazed mountains reached almost twelve thousand feet toward the sky, then mounted and kneed Chief onto the narrow downward trail.

Darkness came quickly to the camp on Castilla Creek. One moment the western sky was awash in reds and golds above the shadowed mountains; the next moment, stars bloomed into bright, cold specks against the blackness overhead.

A gentle, cool breeze rustled the leaves of trees that lined the creek and set the fading flames of the small campfire dancing. Soon, Slocum knew, the air would turn still and a bit sharp; by dawn, it would be chilly enough for a man to savor the warmth of a bedroll, which would brighten the taste of that first cup of morning coffee.

Slocum leaned back against the trunk of a downed pinyon a few feet from the fire, content in the comfortable warmth of Lisa's body as she leaned close against his left side. The clear mountain creek whispered over smooth, worn stones of the streambed, a musical counterpoint to the rustle of leaves in the wind.

The only other sounds at the moment were the soft rip and tear as the picketed horses cropped the rich green grass along the water's edge. Lisa was right, Slocum thought; this would be a good place for a man to spend the rest of his days.

Even as a temporary stopping place, it was a good camp. Dan Waggoner had proved to be a more than competent hand with the skillet and Dutch oven, as Slocum's straining belt attested. Waggoner was even a better cook than Lisa, and far better than Slocum. On the trail alone, Slocum was mostly content with a quick bait of bacon and beans. Maybe even just jerked beef and coffee when time was scarce. Waggoner's camp biscuits were, Slocum granted, a thing of beauty to a hungry man.

"Slocum?" Lisa's voice was soft, barely audible. She sat with her head tilted back, her hand on Slocum's leg. Starlight set pinpoints of light dancing on the near-blackness of her brunette hair. The warmth of her palm brought a stirring to Slocum's groin, along with the mental image of sharing a bedroll with her.

"Yes?"

"It's—I don't know how to describe it." Her voice held a touch of breathless awe. "It's so heartbreakingly beautiful here. The stars—it's as if I could just reach out and gather in a handful, play with them like fireflies. The way I used to catch lightning bugs when I was a little girl . . ." Her voice trailed away; Slocum sensed the sudden tension in her hand against his thigh. It was as if the thought had triggered some bad memories.

"Where was that, Lisa?"

"Northwest Arkansas. On a farm not far from Pea Ridge, where the Civil War battle was fought."

"I know the place."

"Were you in that fight?"

Slocum shook his head. "No. But I've been through the country a few times." He didn't add that he'd left three men dead not a mile from Pea Ridge. "Go ahead, Lisa. If you want to talk about it, that is."

"Maybe it would help at that. I've never told anyone about it before." A note of bitterness crept into her tone. "It was a happy day in my life when I got old enough to leave that place. And my father . . ." Her voice trailed away.

Slocum's brows lifted. He had the feeling that Lisa wanted to talk, to drag some inner demon out into the open. The soft reddish-gold glow from the dying campfire showed fine, dark frown lines creasing her forehead between narrowed eyes.

"Did he mistreat you?" Slocum asked after a moment's silence.

Lisa sighed. "He never beat me. But there are other, more brutal ways to degrade a person." She glanced at Slocum, light dancing from the tears pooled in her lower lids. "I was the oldest of four children, the only girl. Mother died on my ninth birthday. Father blamed me for that. He said she had been sickly ever since I was born—that it was my fault she'd died. He hated me for it."

"That's a heavy load to put on a young girl's shoulders," Slocum said sympathetically.

"He needed someone to blame. Nothing was ever his fault. Even the fact that he refused Mother's pleas to see a doctor. He said doctors cost money and never knew what they were doing anyway. When she died, I was the one he picked to blame." Lisa blinked away the tears and squared her shoulders. "Anyway, he told me that since it was my fault, I'd have to take her place. Be the wife and mother, do the cooking and cleaning. What he called 'woman's work.' God knows I tried, but I couldn't do anything to please him. He never missed a chance to tell me how stupid I was, how clumsy, how ugly."

"For what it's worth, Lisa," Slocum said solemnly, "the man was wrong. On every point."

Her eyes misted again. "Thank you for saying that. I'm still trying to convince myself that I'm not the things he said I was. It's hard. I'd rather he'd beaten me. Bruises to the flesh heal. Bruises to the mind don't."

Slocum nodded in understanding. He had a few lingering bruises of his own. "I know, Lisa. But you have to keep trying."

"I am. Every day. But it's difficult when the only tool I have to work with is a nice body—which, I understand, I inherited from my mother. She was Italian. You've probably noticed the dark skin. I got that from her, not from her husband.'' Lisa sighed. ''He wouldn't let me or my brothers go to school. He believed education was a waste of time for farmers, and especially for girls. That's why I never learned to read and write and do numbers, except for being able to tell the difference between a one-dollar bill and a twenty.''

She fell silent for a moment, staring at the blanket of stars overhead. Slocum didn't push; he'd already learned a great deal about Lisa Barnes.

''I'll make the rest of the story as mercifully short as possible,'' she finally said. ''On my thirteenth birthday—it seems everything bad happens on my birthdays—he came into my room. Apparently, by then I wasn't as ugly as he'd said I was. He told me that since I had done everything else but be a wife, I was old enough for that too.''

''Jesus Christ,'' Slocum said in disgust. ''What a bastard.''

''It got worse, Slocum.'' Tears welled in Lisa's lids despite the cold hate in her eyes. ''After a couple of years, something else—happened. The end of the story is that one day I stole a mule and rode away. I never looked back.''

''Didn't your brothers do anything to help you?''

''No. They were as cowed and frightened of Father as I was.'' She drew in a deep breath. ''Slocum, I have to be honest with you. If Father walked into this camp right now, I'd pull this Schofield and put a bullet through his heart.''

Slocum said, ''If you didn't, I'd do it for you.''

''Since we're trading life stories here, Slocum, how about you? Tell me about yourself.''

A soft footfall behind them brought Slocum's head around. ''Later, Lisa,'' he said as Waggoner strode back into camp, his turn at the cold waters of the bathing pool below camp done. The long rifle rested across the crook of an arm, unsheathed. Frown lines creased his normally smooth forehead.

''Problem, Dan?'' Slocum asked.

''I'm not sure. It seems quiet, but I can't shake the feeling there's something out there, the sensation that we're being watched.''

T-Bone, sitting at Lisa's side, came to his feet, sniffed the breeze, and growled low in his throat, the hairs at the scruff of his neck raised. Slocum's gaze swept the surrounding mountains, senses tuned to the night. Waggoner and the dog didn't see ghosts and goblins. If Dan and T-Bone sensed that something or someone was about, Slocum wouldn't bet against it. For his part, his attention had been so much on Lisa that he wouldn't have heard a company of cavalry pass by.

He mentally scolded himself for his momentary lapse. Out here, a man who didn't keep his mind on the business of staying alert could wind up as coyote bait. He reached for his rifle. "I'll take a look around, Dan. Lisa, keep T-Bone here. Move away from the fire, just in case—and keep a sharp eye out."

Waggoner and Lisa watched as Slocum disappeared into the darkness. One moment he was there, the next he was gone.

Waggoner led Lisa away from the campsite into a stand of pinyons a few yards upstream. They could barely make out each other's shapes in the black shadows, but from there they had a clear field of fire into the camp and for almost a hundred yards upstream and down, Lisa noted. A metallic snick, soft in the night, told Lisa Waggoner had cocked the big-bore rifle.

They stood for several minutes in the still night, the only sounds those of small animals rummaging through the brush nearby, the whisper of breeze through the pines.

"An unusual man, Slocum," Waggoner said at length, his words little more than a whisper.

"Yes, he is," Lisa answered softly. "I know he's a gunman, a loner. He tries to hide it, but he has a gentle side."

"I don't know about the gentle side, but Slocum is a born hunter." Lisa couldn't see Waggoner's face, but she sensed his keen gaze drifting constantly over the countryside. "I thought I had gotten to know him well at the Round Tops. With the possible exception of Sergeant Grace of the Fourth Georgia, Slocum was the best sniper in the Confederate ranks. Every field-grade officer in the Union Army respected him. Many feared him. Just the rumor that he might be in the area sent any general who was short on courage scurrying toward the rear."

Lisa sighed softly. "I'm glad he's on my side."

"So am I, now. It has been quite an experience, meeting him face to face, riding with him, after the pair of us spent two days stalking each other."

"Pardon me for saying so if I'm out of line, Dan," Lisa said, "but it sounds like you enjoyed those two days."

Waggoner half smiled. "Let's just say it was the most intense experience I've ever had. I'm glad I failed."

"Failed?"

"Slocum was the only target ever assigned to me that I didn't bring down." Waggoner sighed. "Strange how the fates turn. Two men who once tried every trick known to kill each other, now riding together."

Lisa frowned. "I would think that, under the circumstances, you two would hate each other."

"No, not at all. Respect, yes—maybe even a bit of mutual awe. Or at least a measure of awe on my part. But hate, no. We were simply trying to do our jobs. Hate blinds a person, Lisa. Hate can only lead the one who hates to grief."

Lisa glanced sharply at the former Union officer, wondering if he had overheard her private conversation with Slocum. Or had he somehow sensed the dark emotions that boiled in her? Was it simply a chance remark? Either the man had extraordinary hearing, or a keen sense of when someone was troubled. She shrugged the thoughts aside. They didn't matter anyway.

What mattered was that Slocum was out there somewhere in the darkness, stalking something that might or might not be there.

"Don't worry, Miss Barnes," Waggoner said, as if reading her mind. "If there's something amiss out there, he'll find it."

Partway up the slope of the mountainside, Slocum crept through the darkness, Winchester at the ready, placing each foot with care. The snap of a twig underfoot, the rustle of clothing against brush, would alert whoever—or whatever—was out there. The thin night air amplified sounds. That worked as much to the benefit of the hunter as the hunted. Slocum trusted his ears and nose more than his vision in the deep blackness of the pines.

He had spent more than an hour covering less than a hundred yards, circling wide onto the hillside away from camp, pausing every couple of steps to listen. He heard nothing—no movement in the brush that seemed out of place—yet he took his time. A man in a hurry was a man who could easily get himself killed.

He eased from beside a thick pinyon trunk, took a half step, and froze in mid-stride.

It was there.

The musky, distinct scent in his nostrils prickled the hair on his forearms. It was the scent of mountain lion. And the cat was nearby. The tickle in Slocum's gut gave way to the familiar calmness of thought and muscle. He was in his element. The cat was in its element. It was simply a matter of which of them wished to press the point.

Slocum knew the odds of a mountain lion attacking a man were slim, but lives had been lost on thinner bets. The big cats, like men, were unpredictable.

What seemed to be a shadow flickered against the darkness on the far side of the small clearing in the pines, barely ten feet away. Slocum couldn't be sure if his eyes were playing tricks on him, but he knew one thing—if he could smell the lion, the cat could smell him. If it came at him, he would have time for only one shot, and that by instinct; there wasn't enough light to pick up the sights.

Time seemed to stand still for Slocum as he waited, alert, senses tuned to every sound and movement in the blackness. He didn't move for a long time, and only then after he heard the faint rustle of fallen pine needles well beyond the spot where he thought he had seen the movement.

Slocum eased forward, rifle at the ready. Across the clearing, he again paused to wait and listen. He heard nothing. The scent of mountain lion grew fainter, finally faded. The cat was gone. Slocum fired a sulphur match and knelt in the bare patch of sandy soil beneath a pine.

The paw print was the biggest he had ever seen, almost as large as his own hand with the fingers spread. The flickering light of the lucifer showed the outside toe of the paw missing. A faint smear of fresh blood stained the nubbed toe mark. It wasn't the most reassuring sight Slocum had seen. A big cat, crippled and enraged by pain, was the most unpredictable of all creatures.

Slocum shook out the match and frowned into the darkness. So much for the peace and quiet of Castilla Creek tonight, he thought. He rose and silently threaded his way through the timber back to camp.

Waggoner and Lisa emerged from the tree line across the way as Slocum strode into the open.

"Find anything?" Waggoner asked.

Slocum nodded, his jaw set. "It's worse than I figured. We've got a bad combination out there—the biggest cat I've ever seen, and crippled to boot."

Lisa crouched to stroke T-Bone. The hairs on the mongrel's

neck rose again. "Easy, T-Bone," Lisa said softly. "It's all right."

Waggoner's frown deepened. "So I wasn't imagining things after all. Slocum, I don't know all that much about mountain lions. My tactical experience has been limited mostly to human predators. What can we expect, and what do we do now?"

"I don't know what to expect, Dan," Slocum said. "There's nothing quite as unpredictable as a crippled mountain cat, especially a big male like that one."

"How do you know it's a male?" Lisa asked.

"I smelled him. Cats are like people in one respect. Each sex has its own distinctive odor." Slocum nodded toward the fire. The flames had all but died away, leaving a bed of glowing coals behind. "Lisa, add some wood to the fire. Usually, a big cat won't come near a blaze. But this one isn't usual. Dan and I will re-picket the horses between our camp and the creek, where we can keep a closer eye on them."

Lisa crouched, pulled a couple of wrist-sized limbs from the wood they had gathered, and glanced up at Slocum. "Will the cat attack?"

"That's the problem, Lisa. There's no way to tell." Slocum turned to study the trees and brush on the mountainside. "He's out there now, close. He's in pain, mad to the bone, and probably hungry. Maybe he'll drift on. I wouldn't count on it."

"How big do you want this fire? I'll put a whole tree on it if it will help."

"Just a normal size, Lisa," Slocum said with a forced smile. "Might as well start a fresh pot of coffee while you're at it." He turned to Waggoner. "Okay, Dan, let's go move those ponies."

Lisa had the fire going again by the time Waggoner and Slocum returned. Slocum nodded his approval. The fire was neither too big nor too small. The coffeepot on the flat stone at the edge of the blaze was beginning to steam. Lisa sat beside the fire, her knees pulled up, arms wrapped around her shins, T-Bone at her feet. The dog's lips rose above fangs in a silent growl. Slocum saw the quavering tension in the mongrel's taut muscles.

"Worried, Lisa?" he asked.

"Not worried. Scared half to death would be more like it. I guess I'm just a sissy female."

Slocum shook his head. "Anybody with an ounce of common sense would be scared, Lisa. Don't worry about it.''

She gazed into his eyes. "Are you scared, Slocum?"

He forced a half smile. "Most of the time, as a matter of fact. The trick is to keep it under control."

"Easy for you to say. My fingers are trembling."

"Slocum's right, Miss Barnes," Waggoner said. "A bit of fear can be a good thing. It sharpens the senses, makes one more alert. Too much fear can be paralyzing. I've seen grown men panic, simply freeze up from sheer terror, on the battle-field. Others who were equally frightened gathered their wits and went on about their business. You'll be all right."

Slocum turned away, waited until his eyes readjusted from the campfire light, and studied the heavy timber and brush along the creek. He saw nothing move, but sensed the weight of a yellow-eyed gaze on him. "That cat's probably got horse meat on its mind. We'd better stand watch tonight. I'll take it from now to midnight. Dan, you've got the duty from then until dawn."

"I'll stand my turn," Lisa said. She stood, squared her shoul-ders, and stepped alongside Slocum. "We're in this together."

"Miss Barnes," Waggoner protested, "that won't be nec-essary. You would be cold and miserable—and jumpy. A frightened sentry is worse than no picket at all."

"I said I'll hold up my end, Mr. Waggoner." Lisa's tone was firm. "I insist on doing my part. And I promise I won't panic and just blaze away at anything that moves." Her shoul-ders heaved in a deep sigh. "Besides, if I'm going to pawed and mauled in a bedroll, I sure as hell don't want it to be by a mountain lion, thank you very much."

Slocum had to grin. He finally shifted his gaze from the timberline; it seemed to grow even blacker as the starlight grew. Slocum would have made a pact with the devil for a nice full moon this night. He turned to Lisa. "Do you know what to do if that cat attacks?"

"Shoot," she said calmly. "If that beast manages to get into the horses, the ones he didn't manage to maul could panic and break loose. I have no desire to be left afoot here in the middle of nowhere. And I've grown rather attached to Duke. No cat's going to have my horse for breakfast."

Slocum nodded. "Fair enough." He glanced at Waggoner and half smiled. "Don't try to talk her out of it, Dan. She can be a bit stubborn at times." The slight smile faded. "Lisa, you take the first watch. Keep a close eye on the tree line and sing out if you see anything bigger than a rabbit move. Dan can take second watch. I'll take over then." He nodded toward the booted .45-70. "Might want to keep the rifle handy."

She shook her head and patted the Schofield at her hip. "I'll stay with the revolver, Slocum. I can shoot better with it, at least at close range. And at night."

Slocum silently agreed. He had given Lisa a ten-shot lesson on the .45-70; she was a good shot with the big-bore rifle, but in darkness, a handgun was quicker. And it held more rounds. "Are you sure you want to do this, Lisa?" he asked.

She squatted beside the fire and poured herself a cup of coffee. "Damn sure. I won't be sleeping much tonight anyway."

Slocum awoke with a start, his right hand instinctively sweeping up the Colt that lay beside his bedroll. He lay for a moment, alert but motionless, his breathing steady, unsure of what had jarred him awake.

Lisa sat near the fire, the big Schofield in her right hand, tension obvious in the stiff set of her shoulders and straight back, staring toward the black tangle of shadows that marked the tree line. She held T-Bone by the scruff of the neck with her left hand. The mongrel bristled, teeth bared, ears backed. The starlight was stronger now; individual pines and brush clumps stood in faint relief.

Slocum glanced toward the horses staked in the open. The hairs on his forearms prickled again. The sorrel palouse lifted his head, nostrils flared as he tested the wind, ears pricked toward the spot that Lisa and T-Bone watched. Lisa's big bay, Duke, also had its head up, the whites of the horse's eyes showing in the pale starlight. Duke snorted and stomped a front foot nervously.

A deep, hoarse cough from the darkness broke the silence. It was a noise Slocum had heard before, one more sinister than the click of a shotgun hammer—the hunting cough of a mountain lion. And it was close.

"Slocum!" Lisa's call was soft against the chill night air.

Slocum's gaze snapped back to the tree line to his right. His heart skipped a beat. Two widely spaced dots glowed at the very edge of the dense underbrush, low to the ground, the yellow gaze fixed on Lisa.

The big cat charged.

# 7

Slocum fired by instinct, knowing the odds for a killing hit were against him; he was lying on his back, shooting in the dark at a target that was little more than a fast-moving blur and with no time for an aimed shot, and there was little more he could do than pull the trigger and hope.

He heard the slap of lead against muscle above the muzzle blast of the Peacemaker. He had gotten lucky. The big cat twisted in mid-leap, its hindquarters knocked aside by the impact of the soft-lead .44 slug against its hip. A hoarse, coughing roar of shock and pain burst from the bared fangs as the lion staggered.

Above the muzzle blast, Slocum heard Lisa yell, "T-Bone! No!"

The cur's body was a swift, dark streak across the clearing. Before the big cat could completely regain its feet, T-Bone launched himself at the lion's throat. The collision of dog and mountain cat was an audible thud; for an instant, T-Bone's jaws closed on the lion's neck. The cat shook free before the dog could gain a solid hold. A massive paw lashed out, sent the dog tumbling.

Slocum slapped another quick shot. The cat twisted and fell on its side, teeth snapping at the bite of lead in its rib cage. Slocum cocked his revolver again—and barked a curse. The lion's fall had carried the animal past Lisa. Her body blocked his line of fire at the cat.

"Lisa, get down!" Slocum yelled in desperation. Ten feet past her right ear, he saw the cat gather itself. The lion struggled for a heartbeat to bunch damaged muscles, then crouched for a final leap, snarling, teeth bared. Hate and rage gleamed in the yellow eyes fixed on Lisa.

The flat blast of Lisa's Schofield came an instant before the lion launched itself. The cat leapt high, half twisted in midair, and fell heavily only a couple of strides from Lisa, its mouth open in a roar of pain and rage.

Slocum bounced to his feet and scrambled two steps to his right, handgun leveled for a final head shot. He didn't need the cartridge. Lisa's second slug ripped into the cat's open mouth and drove into the base of its brain. Huge paws clawed at the soil in the lion's death throes.

Slocum ignored the squeals and stomping hooves of the frightened horses at the picket line and sprinted to Lisa's side. She stood wide-eyed, wisps of powder smoke curling from the barrel of the Schofield as she stared at the scarred, tawny body almost within arm's reach.

A quick glance told Slocum the cat was no longer a threat. Slocum let out a deep sigh of relief. Normally, it took more than one or two shots from a handgun to down an enraged mountain lion. They had been lucky.

"Lisa—are you all right?"

For a couple of heartbeats, she didn't reply. She stood immobile, the Schofield cocked and ready, staring down at the lion as the last involuntary jerks of lean muscle sent tremors over the animal's skin. Then she cried out, "T-Bone!" and sprinted to the downed mongrel's side.

Slocum reached her a moment later. Lisa sat beside the limp bundle of brown fur, the dog's head resting on her thigh, the revolver still in her hand. She looked up, tears spilling down her cheeks.

"He—he's—dead, Slocum," Lisa said, gently rocking the still form.

Slocum knelt beside her, took the Schofield from her hand, and lowered the hammer. He ran a hand over the dog's head and down its spine. A hollow spot opened up in his gut. "I'm sorry, Lisa. His neck was broken," Slocum said softly. "I would say he died instantly, didn't suffer—and he saved your life."

Lisa lifted the dead mongrel's head and lowered her face into the fur. Her shoulders shook as she sobbed.

Slocum left her to grieve. He became aware that the squealing horses had quieted down, except for an occasional nervous snort, and weren't fighting the picket ropes. He realized why as Waggoner strode up. Dan had spread his bedroll closer to the picketed mounts than to the campfire on purpose, to keep the horses from spooking and breaking loose if something happened. Waggoner stared toward Lisa and the bundle in her arms for a moment, then studied the dead lion. His brows lifted.

"That has to be the biggest mountain lion I've ever seen," Waggoner said after a moment. "T-Bone?"

"Dead. The cat got him before I could drop it."

Waggoner nodded solemnly. "I saw. He died well. He was a good dog. Perhaps we'd better help Lisa bury T-Bone. I'll get the trenching tool from the packs. What do we do with the lion?"

"I'll drag him away from camp while you're digging a hole for T-Bone," Slocum said. "I'll saddle up Chief. Be back in a minute." He strode toward the picketed mounts.

Chief didn't like the idea of getting close to the cat; his nostrils flared, the whites of his eyes showed, and his ears never left the lion's corpse. It was a natural fear deeply ingrained in most horses, and especially in the mountain-bred Nez Percé palouse strain.

It took Slocum a good five minutes to coax the spotted sorrel into position, and another twenty minutes to slip a loop around the lion's back leg and drag the dead animal a hundred yards away from camp. Slocum left the limp tawny body downstream, but well away from the creek. There, the breeze wouldn't carry cat smell to the still-nervous horses. And the cat's carcass wouldn't contaminate the water down-creek.

He returned to camp in time for T-Bone's funeral, and stood with his arm around Lisa. No one spoke until Waggoner shoveled the last bit of dirt over the small mound. Finally, Lisa said, "I'm going to miss him. He was a good dog. He gave his life for a friend."

"Yes, he was. And I'll miss him too—but more than that, I'll thank him for what he did here." Slocum led her from the grave back to camp, where the coffeepot steamed on its flat rock beside the fire.

Satisfied that Lisa had regained her composure, Slocum tended Chief and picketed the gelding. When he strode back to the campfire, Lisa handed him a cup of the fresh coffee. The warmth of the first sip chased the lingering chill from Slocum's gut and eased the nip of the rapidly cooling night air.

"I won't be getting much sleep the rest of the night anyway," Lisa said, "so I decided it was a good time to make some coffee." She pulled a pint of bourbon from a saddlebag. "With a sweetener." She added a splash of liquor to her own cup, then a dollop each for Slocum and Waggoner. She lifted her cup.

"Here's to T-Bone," she said huskily.

"To T-Bone," the two men added.

Lisa's gaze slowly swept the valley, the tall mountains. "He has a nice resting place." She sighed heavily. "What now, gentlemen?"

Slocum said, "We'll move on come first light. We've got some men to find. Dan, you said you know where we'll cut Deschamp's trail?"

"I'm reasonably sure."

Lisa's brows lifted in a question. "What trail? Won't their tracks have been long ago washed out or drifted over?"

Waggoner nodded. "We won't find tracks as such, at least not for several days and many miles. But even out here, in this big country, it's difficult for a band of men to move a remuda of stolen horses without attracting some attention. They'll need food, supplies, water." He took a swallow of coffee and stared toward past the range of mountains toward the northeast. "I'd say now they're probably somewhere in southern Colorado. They will most likely sell some of the horses there."

"Why there?"

Slocum said, "Because, Lisa, that's where most of the dealers in stolen horses are these days."

"Will we be able to get our—your—horses back, Slocum?"

"One way or another."

Lisa turned to Waggoner. "If we don't catch up with them there, Dan, where will they go?"

"The Cimarron Strip. It's wild country, rough and broken. It's also totally lawless. Few men who carry badges go into the Strip. And even though it seems foreboding to the eye, if a man knows where to look he can find excellent water, good grass, and an abundance of wild game for the pot." He paused for a moment to sip at his coffee. "If a man doesn't get killed in the Strip, he can live rather well there."

"But it's a big country, Dan. What if we miss them?"

Waggoner shrugged. "We look elsewhere. We have time.

We'll find them sooner or later. If not sooner, then later. Because I know where Deschamp is eventually going to turn up. And I—we—will be waiting."

June Deschamp sat at the heavy, worn oak table, a drink at his elbow, and tried not to move his aching shoulder any more often than he had to. He wondered if the damn thing was ever going to quit hurting. Sometimes it was a sharp pain; sometimes just a dull sting, like a thousand little panfish nibbling at a bait. The little fish were nibbling now.

The sting deepened the frown on his face. It had been two weeks since the gunhawk called Slocum had gotten that slug into him, and the chest muscles below his collarbone still hurt. The son of a bitch with the black hair and green eyes was going to pay for that, Deschamp again promised himself. He was going to pay soon. He forced the thought of Slocum from his mind and studied the man seated across the table from him.

The baby-faced Eldon Lucas's round, smooth cheeks creased in a grin below mischievous blue eyes. A lot of people had mistaken Lucas for a soft, harmless, and genial man over the years. The mistake got them buried. Lucas was a snake with a handgun. He had gotten rich dealing in horses, and he wasn't especially particular whether the animals came with a bill of sale or not.

Lucas hoisted his whiskey with his right hand, a gesture not lost on Deschamp. Lucas was left-handed. Fast left-handed. Which was why Deschamp's handgun lay in his own lap, cocked and ready.

"Here's to horses and the men who buy 'em," Lucas said, hoisting his glass.

"And them what sells 'em," Deschamp said. He tossed back a swallow of whiskey without taking his eyes from the man across the table. "Forty a head the best you can do, Eldon? Those palouse ponies in particular ought to be worth twice that much apiece."

"Forty's a fair offer," Lucas said with a boyish, engaging smile. "There's two spavined horses, one outlaw plug, and a barren mare in that remuda of yours. Those four together aren't worth a dime on the market. I got to show a profit if I'm going to stay in business." Lucas winked at Deschamp. "Besides, June, you and me both know you didn't invest just a whole hell of a lot of money in any of those horses."

Deschamp sighed and forced a grin. "Guess you've got me by the *cojones* again, Eldon. I swear, you skin me to the bone ever time we do business. Don't know why I keep comin' back here."

"I do, June." Lucas chuckled. "Easy money and no questions asked."

"I'd argue with the 'easy' part some." Deschamp put his glass down on the scarred table and lifted an eyebrow. "It ain't that I don't like your company, Eldon, but me and the boys need to be headin' on. How's about fetchin' that cash now?"

Lucas nodded, rose, and strode to the blocky Wells Fargo strongbox sunk into the solid stone wall alongside the fireplace.

Deschamp ran his tongue over his chapped, cracked lips. There wasn't much spit in his mouth, and his gut tickled. There weren't many men June Deschamp was afraid of. Lucas was one of them. Right near the top of the list.

Deschamp all but held his breath as Lucas turned his back to fiddle with the strongbox combination. June's fingers curled around the butt of the cocked six-gun in his lap. Sweat beaded his forehead. Deschamp knew he would get only one chance at Lucas; he wouldn't risk even a backshot if he didn't need more traveling money than the horses would bring. And after another couple of weeks, he wouldn't be needing Lucas's services anyway.

The door of the small safe swung open on oiled hinges.

"Well, now, let's see," Lucas said, reaching inside, "that was forty a head for fifteen—"

Deschamp's slug caught Lucas between the shoulder blades, almost drove his head into the open safe. Deschamp frantically thumbed the hammer, fired twice more. Lucas's body jerked under the impact of each slug. Still, the baby-faced man managed to half turn, a revolver suddenly appearing in his left hand. The handgun swung toward Deschamp. June emptied his pistol into Lucas.

Lucas's mouth opened and closed, like a catfish out of water, a couple of times. The weapon in his hand wavered. Then the muzzle slowly dropped.

"Damn—you—June—" Lucas said, the words gurgling through his own blood, "—never expected—you—backshoot me—" Lucas's knees buckled. He slid down the wall, his blood leaving a red smear on the stones.

Through the ringing in his ears from the concussion of muzzle blasts in the confined space, Deschamp heard the quick volley of rifle shots outside, the answering bark of revolvers, another series of rifle shots. His boys had taken care of Lucas's four hired guns according to plan.

After a brief silence, a single rifle blast outside signaled the end of the ambush. Deschamp's fingers trembled as he ejected the spent cartridges and fumbled fresh loads into his revolver. He never moved his gaze from the crumpled form on the floor, half expecting the moonfaced man to come up shooting.

"June?"

The single word from the doorway jarred Deschamp. His muscles jerked involuntarily. The startled reaction raked fire across his shoulder and chest. He spun on a heel. Bud stood in the doorway, the Bisley Colt in hand.

"What?" Deschamp barked.

"You okay? You nail that horse trader?"

"I nailed him, all right. Dammit, Bud, don't you *never* sneak up on me again like that, or I'll plug you sure before I know who it is." Deschamp holstered his handgun, as much to cover the nervous twitch in his fingers as to stow the weapon. "Wait outside, Bud. I'll be out in a minute."

Deschamp waited until the door closed behind the young gunman, then stepped gingerly over Lucas's body. He sighed in relief at the sight of bundles of cash inside the safe. He grabbed a gunnysack from beside the fireplace, dumped out the handful of potatoes in it, and started stuffing cash into the bag. He didn't know how much he had, and he didn't stop to count it just now; he wanted to get the hell out of there. Before Eldon Lucas got up and started shooting . . .

Deschamp wasn't able to relax until the Lucas ranch lay nearly nine hours behind him to the northwest, across rolling to flat grasslands broken only by an occasional creek or shallow arroyo.

In southeastern Colorado, the main threat was no longer Indians, as it had been when Deschamp first passed through the arid region. The Indians had been moved onto reservations years ago. Out here now, the threat was water. More specifically, the lack of it. Horses and men alike could live a surprisingly long time without food, but not long at all without water.

Deschamp lifted himself in the stirrups, peered toward the horizon, and grunted in satisfaction. The gray-green clump of cottonwood and chinaberry trees was within a mile of where he remembered it to be. Despite the numbness in his saddle-pounded butt and the throbbing ache in his shoulder, he was satisfied. Not many men could navigate the flatlands of prairie grass on memory and instinct and get that close to the best-watered campsite in a hundred miles.

Deschamp settled back into the saddle and turned to the squarely built man riding alongside.

"Camp's right up ahead, Curly. Less'n an hour from now, we'll be settled in at Osage Springs."

Curly shifted the chew in his cheek and spat. A few drops of brown spittle dribbled down the right side of his chin. "How come it be called Osage Springs? Any Osages there?"

"Used to be one of their favorite hangouts, but they're not around any longer. All good Injuns now. Dead or on reservations over in Injun Territory."

Curly's eyes narrowed. A dirty thumb unconsciously traced the thick scar tissue on his neck beneath his right jawbone. "Damn shame. I ain't kilt me near enough Osages to get even yet."

"Could have been worse, Curly," Deschamp said. "Could of been Comanches that got you. Even worse'n that, Apaches. Osages was downright civilized Injuns compared to them."

"Civilized, my ass," Curly rumbled. "Drag a man half to death behind a two-hoss hitch, just on account of some little Injun cunt claimin' I raped her."

"You did, Curly. Just like that little Nez Percé split-tail up on the Lapwai. You was lucky the one you got caught rapin' was Osage. Them Comanch and 'Paches know ways to keep a man wishin' he could die for days."

"Well, I ain't forgettin' it, that's for damn sure."

Deschamp grinned at his surly, thick-shouldered companion. "Just a little longer, Curly, you'll have all the money you need to go huntin' Osages. If there's any of 'em left. Unless Mexico, willin' women, and fine tequila sounds better to you."

"Any Osage Injuns in Mexico?"

"Not as I know about. Could be some, though. Lot of American redskins went 'cross the Rio 'stead of goin' to reservations." Deschamp twisted in the saddle to check the remuda strung out behind the two lead riders, and winced as the movement brought a fresh yelp of pain from the tender shoulder.

The horses were beginning to show the miles, stumbling often, heads down, ears flopped, flanks gaunt. Even the tough spotted-butt horses that had come all the way from the Lapwai had lost a little bounce in their steps.

Three men rode on each side of the strung-out remuda; behind the horses, thick, choking dust swirled around Bud and two other younger riders. Bud would bitch like hell at having to ride drag again tomorrow, Deschamp knew, but the kid was going to eat dust until he earned his way out of bringing up the rear.

"What's your figurin', June?" Curly asked after a time. "Lay up here a few days, then head on down to the Pease country? 'Pears to me there ain't no rush, what with all the grub and whiskey we got from Lucas's place."

The question irritated Deschamp a bit. Curly was the only one left of the original bunch who knew about the payroll money stashed on the Pease. And that was one man too many who knew. Even if he didn't know exactly where it was buried. Deschamp tried to hide his aggravation behind a forced grin. "We'll rest the horses a day or two. But before we head for the Pease, we're gonna drop these ponies off with an old partner of mine down in the Cimarron Strip. Might even do us some huntin'."

"Huntin'?"

"More like waitin'. Keep scouts out on our backtrail. Let that bastard Slocum and his buddy with the buffalo gun ride right into the biggest damn bushwackin' they've ever seen."

Curly frowned and spat. "Reckon that's a good idea, June? Seems like a waste of time, when all we got to do is ride to them red bluffs, pick up our cash, and haul ass for Mexico."

Deschamp shook his head. "No, Curly. I'm gonna get that Slocum son of a bitch first."

Curly instinctively glanced around. "Reckon he's trackin' us, June?"

"Bet on it."

"How do we know he ain't waitin' up ahead of us?"

The question triggered a chill in Deschamp's gut. Unlikely as it was, Slocum and that bastard with the buffalo gun could be lining them up in their sights right now. He pushed the thought away. "Not with the lead we had on 'em, Curly," he said with more conviction than he felt.

"So what we do once they catch up with us?"

"Don't you fret none on that, Curly. I got it all figured out." The lie fell easily from Deschamp's tongue, even while he inwardly cursed Curly for bringing it up. He had been so busy hurting and hating he hadn't even come up with a plan. Deschamp forced a grin. "I'll lay it out for you and the boys when we're ready to trap 'em."

Curly grunted, satisfied. "Whatever you say, June."

"One thing I say is that I ain't spendin' the rest of my life lookin' over my shoulder. Not when I could be sittin' easy and enjoyin' all that whiskey and señoritas that army money can buy us down south of the border." Deschamp squinted into the distance, toward the Chama country. "And that's why, partner, we got to get him first. . . ."

Slocum spotted trouble about the same time the spotted sorrel did.

Chief raised his head, ears perked forward. In the distance beyond the low rise, black dots circled in the sky. Buzzards wheeling, dropping down, rising again, meant only one thing. Death. And with that many carrion eaters in one place, it wasn't just a steer carcass or dead mule up ahead.

He reined in, reached for a cheroot, and fired the smoke as Lisa and Waggoner rode up beside him, the packhorses following on loose lead.

"What is it?" Lisa asked.

Slocum dragged the rich, heavy smoke into his lungs and exhaled slowly. "Up ahead, over the rise. See anything?"

Lisa pushed her hat back and peered into the distance. "Birds," she said after a moment.

"Not just birds. Buzzards. A lot of them."

Lisa frowned. "Something dead?"

"A lot of somethings, Miss Barnes," Waggoner said solemnly. "Perhaps you would prefer to remain here while Slocum and I check it out?"

Lisa shot a quick, hard glance at Waggoner. "For Christ's sake, Dan, will you stop trying to protect my delicate female sensitivity? I'm not going to swoon on you, or come down with the vapors. Dammit, I'm one of the boys now. Let's go." She started to knee the big bay horse into motion.

"Hold up a minute, Lisa," Slocum said. "We can't go riding up there all bunched up. No need to make a nice, easy target for anyone. Dan?"

Waggoner nodded and slid the long rifle from its sheath. "We'll hobble the pack animals here and spread out in a skirmish line. I'll take the center, Lisa the left flank, you the right, if that's satisfactory.''

Slocum nodded. ''Sounds solid to me.'' He swung down, strapped hobbles around the ankles of the pack animals, and stood for a moment, staring toward the blur of buzzards in the distance.

''Just out of curiosity, Slocum, where the hell are we?'' Lisa asked.

''About halfway between the Two Butte and Cimarron Rivers,'' Slocum said. ''That's the Lucas place up ahead. Lucas is the biggest dealer in stolen livestock in four states and two territories.''

Lisa frowned. ''Think the horses are still there?''

''I hope so. We're only two or three days behind Deschamp. Maybe Lucas hasn't had time to move the stolen mounts out yet.'' Slocum palmed his Colt and slipped a sixth cartridge into the weapon. He doubted they would be riding into a gunfight— the buzzards up ahead hinted anything like that was already over—but it paid to be ready anyway. Slocum swung into the saddle. ''Let's go.''

Lisa drifted off to the left, Slocum the right, and they settled into a rough line some fifty yards on each side of Waggoner. They rode without speaking or shouting, the silence broken only by the moan of wind through prairie grass, the creak of saddle leather, or the occasional jangle of bit.

As he rode, Slocum admitted Waggoner had surprised him. The former Yankee officer had said they would cross Deschamp's trail near the abandoned trading post on the Purgatoire River northeast of Raton Pass in Colorado.

He had called it within a mile. Deschamp had followed the Purgatoire northeast for forty miles, then cut cross-country through flat, waterless prairie toward the Lucas place. Slocum idly wondered how Waggoner had managed to climb so completely into Deschamp's head. Slocum thought he knew the outlaw well. Waggoner could read him like a book, it seemed.

Slocum reined in a hundred yards short of the ranch house and studied the layout with care.

Buzzards screeched and hissed, feathers ruffled in quarrels, over three dark, huddled shapes on and around the sagging front porch. Others ripped and tore at another mass along the east side of the house. He could hear other scavengers behind the structure, near the corral.

There was no other sign of life.

He chanced a glance to his left. Waggoner also had reined in, rifle at the ready. Lisa pulled Duke to a stop. Sunlight winked from the barrel of the .45-70 lying across her thighs.

Slocum waited several minutes until he was satisfied that no ambush awaited, then kneed the nervous sorrel toward the house. Most of the buzzards swirled away in a shower of black feathers at his approach. A few lingered, wings flared, hissing at the intruders, unwilling to leave a meal.

Slocum fought back the urge to drive slugs into a couple of the big birds. Until he knew for sure what awaited, he would save every cartridge.

It didn't take long to figure out what had happened.

Slocum knelt beside one of the dead men beside the porch. Or what was left of him. Scavenger birds, coyotes, and rats had plucked the eyes out and stripped most of the flesh from the slightly built man's face and hands. A Smith & Wesson top-break revolver lay beside the dead man's outstretched hand. Slocum picked it up and checked the cylinder. Only one round had been fired. Slocum waved for Waggoner to come in.

"An effective ambush," Waggoner said calmly as he swung from the McClellan saddle to study another torn body lying beside the front door. An old Henry rimfire rifle, the action levered open, lay near the corpse. "Looks like they didn't have much of a chance to fight back."

Slocum nodded silently, his gut churning at the sights and smells. Ma Nature's cleanup crew made a hell of a mess before they finished the job. He glanced up as Lisa strode around the corner of the house, the Schofield now in her hand, leading Duke. The big chestnut gelding's eyes were wide, its nostrils flared, front feet dancing nervously. Lisa's eyes were almost as wide as Duke's, her face drawn and pale.

"There's another one out back," she said shakily. "Good Lord, I never realized what buzzards could do to a body." She shuddered once, then squared her shoulders. "The corrals are empty. Not a horse left there. Or in the barn either. The corral gate's open."

"I'm sorry you had to see this, Miss Barnes." Waggoner's lips drew into a thin, hard line. He turned to Slocum. "I don't know any of these men. They're not Deschamp's troops."

Slocum winced at the foul odor from the bodies and the rank, musky scent of carrion eaters. "I know some of them. Lucas's men. You two stay out here and keep an eye out. I'm going to check out the house."

He looped Chief's reins over a sagging porch rail, stepped between two bloody, half-eaten corpses, and toed the door open.

Eldon Lucas slumped against the blood-smeared wall, sightless eyes staring at Slocum. Dark stains spread from two holes in his shirtfront near the heart. At least the scavengers hadn't been able to get at Lucas.

The body was bloated a bit, but still intact. Slocum slipped a hand under the dead man's shoulder, leaned him away from the wall, and saw at a glance why there was so much blood on his front. He had been shot in the back, from close range. The safe above Lucas's body stood open and empty except for a few papers that fluttered in the light breeze from the open door.

Slocum made a quick tour of the house. Satisfied that no one else was in the building, he lowered the hammer of his Colt and holstered the weapon. He stepped outside, nostrils rebelling against the stench of blood, ripped intestines, and death.

"Lucas won't be buying any more stolen horses," Slocum said. He nodded toward the door. "He's dead. Shot at least twice in the back. He was a tough bird, though. Managed to turn and draw before he was hit three or four more times in the chest."

"Deschamp?" Lisa asked.

"It had to be, Miss Barnes," Waggoner said. "Judging from the condition of the bodies, we're a day and a half, possibly two days behind him."

"Lucas's safe is cleaned out," Slocum said. "Looks like June wanted more than Lucas offered." He glanced at Lisa. "You say there are no horses?"

She shook her head. "I'm no tracker, but I saw a lot of hoofprints headed that way." She tilted her head toward the southwest. Slocum noticed that most of the color had returned to Lisa's face. She stared for a moment at the torn bodies. "Should we bury them?"

Slocum shook his head. "We can't spare the time. Besides, not a one of these men deserve burial. They're hardcases, killers. Leave them for the coyotes and buzzards." He untied Chief and swung into the saddle. "Let's go. We've got some tracking to do."

# 8

Slocum knelt on the sandy north bank of the sluggish stream and studied the tracks in the fading light. After a moment, he glanced at Waggoner, who stood beside him, and shook his head.

"Unless I've forgotten everything I know about tracking, we're losing ground," Waggoner said, a touch of worry in his tone. "What do you make it, Slocum? Two days?"

"At least," Slocum said heavily. "Maybe more. Deschamp's moving mighty fast, considering he's trailing two dozen horses. I expected him to stop here. Any sane man would."

"No one ever said June Deschamp was sane," Waggoner said, brows furrowed. "If I remember correctly, this is the only decent water for at least forty miles."

"More like fifty to Osage Springs," Slocum said. "What little water there is between here and there isn't fit to drink. Loaded with gypsum and salts bad enough to colic horses. What it does to men is worse than dysentery."

"So what do we do now?"

Slocum stood, flexed the weight of miles from his shoulders, and loosened his hat, which had been tugged down tight against the gusting southwest wind. "We might as well camp here. And see if we can guess which way Deschamp's headed."

"Can't we just follow the tracks?" Lisa asked. She was still astride the big bay. The horse's ears were perked toward the water, its flanks gaunt. Lather frothed from beneath the breast-band, cinches, and rear skirt of her saddle.

"There won't be any tracks by tomorrow morning the way this wind is blowing, Lisa. By now, Deschamp's in the sandhill country to the south. Even fresh tracks drift over in an hour out there. Our horses are done in. They need rest."

"They're not the only ones," Lisa said. "I think my butt's stuck to this damn saddle, and I'm not sure my knees work any more. Give me a hand, Slocum?"

It was the first time since they'd left Chama that Lisa had asked for help. He reached up for her. Lisa all but fell from the saddle. Her knees buckled as her boots touched solid ground for the first time in hours. She stood for a moment leaning against Slocum. He didn't mind. Finally, she gathered herself, eased away from him, and massaged her buttocks.

"Need help with that?" Slocum asked with a sly wink.

Lisa winked back. "Later, maybe. Right now, I think we'd better water the horses and set up camp." She shook a finger at Slocum in mock scolding. "You men sure don't take very good care of your women. In case it's slipped your mind, we haven't eaten in more than twelve hours. I'm hungry enough to eat a badger."

Slocum's own stomach rumbled at the idea. He had simply forgotten to call a halt for grub. Following a hot trail kept a man's mind off minor details like that. He nodded toward the low cut in the south riverbank. "We'll camp over there. Should have some protection from the wind."

The sunset had faded to a dull, tan-colored wash laundered by lingering dust by the time the three hunters had eaten their fill. Trail-camp fare wasn't for the timid of appetite. Thick slabs of bacon piled atop fried potatoes, and Slocum's specialty, pan-fried cornbread, washed down by a pot of coffee, sat heavy on the stomach. A fresh pot of coffee steamed at the edge of the fire, moments away from boiling.

It wasn't the best of campsites, but Slocum had been in worse. The fifteen-foot-tall bluffs of the semicircular cut in the creek bank at their backs blocked the wind, and kept the fire from flattening out or spitting sparks into the dry grass along the riverbank. An owl hooted from a stand of cottonwoods upstream, awakening to the night's hunt. A distant coyote's yip and wail answered the owl's sleepy call.

Lisa leaned back, let loose a most unladylike belch, and patted her belly. "God, I ate too much again. I'll weigh as much as a blooded mare at this rate. All I need now is a bath. I smell like a she-goat.''

Waggoner nodded downstream. ''There's a pool deep enough for bathing just beyond the bend, past the wild plum thicket. It will give you privacy, Miss Barnes.''

Lisa leaned close to Slocum and whispered, ''Maybe privacy isn't the most important thing.''

Waggoner glanced up idly, overhearing her statement, no expression in his eyes. If the man felt any resentment or jealousy at all, Slocum mused, he hid it well. The thought flickered through his mind that maybe Waggoner's tastes didn't include women. He pushed the idea aside as an absurdity.

''You two go ahead,'' Waggoner said. ''I'll handle camp cleanup. Don't muddy the water. When you get back, it's my turn. The only real problem with being on the trail is the grubbiness and whisker stubble accumulated over the miles. I've never been able to cope with that well.''

''Me either.'' Slocum ran a hand across his chin and winced at the raspy sound. ''If I could raise colts as quick as I grow whiskers, I'd be a rich man inside a year.''

Lisa tugged at his sleeve. ''Shut up, Slocum, and come on.''

Slocum paused long enough to grab his razor and pick up his rifle, then fell into step beside Lisa. Despite the miles and the stiffness she must feel, he thought, she moved with an easy, relaxed gait, light on her feet.

He stood at the edge of the pool for a moment, senses tuned to the night sounds, and heard nothing to cause worry. He propped the rifle against a chunk of driftwood at water's edge, draped his pistol belt over the log, and straightened.

Lisa already had her hat and boots off, fingers working at the buttons of her shirt. She shrugged out of the garment, stripped down her trousers, and stood naked at the water's edge, her dark hair almost black in the faint twilight and ruffling in the breeze. She stood for a moment staring at him, a teasing smile lifting her full lips.

''Well, Slocum? What do you think?''

Slocum swallowed, felt the heat in his groin, and grinned back at her. ''I think your nipples are hard.''

''Probably just the cool night air. What else could possibly cause such a thing? Now, will you please get the hell out of those clothes before I pounce on you?''

Slocum lifted a hand. ''No pouncing until I've shaved,

woman. Whiskers drain my strength. Promise?''

''Promise. You'll need all the strength you can round up in a few minutes. Riding makes me horny.'' She stepped gingerly into the pool. Her breath whistled between her teeth. ''Dan was right. The water's a bit chilly.''

Slocum didn't notice the chill as he stripped and stepped into the water, which came up almost to his waist. He was too busy noticing Lisa. She played in the pool like a schoolgirl, ducking beneath the surface, emerging to shake her head from side to side. Beads of water dribbled down her breasts with their large, dark nipples, trickled along her rib cage to the narrowing of her waist, and speckled dots of light on the thick, black triangle of hair between her legs.

Lisa glanced at Slocum and frowned playfully. ''Don't just stand there like a stump, dammit. Get yourself cleaned up.'' She waded to his side in the thigh-deep water. ''I'll help.''

Slocum managed to bathe with no serious complications, but he soon found out it was a bit difficult to shave. Not having a mirror wasn't the problem. It was the feel of two firm breasts pressed against his back, their erect tips stroking his skin. And the arms that circled his waist and the hands that toyed with his crotch. He nicked himself a couple of times with the straight razor before the job was done. He tossed the razor onto his clothes at the edge of the pool.

''Turn around,'' Lisa said.

Slocum turned and took her in his arms. Her lips parted to meet his. Her tongue flicked against his. Her throaty moan seemed to vibrate against his lips as his hand stroked, then cupped, the smooth flesh of her breast. His fingers crept upward to fondle her left nipple. She shuddered at the touch, but not from the cold; her right hand cupped his scrotum, then closed around the base of his shaft.

Lisa broke the kiss, tilted her head back, and grinned lecherously at Slocum. ''Ever screw standing up in a pool of cold water, cowboy?'' Her words were husky and low, her breathing rapid; Slocum felt the pounding of her heart beneath the smooth skin of her breast.

''Not that I recall.''

''Me either.'' She lifted her right leg, hooking it around his hips. ''But I'll bet it can be done.'' She arched her pelvis against his, guided him into her, and gasped aloud as he eased his shaft deeper into her tight warmth. The wetness he felt inside her wasn't from the water. She shuddered again as his hips began to move, almost of their own accord; her breath came in short, choppy gasps.

"Jesus, Slocum"—the words were all but inaudible, though her lips brushed his ear—"I never felt—oh, Christ!" Her inner muscles went into spasms, squeezing, releasing, squeezing his shaft again and again, until Slocum could hold back no longer. He felt the pressure build in his testicles, the growing tightness as his shaft swelled even more—and then the deep, almost painful throbs of release. He almost cried out as his fluid spurted deep inside her, his shaft pulsing.

Lisa did cry out, softly, her inner muscles milking him dry, as she came for the second time.

Finally, she leaned against him, spent; he felt his shaft begin to wilt inside her. Slocum gasped in a lungful of air, suddenly aware he had been holding his breath during the explosive orgasm. Her leg was still tightly locked around his hips; he felt her hand slip beneath their bellies and the quick, deliberate contraction of her vaginal muscles, as if to hold him inside her. He let his hand drift to her breast, toying with the erect nipple. After several moments, she sighed.

"Let go of my tit, you horny bastard," she said.

"Let go of my prick and I'll let go of your tit."

"Don't want to."

"I don't either."

"But," she said with a wistful sigh, "if you get stirred up again, I'll keep you here half the night. Which wouldn't be at all bad, except Dan probably would like to bathe sometime before sunrise."

Reluctantly, Slocum moved his hand. Lisa tilted her head back and smiled, her eyes misty. "By damn, it *can* be done."

"What?"

"Screwing standing up in a pool of water." She kissed him, a quick, moist peck on the lips, then drew away. "Guess I wasn't as tired as I thought, Slocum. Son of a bitch, but you're good. I'll sleep like a baby tonight. But for now, we'd better go. I need a smoke and a drink in the worst way. Do you always smoke after sex, Slocum?"

"Never looked, but with you, probably—you're the hottest woman I've ever had."

She chuckled. "That's what I like about you, Slocum. You're such a romantic bastard. Let's go."

Waggoner glanced up as the two strode back into camp. He had a small, thin book in his hand, and had turned his body so that the light from the campfire illuminated the pages. "Was the water cold?"

"Not that I noticed," Lisa said casually. "We didn't muddy it up. It's all yours."

Waggoner placed the book on his bedroll, rose, and strode off into the darkness. Lisa rolled two cigarettes as Slocum pulled a quart of whiskey from the possibles sack and poured a couple of hefty shots into two coffee cups.

They sat silently, smoking and drinking, side by side in the peaceful night sounds. After a time, Lisa sighed. "Thanks again, Slocum."

"What for?"

"Making me feel like a woman."

"The pleasure," he said solemnly, "was all mine."

"Bullshit. What's next?"

"Hanging upside down from a tree limb, like a couple of possums?"

She chuckled. "Now that I don't think even *we* could manage." The soft laugh died away. "Seriously, Slocum. What do we do now? About June Deschamp, I mean."

Slocum sighed. "Get together with Dan and see if we can come up with an educated guess. Roll the dice and hope we catch up with him before we run out of supplies."

Lisa stubbed out her smoke and leaned back on her elbows. "We have to catch up with him, Slocum. And when the son of a bitch is dead, my healing will be complete. Yours?"

"No. Never complete, Lisa. But when I take two scalps back to Lapwai country where they belong, the hurt will ease some."

They sat in silence, smoking and passing a pint bottle back and forth, until Waggoner returned. Lisa handed Waggoner the pint. "There's more in the possibles bag, Dan," she said, "Feel free to empty that one."

When Waggoner had downed the rest of the whiskey and rolled himself a smoke, Lisa cocked an eyebrow at him. She said, "Dan, it's really none of my business, but I'm curious. What did you do before the war?"

Waggoner sighed. "That was so long ago I hadn't even thought about it in years. I was an instructor at a small military academy back in Maine."

"Weapons and tactics?" Slocum asked.

"And English, literature, and math, Slocum. As I said, it was a small school. Emphasis on small."

Lisa snubbed out her smoke, the firelight dancing from hope and excitement in her eyes. "A teacher? Dan, could you—would you—I know it's a lot to ask, but . . ."

"But what, Miss Barnes?" Waggoner prompted.

"It's embarrassing to say it." She took in a deep breath. "Dan, I can't read or write, and can barely do numbers. Could you teach me?"

A spark of light flickered in Waggoner's normally expressionless eyes. "It would be my pleasure. I haven't done anything constructive like that in years."

"When can we start?" Lisa made no attempt to conceal her eagerness.

"Right now, if you're not too tired."

"Out here? We don't have any supplies."

"Sure we do," Waggoner said. "We've got a stick for chalk and a patch of sand for a slate. That's all we need to have you learn the alphabet and how the letters are written and sounded. And I have one book with me. It's boring—the Army manual of officer conduct—but it's full of words."

Lisa shifted her gaze to Slocum. "Can we? Start now, I mean? Would you mind?"

Slocum smiled at her. "No, I wouldn't mind in the least." He picked up his rifle. "I'll stand first watch. You two get busy. Make a smart woman out of her, Dan."

"She already is that," Waggoner said. He brushed a smooth area into the sand and picked up a twig. He glanced at Slocum, the excitement in his eyes mirroring the look on Lisa's face. "We'll find out soon if I've forgotten how to teach."

"I doubt you have, Dan. That's a talent that doesn't fade." He shouldered his rifle. "I'll see you two later," he said as he strode into the darkness.

Slocum worked his way to a vantage point on the riverbank and settled down to stand watch. It wasn't really necessary to have a picket out, he knew, but he didn't want to be in the way of Lisa's learning.

And he needed time to think. Deschamp *had* to be headed for Osage Springs. There was no other option, if the butcher wanted to save his men and horses. Osage Springs could be a fortress; it could also be a trap.

Slocum needed a plan to make it a trap for June Deschamp.

• • •

Deschamp leaned back against the trunk of an ancient cotton-wood tree, its limbs twisted by wind, its crown slivered and blackened by lightning strikes, and downed the last of the whis-key in his tin cup.

The Osage Springs camp might not have the women and other comforts of the Brown Palace in Denver, but to Des-champ, the tree-lined splash of green in the middle of nowhere had never looked better. A half day's rest had partly eased the weight of miles and lack of sleep from the men and horses. Even Deschamp's shoulder felt better. The tenderness of new scar tissue had given way to the itch of healing flesh.

Deschamp had another itch. One that couldn't be scratched, wouldn't let him completely relax. He had kept his best men rotating as scouts, ranging far behind the main force, scouring the backtrail. There had been no sign of the man named Slocum or his buffalo-gun partner. But he knew the long-legged son of a bitch was out there. Deschamp could all but smell him. The feeling left a knot in his gut.

The other men didn't share that queasy feeling, Deschamp thought as his gaze drifted around the campsite. Two stretched out on blankets in the warm afternoon sunshine. Another pair had a nickel-ante knockout poker game going on a blanket spread under a chinaberry tree. Another lazed in the saddle a hundred yards downstream, watching the horses graze in the rich, green grama grass that grew along the banks of the spring-fed creek.

Deschamp's eyes narrowed as he stared at a slender form beneath an overhang halfway up the steep sandstone bluff that formed the north side of the canyon. Sunlight glinted from sil-ver conchas and the hunting knife in Bud's hand as the kid carved his initials in the middle of a symbol of some sort, left behind by some long-ago Indian. If Bud had that much energy left, Deschamp decided, it was time to yank some of the piss and vinegar out of him.

"Hey, Jenkins," Deschamp called, "come here a minute."

A tall, spare man with one cloudy eye and humped nose rose from his blankets and ambled to the tree. "Yeah, Boss?"

"Saddle up and take Curly's place on scout. I want you to stay there a spell, on account of you're the best scout and tracker I've got. You spot anybody or cut sign, hightail it back here pronto. Take Bud with you. See if you can teach the worthless little turd something about readin' sign.''

Jenkins nodded. ''Will do, Boss. How long you want us to stay out as pickets?''

Deschamp winced at the reference to pickets. It brought back too many memories of army days, with some damn pup of a lieutenant yelling at him over something that didn't amount to squat.

''Take enough grub for a couple days. We'll camp here for a spell until the ponies get over that trip through the sandhills. I'll be gone a while. When I get back, I'll have Curly pick a man and spell you on watch.''

''You leaving?''

Deschamp grunted an assent. ''I'll be headin' out at daylight tomorrow. Got to call on my old army buddy at the Slash Y and let him know we've got a cavvy needs watchin' for a spell. If a bunch of us just ride up on him without him knowin' we're comin', he might cut loose on us—and the redheaded bastard can flat shoot. You and Bud scout out at least three, four miles back.''

Jenkins nodded and turned to leave.

Deschamp added, ''Watch out for Bud. The kid's dumb as a stump and half crazy to boot. Don't let him get you into no trouble. Lay a six-gun barrel over his ear if he gets to actin' bullheaded and stupid.''

''Will do, Boss,'' the thin man said. He strode off toward the bluff to lay the word on Bud. Deschamp watched him go. He felt better about things now. If there was anybody out there, Jenkins would find them. He might be one-eyed, but that one eye saw things other men missed. And Jenkins was one of just two men in the whole outfit Deschamp halfway trusted. Curly was the other. It was going to be a damn shame to have to kill them both once they got to Mexico with that army money, Deschamp thought. He didn't dwell much on the matter. It was his money. He didn't intend to share a dime of it. With anybody.

Getting rid of Curly wouldn't be a problem, Deschamp figured. The dumb bastard trusted him. Jenkins might be a tad trickier to take. The one-eyed man was a heller with that old beat-up six-shooter he carried, and he always paid attention to what was going on around him. Maybe in his sleep . . .

Deschamp pushed the thoughts aside. There'd be time to worry about that later.

Right now, he wanted the bastard on the spotted-butt horse. He wanted him dead.

Slocum reined Chief to a stop at the notch of a narrow trail leading into the rough, broken valley below, and studied the rugged country spread out before him.

Deep washes and arroyos gouged tortuous paths through the almost bare red soil. The only spots of green in the ragged land were stunted cedars clinging to the crests of narrow ridges and an occasional patch of Spanish dagger plants.

Slocum saw no sign of life. Not even a coyote, quail, or deer moved in the barren land. No hawks or buzzards circled in the washed-out blue sky overhead.

The first time Slocum had ridden up to the edge of the Cimarron badlands known to Mexicans and Indians as Vale de Muerto—Valley of Death—years ago, he'd had the sensation that he looked out upon an alien land, a place tortured by unknown forces where no man had ever trod.

That sensation was only slightly less strong now.

"My God," Lisa said softly as she and Waggoner reined in beside Slocum, "It's beautiful."

Slocum glanced at her in surprise, then turned his attention back to the mazelike ridges and deep, twisting arroyo slashes. In a way, Lisa was right. A hundred shades of red and brown lanced by light streaks of caliche and sandstone and almost black stripes of volcanic stone spread before his gaze. Shapes and shadows seem to change by the moment, the land twisting and writhing like a thing alive.

"I suppose it is, in its own way," Slocum said after a moment, "but a diamondback rattler is also a handsome creature. In *its* own way." He sighed. "Either of them can kill, Lisa. The snake or the badlands. The snake kills more quickly. Get lost in this country, and it's a slow death from starvation and lack of water. There isn't a fresh spring or flowing creek in the whole area except in the rainiest years. This hasn't been one of the rainy times."

Lisa sat the saddle for a moment in silence, soaking in the vista before her. "When you put it that way, Slocum, it looks a bit different. Should we go around?"

"We should," Slocum said solemnly, "but that would mean backtracking, then traveling through the sandhills—and losing at least one, maybe two days on Deschamp's bunch. This is the quickest route to Osage Springs.''

''And you're still sure he's going there? To the springs?''

''If he isn't already there. It's the only place Deschamp could be headed unless he wants to lose a bunch of horses and men. There's no water or grass between here and the springs.''

Waggoner, leading the pack animals, finally spoke. ''Now that I've seen it myself, I'm wondering if we made the right decision. From a tactical standpoint, this place could be a death trap.''

''It has been,'' Slocum said casually. ''There are probably human bones still scattered here and there. Maybe a halberd, a shard of chain mail, even a Spanish helmet.''

''Spanish?'' Lisa asked.

''A column of *conquistador* foot soldiers exploring the West wandered into this place long ago,'' Slocum said. ''They got lost. Indians and thirst wiped out the entire command in a campaign that lasted thirty days and covered twenty miles.''

''I can see how that could happen,'' Waggoner said. ''Are you sure you remember the trail through?''

''I remember it,'' Slocum said honestly, ''but that was from years ago. It may be impassable now. Wind and flash floods change this country in a hurry, Dan. The trail may be blocked by now. Once we're down there, there's no quick way out. The bluffs are a hundred or more feet high, and almost straight up, for twenty miles. Not even a mountain goat can climb those walls.''

Waggoner nodded grimly. ''It's worth a chance. Lead the way, Slocum.''

Slocum slipped his Winchester from its saddle boot, cracked the action to reassure himself a round was chambered, and nodded. ''Keep a sharp eye out, you two, especially on the rim of the bluffs. I'll be too busy following that trail to be looking up all the time. And one other thing. These badlands draw bad men at times. Be ready for anything.''

He kneed Chief into motion. The spotted sorrel hesitated at first, snorted, then skidded down the steep slope toward the red wasteland below.

June Deschamp downed the last of his drink, reached for the bottle in the middle of the crude pine table, and winced. At least it wasn't a sharp pain this time; more of a sting, or burn, as the red scar tissue stretched. The hole in his shoulder was mending.

Deschamp filled his glass and raised it in salute to the man seated across the table. He and Nate Kimber went back a long way. They hadn't been much more than kids when they'd held up their first traveler. The holdup had netted a silver dollar apiece and their first kill.

"Still got that first buck we made together, Nate?"

Kimber grinned, baring tobacco-stained teeth, and patted his shirt pocket. "Carry it all the time. For good luck."

The good-luck charm obviously had worked for Kimber. He'd survived his partnership with Deschamp on the owlhoot trail as they'd moved up from robbing lone travelers to stage-coaches, trains, and finally banks.

After the Trail City bank job in Colorado, Kimber parted company with June, and parlayed his share into the biggest ranch in the Cimarron Strip. While Deschamp blew his stake on women, whiskey, and poker in Dodge City, Kimber bought into the Slash Y. He now laid claim to better than fifty thousand acres, about half of it in reasonably decent water and grass, the rest mostly badlands, sandhills, or dry prairie. He kept half-a-dozen hands on the Slash Y payroll, most of them gunhawks, a couple of them wanted men.

Kimber let it be known that any outlaws who drifted into the Strip were welcome to hide out in the badlands as long as needed. The only rule Kimber laid down was that there would be no theft of Slash Y livestock or property; violators would be shot or hanged on the spot. Consequently, some of the toughest men in the West knew the Slash Y badlands, the Valley of Death, well.

Only a handful of lawmen knew that country, and they were smart enough to stay the hell out.

There had been times when Deschamp admitted to a bit of envy of Kimber's power and money. That had been before the army payroll job. Now, June had as much as—or more than—Kimber had, at least in terms of cold cash. All he had to do was go get it.

"Nate, I sure appreciate you agreein' to graze my ponies and keep an eye on 'em while I finish up some business," Deschamp said.

"*De nada.* You know the rules. Pick 'em up in a month or

I keep 'em all. Pick 'em before then, I keep one of every four head. My choice.''

Deschamp's neck colored. "But Nate, we was partners so long, I was hopin' you'd just do me a favor.''

"Friends or no, June, business is business. Man's got to turn a profit to meet payroll and expenses.'' Kimber stroked his bushy red mustache and grinned at Deschamp. "Going after that army payroll money, June?''

Deschamp instinctively stiffened. "What the hell do you know about any army money, Nate?''

Kimber shrugged. "I've got sources. Hear a lot of owlhoot trail talk. Wasn't sure it was true until I saw the look on your face just now.''

Anger flared in Deschamp's belly. "Now, look, Nate—''

Kimber lifted a hand. "Don't worry, June. I'm not going to muscle myself in for a share. You earned that money. I'm an honest rancher now. I don't need trouble with the U.S. government.'' He tossed back his drink and poured another. "Besides, with that payroll in your pocket, June, you won't miss a few ponies. Especially since you stole most of them anyway. One question, though.''

"Which is?''

"Why did you kill Eldon Lucas and his boys?''

Deschamp's eyes narrowed. "How'd you know about that?''

"Like I said, I've got my sources.'' Kimber topped off June's glass. "Not that it makes any difference to me personally. I didn't like the thieving sonofabitch myself.''

Deschamp shrugged. "I didn't need him anymore.''

"Fair enough reason.'' Kimber glared for a moment into Deschamp's eyes. "What'll happen when you don't need *me* anymore, June? Backshoot me like you did Eldon?''

"Now, wait a minute, Nate! You know damn well I wouldn't do that! Hell, we're partners—friends.''

"Maybe,'' Kimber said casually, "and maybe not.'' He let the subject drop. "Heard you had a speck of trouble in Chama.''

Deschamp glared at Kimber, irritated. "Damned if you don't know more about my business than I do, Nate. What's it to you?''

"One of my boys just rode back in from Chama. From what he told me, I'd say you've got yourself a peck of trouble. Fellow by the name of Slocum and a rifle shooter called Waggoner took out on your trail after the rain quit.''

Deschamp snorted. ''Hell, I know that, Nate. Matter of fact, I'm hopin' the bastards catch up. I got a score to settle and near a dozen guns backin' me. Ain't worried about two men.''

''If you were smart, you'd sure as hell worry about those two. Slocum's poison. He doesn't like people stealing his horses. Waggoner's a scorpion with a long gun. Word is, it was his army gold you stole. I'd say they've both got reasons not to be just real neighborly toward you, June.''

Deschamp's teeth clenched in anger. ''Two men ain't got a prayer of takin' me, Nate. You ought to know that.''

''Don't underestimate those two, my friend. And they're not alone. There's a woman with them.''

''Woman?''

''Tall, black-haired whore from Chama rode out with them. Word is she's got a score to settle with you too. Gal named Barnes. Know her?''

Deschamp shook his head. ''Never met no Barnes whore, best I recall.'' He grinned and winked at Kimber. ''Reckon it'll be a pleasure to howdy that slut after me and the boys get done with Slocum and this—Waggoner, you said?''

''That's what I said.'' Kimber finished off his drink and grinned. ''Watch yourself, or it could be I'll own all those ponies soon—except Slocum's palouses.''

''Why not them too, since you're already dividin' up my remuda?''

Kimber shrugged. ''If Slocum and his partners put you down, he'll come looking for his horses.''

''And if he does?''

''I'll give them back to him, June. Because I don't want any part of that man.''

# 9

Slocum eased Chief around yet another switchback in the trail through the deep arroyo, then reined in and mouthed a curse.

Twenty yards ahead, a cave-in of soft red soil filled the passageway almost to the crown of his hat. And it was the only through trail Slocum knew. To backtrack and hunt another way through the badlands would take hours, maybe days. Beyond the loss of time, it could also be fatal. Even an experienced trail hand like Slocum could become hopelessly lost in the maze of arroyos and dead-end switchbacks.

This wasn't a good place to be trapped.

The sheer, crumbling red dirt and loose shale walls of the twisting arroyo stood sixty feet high. No horse could climb straight up over loose footing. It was no place for a man who felt distinct unease in small, tight spaces. Worse yet, through a quirk of nature, he could be seen from the south rim of the badlands.

Behind the horseshoe-shaped pocket where he now stood, a bend in the arroyo opened into a fifty-foot-wide clearing within rifle shot of a high point on the rim. A good hand with a long gun could keep them all pinned down here—maybe pick off the horses until they were left afoot—and simply wait it out until they died of thirst.

Waggoner reined in a few feet behind Slocum and studied the blocked path silently for a moment; Lisa, leading the pack mounts and bringing up the rear, rode into view around the bend of the arroyo and eased Duke to a stop.

"This doesn't look too promising," Waggoner finally said. "Is there another way around?"

Slocum shook his head. "Not that I know about."

"Then there's only one thing to do—clear enough of this fall that the horses will be able to climb over." Waggoner's gaze raked the prominent ridge little more than two hundred yards south. "We'd better start digging. I don't like the strategic aspects of this place."

Slocum said, "Me either. The sooner we get clear of this trap, the better I'll feel."

Both men dismounted. As Waggoner dug into a pack and pulled out a short-handled trenching spade, Slocum strode to Lisa's side. She sat astride the big bay and studied the dirt fall ahead, faint worry lines between her eyebrows.

"We've got a problem, Lisa. We can't go back, and we can't go around. We're going to have to dig a passage."

Lisa nodded. "I'll help. I can use a shovel."

"No," Slocum said, shaking his head. "One of us has to stand watch." He gestured toward the bend in the arroyo. "I'd like you to go back there and keep a sharp eye on the south rim. Keep low, and if you see anything move—anything at all—sing out. Take your rifle and canteen. Dan and I may be at this for a while."

Lisa nodded silently, dismounted, and strode toward the lookout post Slocum had pointed out, a canteen slung over her shoulder and the Springfield .45-70 in her hand. He waited until she had settled in behind a smaller dirt fall at the base of the arroyo wall. From there, she would have a clear view of the bluff to the south. The dirt mound would provide a bit of cover.

Then Slocum turned back to the blockage. Waggoner, on hands and knees and sometimes wriggling flat on his belly, fought his way to the top of the fall. Dirt cascaded in miniature avalanches beneath his boots. After a moment, Waggoner slid back down.

"It isn't as bad as it could have been," Waggoner said, relief in his tone. "The fall is only a few feet thick by the east wall. A couple of hours of work and we can have it sloped and cut down enough to get the mounts across. I didn't see any more slides between here and the next bend."

Slocum glanced at the sun, now almost directly overhead. With luck, they could be through here before mid-afternoon.

He reached for the trenching tool. "Might as well get started," he said.

The two men worked in quarter-hour shifts, attacking the dirt fall with measured, methodical strokes. By Slocum's fourth turn at the spade, his clothes were soaked with sweat; the sun bore down hard in the windless arroyo. The burning sensation on his palm and forefingers threatened blisters. Calluses formed from bridle reins and catch ropes didn't match up with the burn points left by a short-handled spade.

The going had been slow at first—heave a shovelful of dirt aside and another promptly avalanched down in its place—but now they were actually making progress. Slocum had to force himself not to rush, not to try to move all the dirt in one shift. Slow and steady was the only way the job would ever get done.

Waggoner reached for the spade.

"My turn, Slocum. Get yourself some water and rest." A wry grin touched the corners of his mouth. "Sort of makes a man glad he doesn't have to do this for a living, doesn't it?"

Slocum sighed his agreement and rubbed at his lower back. "I don't know how miners and railroad men handle it, Dan."

The trenching tool in Waggoner's hands bit into the lowering dirt fall. "Just the way *we* do, I expect," he said. "To stay alive." He heaved the spadeful of dirt aside. "I dug enough shooting pits in my Army days to last a lifetime, but a man can move a big pile of dirt in a hurry when rifle balls and canister shot is flying."

"I know," Slocum said as he twisted the cap off his canteen. "I gave a good impression of a badger myself from time to time under those circumstances." He squatted beside Chief in the cool shade cast by the sorrel gelding. "It was different then. Sheer terror gives a man strength he never knew he had."

Slocum resisted the urge to drain half the contents of his canteen, limited himself to a couple of small swallows, pulled a cheroot from his pocket, and struck a match with his thumbnail. The sulphur-fired flame never reached the thin Mexican cigarillo.

"Slocum!"

The call was soft, but the urgency clear in Lisa's voice.

Slocum shook out the match, grabbed his rifle, and came to his feet all in one motion. He sprinted to her side. "What is it, Lisa?"

"Over there." She pointed toward the south rim. "In the

open space between those two biggest cedars, by the notch. I saw something. Like a glint of light.''

Slocum crouched beside her and studied the ridge. He saw nothing, but that didn't mean Lisa hadn't. "Like sunlight reflecting from a spyglass?''

"No. It was more of quick twinkle. Two tiny bright spots, close together.'' She rubbed her knuckles across her eyes and sighed. "It could be I was imagining things. Maybe it was just an animal.''

"Animals don't wear trinkets, Lisa. And I doubt your eyes were playing tricks on you—'' Slocum's breath caught in his throat. A puff of blue-white smoke flowered beneath one of the cedars. "Get down!'' he yelled, grabbing her shoulder and pushing her roughly into the dirt. An instant later the distinct buzz of a rifle slug snarled past overhead. The whack of lead behind them snapped Slocum's head around.

"Dan!'' Lisa's cry hit Slocum's ears at the same instant as the crack of the distant rifle.

Waggoner hit the ground.

Slocum slapped his Winchester to his shoulder, lined the sights a foot above the spot from where the shot had come, and stroked the trigger. The rifle bucked against his shoulder; through the blue-white cloud of powder smoke, he saw a puff of sand against the rim, inches low of his target. The range was pushing the accuracy limit of the .44-40; the blunt-nosed pistol-type bullet lost a lot of zip past a hundred fifty yards. He racked a fresh round into the Winchester, allowed for more bullet drop, and fired.

At the same instant, a slug ripped into the soil a few inches below Slocum, kicking a spray of dirt into his face. He blinked against the sting of sand in his eyes and worked the action of the Winchester. He wiped a hand across his face, trying to clear his blurred vision.

Through the echoes of the rifle blasts, he heard Waggoner yell, "Cover me!''

Slocum twisted and squinted through watery eyes. Waggoner was on his feet, the long rifle in his hand, crabbing and sliding back toward the top of the cave-in. A slug kicked dirt near Waggoner's boots. The muzzle blast of Lisa's Springfield jarred Slocum's cheek and set his ears ringing; his vision had cleared enough that he could see her slug kick sand a foot below the distant cedars. She flipped open the trapdoor, extracted the spent cartridge, and chambered another round.

"Aim a little higher, Lisa," Slocum said. "You get more bullet drop shooting uphill." The range was a bit beyond Lisa's skills, but Slocum didn't tell her to stop shooting. The main thing now was to lay down enough lead to keep the rifleman from drawing down on Waggoner. Slocum worked the lever of his Winchester as rapidly as he could, firing until the hammer dropped on an empty chamber.

The volley of rifle fire faded to echoes as Slocum thumbed fresh rounds into his Winchester. He glanced at Lisa. She calmly ran a fresh cartridge home and slapped the single-shot's action shut. At least, he thought grimly, they had kept the man on the rim busy ducking; no slugs had come at them during their barrage of covering fire.

The break was a brief one.

Before Slocum could take aim, a palm-sized slab of shale a yard away exploded under the impact of lead. A second slug hummed past his ear, followed by a meaty slap and the scream of a horse. Slocum fired two quick rounds and Lisa one toward the powder smoke smear between the cedars. Slocum chanced a quick glance over his shoulder. The little mustang packhorse was down, its hooves cribbing at the red dirt, blood spurting from its neck.

At the top of the dirt slide, long stacked tubes glinted in the sunlight. A couple of heartbeats later, the heavy roar of Waggoner's big-bore sniper rifle slammed against Slocum's ears; the top of the slide seemed to disappear beneath a boil of powder smoke and dust. Slocum felt, rather than heard, the big chunk of lead whisper past overhead. He snapped his head around in time to see a low limb of a cedar disintegrate. A yelp of surprise reached his ears before the first echoes of the big rifle thundered through the badlands.

Slocum caught a quick glimpse of a slight, dark figure crabbing backward from the cedar. Sunlight glinted from silver spots against the black. He lined the Winchester's sights with care, squeezed, and muttered a curse as the black-clad rifleman dropped below the rim before the slug could reach him.

As abruptly as it began, the firing stopped.

Slocum thought he heard the sound of horse's hooves far away, moving fast. Lisa apparently heard it too.

"Sounds like whoever it was has lit out for greener pastures,'' she said as she reloaded the Springfield and gathered herself to stand.

Slocum put a hand on her forearm. "Stay down, Lisa. Maybe he's gone, and maybe not. We'll stay put for a while. Faking a retreat to set up a shot from ambush is the oldest trick in the bushwhacker's book."

The minutes dragged by in silence. Finally, Lisa said, "Something about that man looked familiar. But I just caught a quick glimpse of him."

"You've seen him before. We all have."

The voice from behind startled Slocum. He hadn't heard Dan Waggoner approach. Waggoner stood erect, his gaze riveted on the far rim.

"Are you hit, Dan? I saw you go down."

Waggoner shook his head. "It was close, but the slug missed. I just lost my footing trying to get to my rifle."

Slocum turned his attention back to the far rim. "The shooter was the dandy from the saloon," he said.

"The same. I got a pretty fair look at him through the scope when he bolted. Slender young man dressed in all black, silver conchas all over." Waggoner squatted beside Lisa and peered through the telescopic sight, sweeping the distant ridge.

"Deschamp man?" Slocum asked.

"Yes," Waggoner said. He didn't look up from the scope. "He's the one I tracked to Deschamp's camp. He's called Bud. Fancies himself a shooter, a fast gun. Some sort of relative of Deschamp's."

Slocum said, "I don't remember seeing this Bud fellow during the little fracas we had with Deschamp outside Chama."

"He wasn't there." Waggoner snorted in disgust. "Dammit, if I'd had another second, I could have dropped him when he stood up to run."

Slocum said, "Don't fret it, Dan. If you hadn't gotten in position to put a slug close to him, he could have kept us pinned down here till kingdom come."

"It wasn't the first time I've missed, or probably the last," Waggoner said with a sigh. "No matter how good the rifle, the shooter has to give it a chance."

"Been meaning to ask you, Dan—what kind of weapon is that?" Slocum asked.

"Custom-built job," Waggoner said. "Based on the forty-four-ninety Sharps-necked cartridge, but a bit longer case to handle a hundred grains of powder. Throws a four-seventy-grain bullet from a beefed-up Remington rolling-block action, Creedmoor barrel.''

''Range?''

''I've won some thousand-yard matches with it—even though you certainly couldn't tell it from my shot just now—but for precision shooting, I don't like to push it more than six hundred yards.'' He snorted in self-disgust. ''And here I touch off a clean miss at less than two-fifty. The worst part about it is that now Deschamp's going to know where we are. I think it's safe to assume Bud's spurring back to Deschamp now.''

''Which means Deschamp's camp isn't far away,'' Slocum said, his gaze drifting around. ''Which also means we'd better get the hell out of here. If this Bud comes back with a dozen men, we're dead.''

Waggoner lowered the hammer of the big rifle. ''I was thinking the same thing.'' He glanced at the downed horse. ''We'll lose a few minutes switching packs off the dead horse to the live one. Shame that had to happen. Maybe he wasn't much of a horse, but he didn't do anything to deserve getting shot.''

Slocum also felt a twinge of loss, and not just because they were now short a pack mount. He hated to see anything happen to a horse, but there was a bright side. ''At least it wasn't Chief, Duke, or your black that stopped the slug, Dan.'' He stood. ''Let's get to it. We've got to make some dirt fly.''

A half hour later, Slocum and Lisa waited on the far side of the dirt fall as Waggoner coaxed the remaining packhorse over the treacherous footing. The horse wasn't heavily loaded. Their supplies were depleted to the point that one animal could carry the load without a problem.

Slocum's palouse, Chief, and Waggoner's black had had little difficulty climbing the still-steep and loose footing of the path left by the men's shoveling. Both the spotted sorrel and the Tennessee racer were sure of foot.

Lisa's heavily muscled chestnut had had to fight his way across with brute power instead of delicate balance. Duke stood now at Lisa's side, half winded from the slipping, sliding climb, sweat darkening his shoulders and neck. Lisa unconsciously reached out to pat the big horse on the mane just in front of the withers.

Waggoner, sweating and covered with red dirt, finally urged the laboring packhorse over the crest and skidded to a stop beside Slocum. He removed his hat, pulled a bandanna from his back pocket, and wiped his brow.

"What now, Slocum? We could turn this trap to our advantage. Wait for them to ride in and cut loose on them."

Slocum shook his head. "Too risky, Dan. Deschamp has too many men. We could drop some of them, maybe most. But not all. I'd rather go into a fight on terrain of my own choosing. Fight a guerilla campaign, hopefully cut the odds a few at a time, wear them down. Then make our big raid when the time is right."

Waggoner nodded, eyes narrowed. "Like when you rode with Quantrill."

"An episode I'd as soon forget," Slocum said, bitterness in his voice. "Every man makes mistakes. I made a big one when I threw in with that bunch of cutthroats." He lifted an eyebrow at Waggoner. "Didn't realize you knew about that."

"I've followed your career ever since we faced each other at the Round Tops." Waggoner's tone was calm, non-judgmental. "At least something good came of it, Slocum. I don't know that much about guerilla tactics. You do. So what's your pleasure?"

Slocum turned to stare down the twisting ribbon of trail that led out of the badlands. Or at least it had at one time. "We've got at least another day's ride to reach Kiowa Canyon. It's the nearest pass out of here. After that, Osage Springs. Our horses have their wind back now. Mount up. We'll be moving as fast and as long as the horses can take it until we make camp in Kiowa Canyon." He cut a quick glance at Lisa. "It's going to be a tough ride."

Lisa swung into the saddle. "I can handle it, Slocum. If you're waiting on me, you're wasting time."

"Dammit, Bud!" June Deschamp yelled, hand balled into a fist, "you find more ways to piss in my whiskey than a man can count! I'm half a mind to beat hell out of you and then put a slug in your gut!"

"Now, wait a minute, June," Bud pleaded. "I had that jasper right in my sights—"

"Shut up, you little shit!" Deschamp turned to the tall scout at Bud's side. "Jenkins, I told you not to let this skinny bastard screw up. How come you let him?"

Jenkins shrugged. "I told him. Several times. Told him that

if he found a track, to get his skinny ass back here. We split up to scout. By the time I heard the shooting it was too late to stop him."

Deschamp's beet-red face twisted in disgust. "Ought to lay a six-gun barrel alongside your head, you one-eyed son of a bitch!"

"Any time you're ready, June." Jenkins's voice was calm, collected; he stood relaxed, one hip cocked, but fire danced in the one clear eye.

Deschamp forced himself to regain a measure of composure. For two reasons. First, he didn't want to tangle with Jenkins. The man wasn't Bud. Jenkins was dangerous. Second, what was done was done and couldn't be undone. He sighed heavily.

"All right, Jenkins, maybe it wasn't your fault." Deschamp leveled a stare that would have wilted a cactus at Bud. "What I've got to do now is figure out how to cover up another of Bud's dumb-assed mistakes."

Bud scuffed a toe in the dirt, anger replacing the sting of the tongue-lashing in his expression. "Dammit, June," he said, "let me go back there and finish the job. I'll get them sure this time."

Deschamp snorted. "In a pig's ass you will. I'm keepin' you right at my stirrup from now on, Bud. You step in it one more time and I'll peel your hide for sure."

"I don't know what you're so stirred up about, June—"

"What I'm stirred up about," Deschamp interrupted bitterly, "is that you two tipped Slocum and his buddy off that we're around here. Hell, they're probably tracking you back here right now."

Jenkins spat and shook his head. "Doubt that, Boss. There's not but one trail out of that stretch of badlands for miles. We can easy bushwhack them when they start up Kiowa Canyon."

Deschamp pursed his lips. Jenkins had a point. Catch Slocum and that buffalo gunner, Waggoner, in a cross fire. One rifle volley would take care of the problem. June would like to save the whore to play with later. But if she got in the way, no big loss. "All right, Jenkins. We might just work it that way. Let me study on it a few minutes."

Jenkins and Bud turned to walk away.

"Bud!" Deschamp snapped, "Get your ass back here. I don't want you out of my reach till you prove to me you can do something right! Jenkins, take care of Bud's horse."

"June, I—"

"Shut up and sit down, Bud. Don't say one word or even break wind until I tell you it's okay. I got thinkin' to do."

Bud, his lower lip stuck out in a pout, plopped down beside Deschamp. That stupid kid's going to get everybody killed, June thought, unless . . . He shoved the idea aside for a moment to study the men lounging around the Osage Springs camp.

For the time being, anyway, he had a decent mounted force. The whiskey was gone, and the ones who had been drunk would be hungover and mean, itching for a fight. The horses were rested. His gaze flicked over the bluffs and timber along Osage Springs. The place wasn't good for defense. They didn't want to be caught here, not by men who could shoot like Slocum and Waggoner.

Deschamp called to a wiry young rider with greasy, shoulder-length blond hair. "Sandy," he said as the youth strode up, "you and Tularosa move these horses down to the Slash Y and wait for the rest of us there. You know where it's at and how to get there. Tell Nate we'll be along in a day or two."

Sandy nodded silently and strode toward a small knot of men involved in a halfhearted poker game under a cottonwood tree.

"All right, Bud, here's something not even you could screw up," Deschamp said. "Tell the other boys to grab every gun they've got and saddle up. We're goin' huntin'."

Slocum strode along the sandy gully, Chief ambling a step behind on loose rein.

Slocum glanced at the mid-morning sun. Everything considered, they had made decent time. Behind him, Lisa and Waggoner also had dismounted, partly to stretch the stiffness from saddle-numbed legs and buttocks, but mostly to give the horses a break from carrying their weight. So far, so good, Slocum thought.

Throughout the night, he had fought the black shadows cast by a pale quarter moon overhead, straining to identify landmarks he had not seen for years. At night, everything looked different. But they were still on course, or so he thought. At least they weren't hopelessly lost. Not more than four or five miles ahead they should come up on the stand of cottonwood trees that marked the mouth of Kiowa Canyon.

Slocum ran his tongue over chapped, dry lips. The thought of water such a short ride away seemed to parch his mouth and throat even more. The first waterhole inside the canyon wasn't much—a stale seep, stagnant, muddy, ringed with weeds and tasting slightly of frog piss—but to Slocum it would be sweet as a pure mountain stream. It would see them and the horses through until they reached the clear spring deeper inside the canyon.

Waggoner and Lisa had probably suffered more than he had, Slocum knew. Lisa in particular; she wasn't accustomed to long days and nights in dry, dusty country that sucked the moisture from a person's skin and gut. It had been four hours since their last drink, and that less than a quarter of a cupful. Most of their water had gone to more important beings—the horses. In this country, a person afoot didn't stand a chance.

Chief fluttered his nostrils and tossed his head, jingling the curb chain. Slocum doubted that the horse could smell the water up ahead. What breeze there was now blew from behind him. But the horse's ears were up, eyes alert.

Slocum loosened the Colt revolver in the cross-draw holster. He had learned to trust a horse's sense of smell and eyesight over the years. A horse wasn't as reliable a watchdog as a burro, or even a mule, but only a fool or a soon-to-be-dead man didn't pay attention to the actions of a good horse.

A few yards ahead, the trail twisted sharply back toward the north. Slocum didn't recall this particular bend in the trail. The uneasy feeling that maybe he had missed a branch or turn wormed in his gut. The narrow, deep arroyo did little to warm his belly. Almost vertical walls of sand and shale, barren of even stunted weeds or dry bunch grass, flanked the gash in the earth. Here, there was barely room enough for a single horseman to pass. The overall sensation of being squeezed from both sides rode heavy on his shoulders.

He breathed a bit easier as he led Chief past the sharp angle of the trail. The arroyo widened abruptly, the walls to the left lower now, less sheer. And in the distance, the tip of a single tall butte came into view, dusted in a blue haze. Kiowa Peak. He hadn't lost the trail.

Slocum toed the stirrup, swung back into the saddle, and turned to look over his shoulder. Leather creaked as Lisa and Waggoner mounted again.

"Just a little farther, Lisa," Slocum said with a reassuring smile. "A few more miles and we'll be in the canyon. There's water there—'' His words abruptly broke off; Lisa's eyes had gone wide. She stared past Slocum's shoulder.

''Slocum . . .'' Lisa's voice came out a hoarse croak.

Slocum's head snapped around.

Five horsemen, scruffy, trail-worn, and dusty, fanned out across the growing width of the arroyo, barely a dozen yards away.

They all had guns in their hands.

# 10

Slocum studied the five men spread out before him.

They wore the outlaw stamp—tough, hard-edged men, tanned from wind and weather, unshaven, and coated with trail dirt. Slocum pegged the paunchy man in the middle as the leader of the bunch. A white slash of scar tissue ran from hat brim to cheekbone above a wiry, untamed brownish-red beard. Piggish, close-set gray eyes glittered beneath the brim of a battered and sweat-stained hat. A lever action rifle rested in the crook of one arm, and he wore a handgun on his right hip.

The rider to the beefy man's left—Slocum's right—would be the most dangerous of the bunch, Slocum knew. The man was barely past the smooth-cheek stage, whip-lean and wiry, and the cold set of dark eyes marked him as a gunhawk who knew how to handle the Peacemaker in his left hand.

Slocum tagged the middle-aged man to the leader's right as the second most dangerous, because of the double shotgun he held, muzzles aimed skyward, hammers cocked, the buttstock propped casually against the thigh of scarred shotgun chaps. He had the look of a confident man about him—the confidence of a man who knew what a double charge of buckshot would do at close range.

Slocum didn't pay that much mind to the others. They might be capable shooters, but Slocum couldn't watch five at once. He'd have to trust Waggoner to fret over them if they were hunting trouble.

"Howdy," the man in the middle said, his voice like the sound of a shovel grating across gravel.

Slocum nodded a greeting, but didn't speak. He kept his gaze focused halfway between the speaker and the young gunman. That way he could see which one moved first, and react. Slocum put a mental bet down on the kid making the first try.

"Looks like you all took the wrong road, feller," the beefy one said. "I'm Wes Worden. Reckon you've heard of me?"

"Can't say as I have," Slocum said casually. He heard the shuffle of hoofbeats and creak of leather as Waggoner and Lisa drifted apart, Lisa in the middle, Dan on the far left flank.

"Must not get around these parts much," Worden said, "or you'd know this here's my road. It's a toll road."

"It wasn't the last time I came through," Slocum said.

"Things change." The bearded man turned his head and spat. "Cost you now."

"How much?"

Worden's gaze drifted from Slocum to the others, then back. A twisted grin twitched the tangled beard. "Good-lookin' ponies you folks are ridin'. That'd be a start."

"That's a mighty steep price, Worden," Slocum said.

"And the woman." A leer twisted Worden's weathered features as his gaze raked Lisa briefly, then drifted back to Slocum. "Mighty prime stuff there." He thumbed the hammer of the battered Kennedy rifle to full cock. "You two fellers just step down off them ponies and hand 'em over—along with your guns and the woman—and you might live to see sundown."

"I doubt that."

"What's the problem, mister? You think my word's no good?"

Slocum drew a slow breath. "Mine wouldn't be if I were in your boots," he said. "Which means we have a problem, Wes. You and your men stand aside, let us pass, and nobody'll get hurt."

Worden laughed aloud. "I'll say this, stranger. You got bigger balls than a Mexican stud hoss. You think you two can stop me and my boys?"

"Maybe. Maybe not. If you think it's worth—"

His words drowned under a sudden, high-pitched yell; Lisa's big chestnut lunged past, in a full run by the third jump, headed straight for Wes Worden's mount.

The kid on Slocum's right moved. He was fast.

Slocum whipped the Peacemaker from his holster, thumbed the hammer as he drew, held back the trigger, and let his thumb slip as the muzzle snapped into line. A slug ripped past Slocum's ear half a heartbeat before his own lead took the kid low in the side. The lean youngster jerked in the saddle and gamely tried to bring his revolver into play. At the edge of his vision, Slocum saw Lisa's big chestnut ram chest-first into Worden's horse, staggering both mounts. Slocum took his time, thumbed the hammer, lined the sights, and shot the kid in the chest.

Worden's horse regained its footing. The scarred man swung his rifle muzzle toward Slocum. The shot never came. Worden's hat went flying beneath a pinkish haze as his forehead blew apart. The slug from Lisa's Schofield had taken him squarely in the back of the head.

At Slocum's left, the shotgunner swung the weapon toward Lisa, only a few feet away. Slocum thumbed the hammer, but his heart leapt in his throat as Worden's panicked horse reared between Slocum and the shotgunner. Slocum knew he'd never have a chance—

The heavy blast of a big-bore revolver and the solid whack of a lead ball against flesh hammered Slocum's ears. The shotgunner seemed to lift from the saddle, the smoothbore spinning from his grip. The man fell from sight on the off side of his mount. Slocum chanced a quick glance at Waggoner, barely visible through the cloud of powder smoke. Waggoner held a big Dragoon percussion revolver in his fist; he had drawn the oversized weapon from the saddle scabbard only a bit slower than Slocum's draw from belt leathers.

Slocum touched spurs to Chief. By the quick sorrel's second lunge he had cleared Worden's pitching, riderless mount. Three men down, two left. Slocum skidded Chief to a stop, lined the sights, and drove a slug into the nearest gunman. The man jerked once, again as Lisa's Schofield barked, and yet again as Waggoner triggered the Dragoon, and after what seemed an eternity, fell from the saddle. The man's horse bolted and ran, empty stirrups flapping, following the other spooked horses that raced away up the arroyo.

The fifth man abruptly lost his taste for the fight. He spun his horse about, leaned over the animal's neck, and spurred hard. Slocum reined Chief after the fleeing man, but kneed the palouse to one side at Waggoner's yell.

Slocum glanced over his shoulder. Waggoner stepped from the saddle, knelt on one knee, aimed for a good two seconds with the Dragoon, and fired. Half a heartbeat later and almost a hundred yards away, the fleeing rider straightened, then slowly slid from the saddle and tumbled to the ground.

"Damn, Dan," Slocum called, "I thought you said you couldn't use a handgun!"

"Didn't say I couldn't use one. Just that I wasn't as good with a pistol as I am with a rifle." Waggoner reloaded the Dragoon, his fingers almost a blur. Slocum was impressed; he'd worn out a number of percussion revolvers in his life, and he didn't think he'd ever reloaded one as quick as Waggoner did.

Waggoner swung into the saddle. "Check on these men. I'm going after those horses."

Slocum almost called Waggoner back; they had all the horses they needed. But he didn't. Dan obviously had something in mind.

His ears ringing from the concussion of close-in gunfire, Slocum reined Chief alongside Duke. Lisa's face was a bit pale beneath the coat of dust and powder-smoke residue. She still held the Schofield in her right hand.

"Are you all right, Lisa?" Slocum asked.

"I'm okay. A little scared, maybe, but not hurt. You?"

"Not a scratch. By all rights, we should all be dead. That was quick thinking on your part," Slocum said solemnly.

Lisa flipped the Schofield's top strap catch, broke the weapon open, ejected the spent brass, and reloaded. "It didn't take a lot of brains to see that those men were concentrating on you and Dan, and paying no mind to a mere woman," she said. "And that they were going to kill us anyway, so what the hell was there to lose? I just did the one thing they were least likely to expect."

"And did it well." Slocum also reloaded as he spoke. "Let's see if any of this bunch is still alive."

"And if they are?"

"Then we fix that oversight."

As if to punctuate Slocum's words, a distant pistol shot sounded. He glanced up the arroyo in time to see Waggoner ride past the man he had downed, a puff of blue-white powder smoke swirling in his wake. Waggoner hadn't even reined in, just plopped a slug in the outlaw's back as he rode past, the black moving in a long lope. Before Waggoner passed from sight in a bend of the arroyo in pursuit of the fleeing horses, Slocum saw him shove the big Dragoon back into the saddle holster.

"That's one of the five we won't have to worry about," Lisa said, her tone cold. "Let's see to the rest of them."

There wasn't that much left to see to. The youngest gunman had died seconds after Slocum's second slug shredded his heart. Worden had gone even quicker. Most of his forehead was gone, blown outward by the exit of the soft-lead .45 slug from Lisa's Schofield fired almost point-blank into the back of his skull.

The man with the shotgun coughed his last and died as Lisa and Slocum rode up. Frothy pink bubbles at the corners of the man's lips told Slocum that Waggoner's Dragoon ball had torn through both the man's lungs.

Slocum was a bit surprised that the fourth man was still alive. He had taken three close-range hits from large-caliber handguns through the body. The outlaw made a feeble effort to reach the rifle near his side. Slocum shot him in the head.

"Guess that's it," Slocum said. He paused long enough to reload the fired chamber, then holstered the Peacemaker. "This bunch collected their toll, all right, but the price wasn't what they had in mind."

Lisa sheathed her Schofield and lifted an eyebrow at Slocum. "Wonder what Dan's up to?"

Slocum reined Chief about and glanced up the arroyo. A riderless horse came into view around the bend, its head held sideways, hooves mincing as it tried to keep from stepping on the trailing reins. Another horse trailed close behind.

"We'll find out soon enough," Slocum said. "Looks like he's got the ponies rounded up."

Lisa helped Slocum bring the leading mounts of the outlaw band to a stop. A few minutes later, Waggoner rode in, hazing two horses and leading a third.

Slocum lifted an eyebrow at Waggoner. "Since we all know we don't need any more horses or saddles, Dan, it's pretty obvious you've got something in mind." It was a question as much as it was a statement.

Waggoner nodded. "I think we can concede that Deschamp knows we're coming."

"I wouldn't bet against it."

"And you said Kiowa Canyon was the only good watering place between here and Osage Springs?"

"It is," Slocum said.

"So," Waggoner said, shifting his weight in the saddle, "if you were in Deschamp's boots, what would you do?"

Slocum said, "Ambush us when we ride into the canyon. A few good riflemen on both sides could wipe us out in a cross fire in a matter of seconds. Minimum chance of casualties themselves."

Lisa said, "Excuse me for butting in, but would you fellows mind dealing me in on this game?"

"A standard military tactic, Lisa," Slocum said. "We're going to set an ambush for the men who'd ambush us. Right, Dan?"

"Precisely. Now, let's get lead ropes on these horses. We've got a lot of work to do here, and not much time to do it in." Waggoner inclined his head at Lisa. "You don't have to help with this, Miss Barnes. It won't be a job for queasy stomachs."

Lisa sniffed aloud. "Did you ever have a baby, Dan?"

"Of course not."

"Then don't talk to me about queasy, my friend. That project's as gory as any you men have ever seen. Let's get started."

Slocum frowned, puzzled. "You never mentioned having had a baby, Lisa."

The lines around Lisa's mouth tightened. "I'll tell you about it later. For now, we've got more important things to do."

The sun was little more than a handspan above the western horizon when Slocum finally reined Chief to a halt in a dense thicket of salt cedars a quarter mile from the mouth of Kiowa Canyon.

Slocum was satisfied no one had spotted them before they reached the stand of willowy, thin-leafed trees. The thicket sprawled behind them for better than a hundred yards. The cover along the route Slocum had chosen was thick enough that horsemen could approach Kiowa Canyon unseen from the rimrock above.

It had taken longer than Slocum had hoped to get the dead men tied in the saddles. Their horses had fought against accepting loads that smelled of blood and death. But after a while on the trail, they had settled down reasonably well.

They had ridden for an hour before Waggoner finally found a fallen cedar tree and a raft of suitable driftwood. They took the time to rig props that held three of the bodies upright—or nearly so—in the saddles. The other two dead men, tied across their horse's backs, would resemble supply packs in poor light.

The three propped erect didn't resemble Slocum, Lisa, and Waggoner all that much in daylight, but in the shadow of dusk it wasn't likely an excited rifleman would study them long enough to realize the difference.

It wasn't the best ruse Slocum had ever seen, but it would do. Especially when the horses went into and up the canyon on a dead run. A literal dead run, he thought.

"Slocum?"

He turned to Lisa, who had nudged Duke alongside Slocum's spotted sorrel.

"Yes?"

"Will it work? I mean . . ." Her voice trailed away.

"It has to," Slocum said solemnly, "or we'll all be dead in a few hours. You might as well get down and rest a bit, Lisa. We won't make our move until just before sundown. Any time sooner than that, Deschamp's gang won't fall for it—provided they're there, which I'm about to go find out." He handed Chief's reins to Lisa. "I'll be going on foot. There's water in the dead men's canteens. Give our horses a drink, but go easy on it yourself. If anything goes wrong and we don't make it to the springs, it's a long haul to the next waterhole."

Waggoner asked, "Are you positive you don't need me on scout detail with you, Slocum?"

"I'd rather you stayed here, Dan. One man can move quieter than two, and us Johnny Rebs always did sneak better than you Yanks."

A wry smile touched Waggoner's lips. "Can't argue that point. You gentlemen showed up a lot of times when you weren't supposed to be within fifty miles."

"And sometimes, we shouldn't have showed up at all," Slocum said with a sigh. He slipped the holster tie-down thong over the Peacemaker's hammer to hold the weapon firmly in place, then slid his Winchester from the saddle sheath. "Dan, if something goes wrong, Lisa might need your help here. Don't try to be a hero and come after me, and don't fight them unless you can't get away." He nodded toward the rim that towered above his right shoulder. "See that switchback game trail and the notch it leads to?"

Waggoner studied the terrain for a moment, then nodded.

"I don't plan on getting spotted," Slocum said, "but if I do, I'll try to keep them busy long enough for you and Lisa to make it up the trail. From the top of the notch, cut due southwest. In a few hours you'll come to the old Southern Trail. It'll take you back to Santa Fe, or to the Dodge City trail at Tascosa to the northeast.'' He started toward the canyon rim, stopped at Lisa's touch on his arm.

"Watch yourself out there, Slocum," Lisa said. "I'm not quite through with you yet."

Slocum touched fingers to his hat brim. "In that case, ma'am, I'll make damned sure nothing goes wrong. I'll be back a bit before sundown."

Slocum's shirt was soaked with sweat, his lungs laboring, the sting of abused thigh muscles and shaky knees testifying to the steep, twisting canyon wall.

He paused near the top and pressed his body close to the reddish-gray sandstone wall beside the narrow trail. He waited patiently for a few minutes until his heartbeat slowed, his breathing caught up with his need for air, and strength flowed back into his legs.

A couple of cautious strides brought him to the final switchback in the trail, less than thirty feet from the notch in the rim. He glanced back down the hillside. From here, he had a clear view of the hundred yards or so of open ground between the edge of the salt cedar thicket and the grove of cottonwoods at the entrance of Kiowa Canyon.

Deschamp might be crazy, Slocum knew, but the man wasn't dumb. Any field commander with an ounce of savvy would post a sentry here, where an opposing force would be easily spotted on its approach.

Seconds later, a pinpoint of light flickered above and to his right, a quick, moving dot, like sunlight working its way down a rifle barrel. Slocum didn't move, his gaze riveted on the juniper from where the wink of light had come. A match flared in the shadow of the tree beside the notch, then died away. A faint puff of cigarette smoke dusted away on the breeze.

Slocum had found the sentry. And the whole operation depended upon his taking the man down—quickly and quietly. A yell or a gunshot and Deschamp's men would be on them like a rooster on a grasshopper.

Slocum pulled his thin-bladed skinning knife from its belt sheath and tested the edge with a thumb. The razor-like edge of the blade was reassuring to the touch. Still, Slocum winced inwardly as he sheathed the knife. There was something about killing a man with a blade that chilled the blood. Steel was more personal than a bullet. He pushed the uneasy sensation aside and began the final, silent stalk, a slow, careful step at a time, senses tuned to the soles of his boots. A snapped twig or a loosened stone now would bring a warning shout. Or the wallop of a rifle slug.

No shout or gunshot came. He was almost within arm's reach of the man on the far side of the juniper now, close enough to smell the man, hear his every move. He eased the skinning knife from its sheath.

The sentry stretched and stepped away from the juniper, his back to Slocum. The lookout was a big man, over six feet tall and thick through the shoulders. Slocum knew he had to time his move right, make it count, or it could be his last—and possibly the end of Lisa and Waggoner.

The big man leaned his rifle against the juniper and stepped away from the tree. His right shoulder twitched a few times. Slocum offered up a silent thanks for the blessing of full bladders. He eased the final step forward as the sound of a steady stream of urine turned to short, spastic spurts and he heard the man's sigh of relief.

Slocum's left arm whipped out, his hand clamped over the big man's mouth, and he yanked his head back. With his right hand Slocum swept the keen blade across the exposed throat. A strangling gurgle sounded beneath Slocum's left hand; the convulsive, desperate jerks of powerful muscles threatened to break Slocum's hold for a moment. The big man's fingers clawed at Slocum's hand; Slocum gritted his teeth and tightened his grip with all the strength in his arms and shoulders. He knew that sometimes a minute, often more, passed before a man with his throat slashed bled to death.

Slocum's heart hammered against his ribs. A flailing boot heel cracked painfully against his shin. An elbow rammed into his ribs, almost knocking the air from his lungs. The sentry's struggles weakened as blood pumped from severed arteries. It seemed to Slocum that an hour had passed, rather than a minute or so, before the huge body went limp. A final gurgle from the severed windpipe marked the man's dying gasp.

Slocum eased the sentry to the ground, knelt for a moment to rasp air back into his own lungs, then let the man's head drop. Slocum winced inwardly at the sight; he had never gotten used to the idea that a single body—even one this big—could hold so much blood. Finally, he stood and sheathed the knife; the blade showed no bloodstains. The fatal cut had been quick and clean.

Slocum dragged the dead man behind the juniper and silently hoped there would be no sentry change for the next hour or so. He glanced at the sun. There wasn't much time left. . . .

Deschamp squinted into the shadows creeping into the Kiowa Canyon floor from the west, brows furrowed. He glanced at the one-eyed man at his side.

"Dammit, they should have been here by now, Jenkins. You sure Bud wasn't just seein' boogers out there?"

Jenkins tongued his chew and spat. "He wasn't, June. I saw them myself when I went to get Bud down off that rimrock before the shooter with the buffalo gun nailed him."

Deschamp snorted in disgust. "You should of let him get shot. That damn kid was born dumb with a capital D and gets dumber ever year. Christ, if he'd done like he was told, it'd be over with by now. Slocum and that long gunner'd be coyote bait and we'd be spreadin' that whore's legs right now."

"June, you got about as much patience as a badger with a hard-on," Jenkins said. "Don't get your guts in a boil. They'll be along directly."

"Patience is for buzzards," Deschamp snorted. But mentally he conceded Jenkins's point. Waiting never had been June's long suit. See something you want, take it now and don't look back. The philosophy had served him well in the past.

The stone digging into Deschamp's belly seemed to get bigger and sharper by the minute. With the lowering sun, the air had lost its oppressive heat, but sweat still slicked the receiver of the rifle in his hand. The idea that right now the jasper with the big rifle might have the sights lined right on his head gave Deschamp's bladder a twitch. The old Army story was that a man never heard the shot or shell that killed him. June didn't want to find out if it was true or not.

"Dammit, Jenkins, if they don't show soon, we're gonna run out of shootin' light," Deschamp said.

Jenkins spat out his used-up chew. "They'll show. No place else they can go for water and grass, and their horses need both." The hawk-nosed man's one good eye swept the canyon walls. "When they do, we'll have them cold. They won't stand a chance."

Deschamp grunted in agreement. He had two men stationed on the far canyon wall across the way, with him and Jenkins on this side and two more further back Slocum, Waggoner, and the whore would be in a cross fire from half-a-dozen men who could handle rifles. He had reserves too—Big George, standing watch on the one trail up from below, two men back at Osage Springs, guarding the camp. And Bud.

Deschamp had told his men not to shoot the woman if they didn't have to. He wanted her alive. He wasn't all that greedy. When he was done with her, the rest of the boys could have their turn.

All except Bud. The dumb little shit hadn't earned the right. Just to make sure he didn't screw up worse than he already had, Deschamp had left the kid to hold the horses well back of the canyon rim. Bud didn't even bitch about being left out of another fight. He might be dumber than a stump, but he knew when not to argue if he didn't want to get a six-gun laid alongside his head.

The sundown shadows crept further onto the canyon floor. Across the way, a match flared in the growing dark halfway up the rocky bluff. Deschamp muttered an oath; he'd told everybody to lay off the smokes until the job was done. On an ambush patrol, a fire even the size of a match could spoil the whole plan.

"Dammit," Deschamp muttered, "where the hell are they?"

Slocum knelt in a small clearing at the edge of the salt cedar thicket.

"They're there, all right. Half a dozen riflemen in the canyon itself. The young dandy's holding the horses a hundred yards back." He didn't mention the man he'd left dead at the top of the trail. "I didn't see any others. Deschamp's smart enough to have left at least a couple of men back at the camp."

"No problem," Waggoner, crouched beside Slocum, said. "I'll take care of anyone left at the springs."

Slocum turned to Lisa. "The whole thing depends on you and your sense of timing. You understand what to do?"

Lisa nodded grimly, her jaws clenched. "I've got it. Don't worry about me."

"Just don't take any chances. The one thing we don't want is to get someone hurt." His tone softened. He put a hand on Lisa's forearm. "Especially you. Be careful." Slocum stood and peered into the deepening gray dusk. "All right, let's mount up. It's time we cut the odds down some."

# 11

Slocum knelt beside a clump of Spanish dagger plants at the neck of the trail leading down into Kiowa Canyon, his frown deepening with the passage of each minute.

The light was fading fast. Slocum figured he had, at best, another twenty minutes of decent shooting light. After that, it would be a matter of instinct—slapping shots without the advantage of being able to draw a bead.

He was satisfied with his field of fire, despite the brush and boulder cover in the canyon below. He held the high ground on the only easy passage out of Kiowa Canyon. With any luck at all, he could hold Deschamp's bunch off long enough to allow Lisa to climb the switchback trail he had followed twice.

The second time up had been easier than the first. He had led Chief and one packhorse up the trail, Waggoner following with his black and the second pack mount. They'd had only one scare, when the packhorse Dan led lost its footing for an instant, almost fell, and sent a shower of shale, dirt, and stones down the canyon wall.

Slocum drew in a deep breath of the juniper-scented air and glanced over his shoulder. Waggoner should be in position on the high bluff overlooking the Osage Springs camp by now, or at least near it. Splitting forces like this went against the military manuals and common sense, but when you had only three people in your army, there weren't many options.

He turned his attention back to the canyon. All but two of Deschamp's men were out of his line of sight, beyond a twist in the trail. One of the Deschamp men on the east wall was within easy range, a bit under a hundred yards, his back to Slocum. His companion was fifty yards farther downrange, with good cover behind a rock slide. He would be harder to take down.

Deschamp and his partner were out of Slocum's field of view, off to his left on the west wall, beyond the turn in the trail. Slocum didn't waste his time fretting about it. A man played the cards the way they were dealt.

Sounds carried well on the windless autumn air in the deep confines of the canyon walls. Slocum would know when the fight started—and it had to be soon, if the plan was going to work.

At the moment, the only sounds were the soft flutter of Chief's nostrils and the swish of a nighthawk's wings overhead. The sorrel gelding, tied a few yards back of Slocum's post and out of the way of a stray slug, had quickly recovered from the tough climb up the twisting game trail. Slocum could only hope that Lisa's big chestnut, obviously no mountain horse, had the wind for the climb.

"Any time now, Lisa," Slocum whispered aloud.

"Dammit, Jenkins," Deschamp growled, "they're not comin'. We're just wastin' time—"

The sudden stiffening of the one-eyed man's body cut short Deschamp's complaint. Jenkins cocked an ear, listening. "They're coming, June. Four, five horses. Moving fast."

Deschamp heard it then. The distinct rumble of hooves just past the canyon mouth boosted his heart rate. He shouldered his rifle. "Now we've got 'em!"

Three horsemen thundered around the bend, two pack animals trailing behind, and raced into the open floor of the canyon. They had covered barely twenty yards before the first crack of rifles boomed from the ranks of the ambushers. The initial shots triggered a withering volley of fire. One of the packhorses stumbled and went down.

Deschamp drew a bead on the lead rider, fired, and muttered a curse; even in the fading light and shooting at a moving target, he knew he couldn't have missed that shot. At his side, Jenkins fired twice, levering his rifle as rapidly as he could.

Above the crackle of gunfire, Deschamp heard the frequent thump of lead against flesh—but still, the riders came, as if untouched by the hail of lead. A second horse fell, tumbled end over end, and lay kicking in the sand, the rider still in the saddle. That didn't make sense. No man could go through a fall like that and still be astride his horse.

"June, something's not right," Jenkins all but yelled in Deschamp's ear. "They don't ride right or look like—" His words faded under a barrage of rifle shots and the deeper cough of a shotgun.

Deschamp aimed through the haze of darkness, dust, and powder smoke and squeezed the trigger. The dark shape of the lead horseman was less than sixty feet away. The body twitched, but stayed upright in the saddle.

"Dammit, what's—" Deschamp realized with a start that none of the horsemen made any attempt to shoot back. The remaining two rode stiff, unbending, upright in the saddle, an unnatural posture for men under fire.

The lead horse charged past Deschamp. He didn't recognize the rider. It was not Slocum or the woman, and too short to be the buffalo gunner. Deschamp ducked and cursed as lead slugs spanged from the rocks beside him, shots fired by his own men.

"Quit shooting!" Deschamp yelled. "You idiots damn near hit me!"

Deschamp pulled his handgun and sent a round into the body of the second rider. Nothing happened, but he knew he couldn't have missed—he dropped the muzzle of his revolver and fired into the horse's shoulder as the animal raced past. The horse made four strides, then staggered to a stop near the top of the trail. The animal sank to its front knees, then toppled over. The rider stayed in the saddle.

The crackle and echoes of gunfire from the canyon seemed to ruffle the dagger-shaped leaves of the yucca plants at Slocum's side. He ignored the distant shots, his concentration on the rifleman farthest away—the most difficult target.

The man made a mistake.

He stood and peered down the canyon, his back exposed to Slocum, his attention elsewhere. Slocum steadied his rifle, lined the sights two feet above the X where the man's suspenders crossed, slowly let out his breath, and squeezed the trigger. The .44-40 thumped against his shoulder. He didn't wait to find out the results of his first shot. He racked another round into the chamber and swung the muzzle toward the nearest man. The gunman had spun around at the unexpected shot from behind, rifle raised, his head swinging from side to side as he tried to locate the spot the shot had come from.

Slocum took his time, a couple of heartbeats, and drove a slug into the man's upper chest. The man went down, rifle spinning from his grip. Slocum glanced toward the first man he'd fired at; the outlaw was no longer in sight. Slocum forgot about him as well. They would be no problem in this fight.

He thumbed two fresh cartridges into the loading port of the Winchester and shouldered the rifle as the sound of hoofbeats approached from just beyond the bend in the canyon. Slocum lined the sights—then lowered the weapon as the horse came into view, Wes Worden's body flopping in the saddle. As the lathered and winded horse stumbled past, half trotting, half loping, Slocum saw why Worden's corpse no longer sat upright. The driftwood fork Waggoner had used to prop Worden in the saddle had been shot into two pieces.

Slocum felt a momentary twinge of guilt about the horse. The animal was all but dead on its feet. It would never be worth anything as a saddle mount again, even if it lived.

He pushed the feeling aside. There were more important matters at hand. He chanced a quick glance around the broken, rocky ground. There was no sign yet of Lisa. She should have been here by now, he thought worriedly, and time was running short. It wouldn't be long until Deschamp figured out they'd been wasting lead on dead men down in the canyon. Then he'd gather his force and come up this trail. Slocum had to hold his position until Lisa showed—or until he knew for sure that she hadn't made it.

The latter thought chilled his blood.

He settled in to wait. There was nothing else he could do.

Deschamp realized the shooting had stopped. The echoes of gunfire still rattled through the canyon, but no new rounds were fired. One horse and rider, apparently unhit, rounded the bend and raced from sight, straight toward camp. Dade and Turner would take care of him. That was why he'd left a rear guard at Osage Springs in the first place.

Deschamp thought he had heard, over the near-constant rifle and shotgun blasts in the canyon, a couple of shots from back uptrail. He dismissed the idea from his mind. Probably just echoes. Or worse, Bud deciding to deal himself into the game.

Nothing about this operation made sense. Deschamp's mind

whirled, his empty rifle forgotten. "What the hell's going on here?"

Jenkins casually thumbed fresh loads into his revolver. "I don't know what happened, June, but none of those riders were the ones we're after. Could be we've been suckered."

"But—where are they? Where's that damned Slocum?"

Jenkins and Deschamp clambered from the rocks and strode to the downed horse, still kicking its death throes. Jenkins stared at the body for a moment, then shook his head. "This sure as hell ain't Slocum. It's a young kid."

"I know him," Deschamp said. "Name's Fargo. Ran into him once down in Fort Davis. Heard he joined up with Wes Worden's bunch about a year ago. But, hell, Wes's gang's supposed to be in Missouri. . . ."

"Where this kid's supposed to be doesn't matter now, June," Jenkins said, kneeling beside the bullet-torn body. "He's been shot more than a dozen times, but he's not bleeding."

"Not bleedin'?"

"Nope. This man was dead quite a spell before we cut down on him. He's tied in the saddle. We've been foxed, sure enough."

"Then where's Slocum?"

Jenkins shrugged. "Likely went around while we were busy here. No telling where he is now. Maybe slipped past the canyon during the fracas and headed on east. Maybe doubled back, maybe went around some other way. Could be he's behind us right now."

Deschamp checked the quick surge of raw fear, the urge to dive behind the nearest cover. In his mind's eye, he could see himself—in the buck-horn sights of a Winchester or the center of a telescopic sight on a buffalo gun. It wasn't a comfortable feeling.

Jenkins's next comment didn't help the wiggle in Deschamp's gut all that much. "Thought I heard a couple of shots from back on the trail we rode down on. Hard to tell, as much shooting as was going on." The one-eyed man pulled a plug of tobacco from his pocket and gnawed off a fresh chew.

If Jenkins was worried about being in somebody's sights, he wasn't showing it, Deschamp thought. One by one, Deschamp riders filtered on foot down the canyon walls and strode to where the two men stood over the kid's body. Deschamp glanced around, his face twisted in disgust and rage.

"Somebody tell Bud and Foley to bring the horses." He waited until a lithe young man strode away, then signaled to the others to gather around closer. "Boys, I don't know what happened here, but somethin' tells me we better get back to camp *muy pronto*. I ain't likin' the looks of this. I ain't likin' it a bit."

"You know, Boss," Jenkins said softly, "might be a good idea if somebody went to check on Big George. He was supposed to signal us if anybody rode past him. That notch he's watching is the only trail up out of the badlands for miles. Except the one we rode down here on."

Deschamp snorted in disgust. "Big George. The bastard probably snuck a bottle with him and passed out." But he turned to one of the men at the edge of the group. "Ned, go fetch George. You find him drunk, shoot the damn fool on the spot. The rest of you, reload your guns and get ready to ride. The hosses'll be here any minute."

Slocum's heart skipped a beat, then steadied, as the creak of saddle leather, muffled voices, and hoofbeats drifted up Kiowa Canyon.

They were coming. Slocum shouldered his rifle, unconcerned about the odds he was about to face. He was gambling that they would scatter and take cover when he opened fire. If they didn't, it wouldn't matter. He'd go down before the charge.

Every man died, eventually. Slocum figured when his time came, it came, and the where of it wouldn't matter. Kiowa Canyon was as good a spot as any to leave his bones.

Slocum could barely make out the sights of the .44-40 now. The horsemen rounding the bend were dark lumps against a deep gray background.

And still, no sign of Lisa.

He forced the worry from his mind and picked his target from the dark figures below. Not Deschamp. The bastard didn't deserve to go that easy. Slocum lined the sights as best he could on the stocky rider at Deschamp's side and squeezed the trigger.

The muzzle flash of the Winchester half blinded Slocum; he couldn't see the man go down, but he heard the solid whop of lead on flesh an instant after he pulled the trigger. The sound told him his slug had found the mark.

He levered a second quick, unaimed shot into the group of

riders. Startled yelps and confused shouts sounded over the echoes of Slocum's shots. Slocum ducked from beneath the juniper, sprinted two steps to his right, and flung himself behind the cover of a low boulder. He had barely hit the ground before fire flashed from half-a-dozen guns below. Lead sprayed limbs from the juniper; other slugs whined overhead or fell short, hit the hard-packed trail, and screamed away.

Slocum fired by instinct at the spot where one muzzle flash bloomed, and grunted in grim satisfaction at the sharp cry of pain that followed. Slocum winced as a slug spanged from the top of the boulder near his shoulder and whined into the blackness. The men below were firing wildly, unsure of how many and where their foes were. With any luck, they'd think at least two men held the high ground on the canyon trail.

Slocum slapped another round downrange, knew the round hit nothing, and dropped behind the boulder. A flurry of pistol and rifle shots raked the trail. Slocum chanced a glance over the boulder, and saw the dark shapes below scatter and dart for cover, some afoot, others still in the saddle.

Four of the riders didn't bolt. They leaned over their mounts' necks, dug in the spurs, and charged.

Slocum put down his rifle, pulled his handgun, and waited. In close-quarter fighting in near-darkness, the six-gun had the edge on the rifle. The first two men neared the boulder fall, bent low, riding hard. They were within twenty yards before Slocum fired, deliberately holding low. A horse squealed and went down under his slug. The rider tumbled free, rolled to his feet, and came up shooting.

The man was good. Stone shards dug into Slocum's cheek, a slug tugged at the crown of his hat, and another whipped past his ear so close he could hear the hum of the bullet.

The other three were almost on Slocum now. He steeled himself for the shock of lead, his jaw set in grim determination to take as many with him as he could. He spun away from the boulder into the open, rolled to one knee, and fired. The slug knocked one man over the rump of his horse. Then Slocum was looking at certain death, the twin bores of a sawed-off shotgun less than twenty feet away—

The shotgunner suddenly threw both hands in the air, the weapon spinning away. The familiar, flat blast of a Schofield .45 sounded, then again, and the remaining horseman abruptly spun his mount and spurred away.

Despite the buzz of a slug past his ear, Slocum sighed in relief. Now he knew for sure where Lisa was. Backing his play. Except for random, wild shots from the canyon below, the only real threat now was the man afoot in the rocks. Slocum turned his full attention to the rockfall where the man crouched. Flame spurted from the rocks. Slocum emptied his Peacemaker, and heard the muzzle blasts of two Schofield shots from off to his left. A second later, a dark form slid from the rocks and lay still.

The battle stopped. Slocum heard the confused shouts from Deschamp's men and the bellow of the leader's voice as he tried to organize his force.

"Lisa," Slocum called softly.

"Over here." The reply came from behind a black earth mound across the trail.

Slocum reloaded his Colt and Winchester quickly and sprinted to Lisa's side, keeping low to the ground. No shots came from the canyon floor, only the sound of loud voices raised in argument and the fidgeting hoofbeats of frightened horses.

"Are you all right?" Slocum said.

"I'm fine." Even in the near-blackness, Slocum could see the firm set of Lisa's jawline. "You?"

"Thanks to you, never better. You pulled my skillet out of the fire just now."

Lisa slid a sixth cartridge into the Schofield and snapped the weapon shut. "I told you earlier I wasn't through with you yet, remember?"

"I remember. Thanks anyhow. Let's get out of here. I doubt Deschamp and his men will be in any real hurry to come after us. We can be with Dan before those fellows get organized and work up the guts to scout the place out. Is Duke up to a hard three-mile ride?"

"He'll manage," Lisa said. "He's tougher than he looks." She reached out and stroked Slocum's cheek; her fingers were chilled. "Let's go. And Slocum, don't get us lost. I can't tell up from down or north from south in the middle of the night."

The first mile or so passed in silence, Slocum concentrating on keeping his bearings and following the faint trail toward Osage Springs while moving as rapidly as they could, alternating the horses' gaits between fast walk and trot.

Finally, the stars began to throw enough light that Slocum

was able to turn part of his mind from the problem of navigation through country he hadn't seen in years. Now he was satisfied they were on the right track. The position of the North Star, the trail becoming more distinct in the starlight, and the occasional black mass of a familiar landmark let him relax a bit.

He turned to Lisa. "It's none of my business, so don't answer if you don't want to," Slocum said, "but it caught me a bit by surprise when you mentioned having a baby."

Lisa removed her hat and ran a hand across her face. The starlight seemed to bathe her skin with a pale velvet cloth. She sighed.

"I've never told anyone about it since it happened," she said, her voice soft. "It was six months after I stole the mule and left home. I made it as far as Dodge City. The baby was born there—three months early. Born dead."

"I'm sorry to hear that," Slocum said sincerely.

Lisa fell silent for a moment, then said, "It was probably for the best. The midwife said the child was—not whole. She said it—he—a boy—had almost no brain. For most of my life, I thought it was my fault. It wasn't until just a few years ago that I found out from a doctor that those things happened sometimes." She took a deep breath and stared into Slocum's eyes. "He said it wasn't uncommon in cases of inbreeding. Especially incest."

Slocum's jaw clenched. "That son of a bitch," he muttered grimly. "How could anyone do that? To his own daughter—"

"What Father did to me personally isn't the worst of it, Slocum. You might as well know the whole sordid story. Then maybe you'll understand why I hate June Deschamp so much." Lisa squared her shoulders with an obvious effort. "After a while, Father got to drinking so much that he couldn't—couldn't get it up again. It was a blessing to me, for a while. Then it got worse."

"Worse?"

"Yes." Lisa's voice tightened even more. "That was when he decided that if he couldn't use me, somebody else might as well. That somebody else was his brother. He's the one who made me pregnant. And as a result, left me unable to ever have children."

Her words put a hard, cold knot in Slocum's gut. "God, Lisa. I don't know what to say—"

"Let me finish, before I lose my courage," she interrupted. "My last name hasn't always been Barnes. Before I changed it, it was Deschamp. June Deschamp is my uncle. The father of my dead baby."

Slocum rode in silence for a quarter mile or so, trying with little success to check the rage that boiled in his gut. "My God, Lisa," he finally managed to say, "I understand now. And as much as I'd like to, I promise you I won't kill him. At least not until you face him."

"Thank you. You once said a person had to face his or her own demons, Slocum. That's what I have to do. It's the only way I can put all this behind me, get a fresh start on a real life." She sighed, her breath soft in the cool night. "I already owe you for giving part of myself back to me."

"I did?"

"Yes. Until you came along, I never knew that I could be a real woman—able to—I don't know how do I say it. Lie with a man, feel true pleasure. To know how it feels to—to share instead of just be used for money." She reached out and put a hand on Slocum's forearm. "I was a whore, Slocum. In body, at least. In a way, I suppose I was punishing myself by spreading my legs for anyone who had the price. There was no pleasure in it for me, only money. I told myself that if I was going to be used like that, I might as well make it pay."

"I understand, Lisa. Or at least, I think I do. No man could really understand what you went through."

Lisa turned to face him, her head held high. "That's over, Slocum—that part of my life. Now, thanks to you—and Dan's teaching—I know I can be more than that."

Slocum said softly, "You already are, Lisa."

After a moment she said, "Slocum, now that you know the truth, will you ever be able to come to me again? To see me in the same light?"

Slocum nodded. "What happened wasn't your fault, Lisa. It's what you are now that counts. It doesn't matter a whit to me. As you say, the past is history. Today and tomorrow and the years after that are the only things that matter."

Starlight glinted from the tears on Lisa's cheeks. "I'll never be able to completely forget, and I'm sure as hell not ready to forgive," she said. "But at least, when June Deschamp pays for what he did to me, I'll be on my way to learning to handle it. Slocum, is revenge ever a cure?"

"Maybe not a cure," Slocum said honestly, "but it can be satisfaction. You can have Deschamp, Lisa. You have the right more than I. What he did to you was worse than what he did to Quill and Joe. At least he didn't leave them alive to suffer."

After a moment, Lisa cleared her throat. "Did you love her, Slocum?"

The question caught him a bit by surprise. He reached into his own mind, frowning, searching for the answer. Finally, he shook his head. "I don't know, Lisa. I felt different when I was around Quill—and Joe Summerhawk. More relaxed and happy than I have been in years. But love her? I can't say, because I'm not sure what love is."

Lisa sighed. "Please don't take this wrong, Slocum, but it's possible that you've suffered more than you realize. If you don't know what love is."

Slocum squared his shoulders. "Maybe you're right. The trails I've ridden didn't give me much of an opportunity to get really close to any woman. At least not close enough to want to spend the rest of my life with her. But I know I felt enough for Quill that there's an empty spot in me that won't be filled until I take her scalp, and Joe's, back home to them. Maybe that emptiness will never go away. But I'll find some comfort in the fact that they will then be able to rest in peace."

"I think you did love her," Lisa said. "But Lord knows, I'm no expert in that." She fell silent again for a while, then finally said, "Slocum, I'd like to know more about you. You mentioned you were originally from Georgia, I recall, and I have the impression the war did something to change your life. I know you have a reputation as a dangerous man, a loner."

Slocum lifted a hand and reined Chief to a stop. "I'll tell you about it later, Lisa. Right now, we're almost within rifle shot of Osage Springs. Dan should be nearby."

"He is." Waggoner's voice from nearby gave Slocum a start. Slocum had to squint to make out the lean man's shape against the darkness of a juniper clump at the edge of the trail. "Everything go all right?"

"According to plan. You?"

"No problem here." Waggoner stepped from the shadows. "Care for some coffee?"

"I'd kill for it," Lisa said emphatically, "and a smoke. I've been dying by inches all the way here for a cigarette and a cup of hot, strong coffee."

"Then get down and follow me."

Waggoner led them down a narrow side track into a shallow, rocky bowl below the line of sight from the canyon trail above and the camp beneath.

Slocum smelled the coffee minutes before they squatted beside a small bed of coals and took the cups Waggoner filled from a battered pot. "It's safe to smoke here too," Waggoner said. "Anybody would have to be right on top of this place to see a match flare or smell tobacco."

Slocum sipped at the coffee, sighed in satisfaction, and lit the cigarettes Lisa rolled. The rich, heavy smoke soothed his nerves and stroked his lungs. After an appreciative moment, he raised an eyebrow at Waggoner. "Want to tell me what happened here?"

Waggoner shrugged. "As I said, no problem. The two men left behind weren't very good sentries. I have the surviving one bound, gagged, and staked to a cedar tree a few yards from here."

"The surviving one?" Lisa asked.

"The other decided to put up a fight. I'm afraid I hit him a bit too hard with the Dragoon. I dragged the body out of sight, away from Deschamp's camp."

"Oh," Lisa said.

Slocum asked, "So what's the tactical situation?"

Waggoner topped off their cups, poured the remainder of the pot into his own mug, and dumped the coffee grounds on the fading coals. The faint red specks sizzled and went black.

"I hope you don't think I overstepped the bounds of the plan, Slocum," Waggoner said, peering over the rim of his cup, "but the situation that presented itself here was simply too inviting to turn down." He sipped at his cup and half smiled. "I analyzed the situation and came to the conclusion there might be a better way than try to ambush the lot of them here."

"Let's hear it," Slocum said.

"It seemed that I had sufficient time to play around a bit, so I took the liberty of scattering Deschamp's spare mounts from hell to breakfast, as you Westerners say. Except for the horses they're riding now, Deschamp's men are afoot."

Slocum nodded his approval. "Good thinking, Dan. It will slow him down."

"Unfortunately," Waggoner said, "they'd already moved your palouse string and the other stolen animals. They're being held at a ranch called the Slash Y a short ride from here. We could pick them up on the way to the Pease.''

Lisa frowned. ''Won't trailing a bunch of horses slow us down?''

''Not if what I have in mind works out,'' Slocum said.

''You have a devious look in your eyes, mister,'' Lisa said.

Slocum grinned at her. ''Only because I *am* a devious son of a bitch at heart, girl. Dan's the tactician. I'm the sneaky ace of the deck.''

Waggoner rolled and lit a cigarette. ''I also liberated what supplies we could use from their stores, weighted the rest with rocks, and threw them into the deepest part of the spring. I slit their water bags, bashed in canteens, and appropriated some two thousand dollars in cash. I suspect it came from Deschamp's raid on the Lucas ranch.''

The half smile on Slocum's face spread to a full grin. ''The best offense of a campaign. Deny the enemy supplies, funds, and transportation, and he's yours. Those tactics worked well for the Union.'' Slocum's grin faded. ''One question, Dan— why did you leave one sentry alive?''

Waggoner downed the rest of his coffee and sighed. ''I thought it to our advantage to interrogate a prisoner. Again unfortunately, he didn't know the precise spot on the red bluff of the Pease where the army payroll is hidden. Slocum, would you consider a slight alteration in plans?''

''Let's hear it.''

''We continue to harass Deschamp, thin his ranks at every opportunity. Keep them basically afoot with no supplies. We get to the red bluff before Deschamp and his gang—and leave his man here alive to tell him where we're going. A few days under those conditions, Deschamp will be a desperate man. Desperate men make mistakes.''

Slocum finished his smoke, ground the butt under a heel, and grinned at Waggoner. ''Looks like I owe you an apology, Dan.''

''How's that?''

''You sneak better than I thought.''

# 12

Slocum sat easy in the saddle, forearms crossed over the horn, and smiled pleasantly at the stocky, red-haired man on the Slash Y porch.

Nate Kimber's weathered face had turned two shades darker in the last few seconds.

"I'll give you one thing, feller," Kimber said, his voice low and menacing, "you got one hell of a set of *cojones,* riding in here and telling a man he's got stolen stock on his place. One word from me and you'd catch so much lead they'd have to hire a freight wagon to lug you to the graveyard."

Slocum glanced at the three other men on the porch, hands near holstered weapons, and at the rifle muzzle sticking over a windowsill. "I guess you could at that. But it would cost you more than I think you're willing to pay."

"What the hell are you talking about?"

Slocum's smile faded. His eyes narrowed. "Just that if you or any of your men try to point a weapon at me, I'll kill you on the spot. And my friend on the ridge back there will put a big chunk of lead in the man with the rifle at the window. At the same time, the lady standing behind that cottonwood tree over there will take down a couple more Slash Y men."

Kimber peered past Slocum at the silhouette on the low hill almost a quarter of a mile away, glanced toward the tree, and snorted. "One gun so far off a man can't see it. And a woman?"

"Don't underestimate the lady. Or the fellow on the hill. That could be a bad mistake."

"I don't bluff, mister."

"I don't either," Slocum said. "So what's it going to be, Kimber? Do we talk it over or start shooting? It would be a shame for you to get killed because June Deschamp can't keep his hands off other people's horses."

Indecision flickered in Kimber's eyes. His gaze again flicked toward the distant form kneeling on the ridge, to the cottonwood tree, then back to Slocum. "You know June?"

"You might say we've met. Well, Nate?"

"Who the hell are you, mister?"

"Name's Slocum."

Kimber's ruddy face paled. After a moment, he shrugged and sighed. "What the hell. You're June's problem, not mine. Take your damned horses. They're in the holding pasture just north of here."

"I know where they are, Nate." Slocum straightened in the saddle and uncrossed his arms. His right hand remained on the horn, inches from the butt of the Peacemaker at his left hip. "You know, it would be mighty neighborly of you and your boys to give us a hand. Might take a few miles to get those forty ponies settled in to trail—"

"Forty!" Color flamed back into Kimber's cheeks. "What the hell are you talking about, forty? Christ, that's my whole remuda!"

"Oh, don't worry about that, Nate. We're not horse thieves. That's yours and June's specialty. We'll leave the Slash Y mounts at Tascosa."

"Slocum, you can't—"

Slocum glared hard at Kimber. "The hell I can't. We have no intention of leaving fresh horses behind for your buddy June. You can pick up your horses from Sheriff Jim East and Texas Ranger Captain G. W. Arrington at Tascosa. I expect they'll want to see proof of ownership. Bills of sale and the like."

A muscle twitched in Kimber's jaw. "Dammit, Slocum, you've pushed me about as far as I'll push! I've got hundreds of dollars tied up in those horses!"

"If you bought them fair and square, you have no problem, Nate. Now, time's wasting. Unless you'd like to be looking up at six feet of dirt, call off your wolves and I'll call off mine. Otherwise, I'll drop you where you stand before you have time to break wind."

For a moment, Slocum wondered if he'd pushed too hard and too far. The Slash Y owner was about a whisker away from going for the Colt at his hip.

"Wes Worden wasn't a good neighbor," Slocum said.

"What about Wes?"

"He wanted to argue with us yesterday. We had to kill the whole bunch."

A surprised expression sifted over the outrage in Kimber's face. "Wes Worden? You three took Wes and his boys down?"

"He and his men weren't as good as they thought."

After a moment, Kimber's shoulders slumped.

"All right, dammit, you've got the whip hand. For now." A bit of defiance returned to Kimber's tone. "But you haven't heard the last of this, Slocum. By God, I'll hunt you down like a dog for this."

Slocum shrugged. "Now or later, Kimber. It makes no difference to me. Neighborly sort, or dead man. Your call."

Kimber blinked, tried to hold Slocum's steady gaze, and failed. Finally, he turned to the other Slash Y riders.

"All right, boys, mount up. We'll settle accounts another time."

"One more thing, Nate," Slocum said casually, "you and your men leave your weapons here. You won't be needing guns to gather and trail a few head of horses."

Kimber glared at Slocum, a fresh surge of rage flickering in his eyes. "Why the hell should we do that?"

"It's pretty simple. I'd feel a lot better if we didn't have to watch our backs. And I'm in a bit of a hurry, friend. Let's go."

"Nate," one of the riders barked, "are you gonna stand there and let that horse's ass hooraw you like a greenhorn?"

"As a matter of fact I am, Bill," Kimber said, "on account of I'm not in any real rush to get shot. I don't plan to tangle with anybody who's gun savvy enough to take Wes Worden. Not when they've got us cold, and sure as hell not when this particular horse's ass is named Slocum. Do as the man said."

Slocum waited until the men on the porch and two more from the house stacked their rifles and shucked out of their gunbelts. Kimber's side arm was the last one on the pile. Slocum knew from his predawn scout that the six men accounted for the Slash Y headquarters crew. Kimber glared bleakly at Slocum, then shook his head. "Damned if you don't blow the suds off the brew, Slocum. Got to admit I admire a man with sand.''

Kimber turned to the waiting men. ''Mount up, boys.'' He stepped to the hitch rail and untied the reins of a tight-twisted little sorrel mustang. ''June won't like this much, you know. He'll be after you like stink on a skunk.''

''That,'' Slocum said calmly, ''is *his* problem, not mine. Now, if you'll lead the way?''

Three hours and a dozen miles later, Slocum called a halt. The horses were more trail savvy than Slocum expected. They'd probably had been stolen so many times they knew every landmark from El Paso to Montana, he mused.

The forty mounts moved at a steady, ground-eating walk behind Waggoner's black. Dan had taken the point; he knew the faded track of the Southern Santa Fe Trail, with its faint wagon ruts still visible in the rolling prairie soil south of the Canadian River in the Texas Panhandle.

Slocum turned to Kimber.

''Call in your men, Nate. This is as far as you go.''

At Kimber's yell and wave, the Slash Y riders peeled away from the remuda and rode to the boss's side.

''All right, all of you step down,'' Slocum said. ''You too, Nate. Strip the saddles. You can pick up the horses you're riding at Tascosa along with the rest.''

''What!'' Kimber yelped, his face darkening in rage. ''You're going to leave us out here afoot?''

Slocum shrugged. ''The Apaches say a good long walk puts a man's soul at peace. If you don't dawdle too much, you can be back at the ranch by, say, midnight.''

''Damn you, Slocum. Damn you straight to Hell.''

''I'll meet you there or greet you there, depending,'' Slocum said. ''Now, strip the saddles and tack.'' He kept a close watch on the man called Bill as the Slash Y riders unsaddled. The swarthy man was as mad as a stepped-on rattler, and Slocum knew the type. Hot tempered to the point of stupidity, and usually carrying a backup gun—

Bill's hand snaked into his saddlebag, came out holding a snub-nosed revolver. Slocum whipped his hand across his body, drew his Peacemaker, and drove a slug into the man's chest before Bill could even swing the short handgun toward Slocum. The rider staggered, spun, and went down on his face under the impact of the .44-40 slug.

"Jesus," Kimber muttered. "He never even got off a shot."

"Too bad about Bill," Slocum said as he holstered the handgun. "You'd think a man would have more sense than to commit suicide like that." He called Lisa over and told her to go through the other saddlebags. She found no additional hideout guns.

Slocum turned to Kimber. "We'll loan you a trenching tool if you want to bury your man."

"Nah. Bill was a dumb son of a bitch. I'm surprised he didn't get killed sooner. Let the coyotes have him."

Slocum nodded and touched fingers to his hat brim. "Adios, Nate. Appreciate your help."

"We'll meet again, Slocum."

"Maybe. Maybe not. Who knows where trails lead for men like us, Nate? You boys better head on back now. It's a long walk back to the ranch."

Slocum watched as the Slash Y riders trudged away, a couple of them already limping in high-heeled riding boots that never were meant for walking.

"Slocum?" It was the first time Lisa had spoken since before the showdown at the ranch headquarters. "Did you have to leave those men afoot? I mean, to embarrass them like that? I know enough about stiff-necked male pride to put down a bet that they're not likely to ever forget it."

"They won't," Slocum said solemnly, "but it's six more horses Deschamp won't have access to. That means Deschamp will be on tired horses that are as sore-footed as Kimber's men will be. That will give us the main advantage we need. Time."

Lisa's brow furrowed in thought. "But won't Deschamp just steal some more horses? From another ranch?"

"That'll take time too," Slocum said. "The one thing that makes the Slash Y a horse thief's heaven is that it's so isolated. There isn't another ranch within two days' ride of the place. And I know how to take care of that problem too."

"Do you always have an answer, Slocum?"

"Not always. But I've ridden so many owlhoot trails I can think like an outlaw. Most times." He lifted Chief's reins. "Let's get these ponies on the move again. A couple of hours up the trail there's a creek with good grass and water and a decent campsite. We'll rest there a while, let the horses graze and water, and change mounts." He glanced at Lisa's chestnut gelding. "Old Duke there looks like his tired's hanging out."

Lisa lifted herself in the stirrups and rubbed a nicely shaped buttock. "He's not the only one."

Slocum wanted to rub her butt for her, but decided to put it off until later. There was work to be done first, and he needed a bath and shave. He figured he probably smelled like the downhill end of a climbing mountain goat, and the stubble on his jaws scratched his own neck.

He said, "We'll reach Tascosa in two days and drop off the horses. There's too many for us to wrangle and still have the mobility we need. I'll board the horses stolen from the Nez Percé land in Tascosa. We can rest up a night there, in a real hotel with a real bed and bathtub, and still be able to reach the red bluff on the Pecos in two or three more days."

"Then you were serious about leaving Kimber's horses with the law?"

"Yes. I may be a lot of things, Lisa, but I'm no horse thief. Jim East and Cap Arrington are hard men, tough but fair, and probably the best lawmen in Texas. They'll sort out the remuda and return the stolen horses to their rightful owners. It's going to be an expensive summer for Nate Kimber."

They rode in silence for a moment, trailing behind the docile horses, before Lisa spoke again, a faint smile tugging at her lips. "I was just thinking about what happened back at the ranch. Slocum, you run a hell of a bluff. Remind me never to play poker with you."

Lisa snuggled against Slocum's chest as dawn lightened the window of the Exchange Hotel room to a soft gray rectangle.

The one-story adobe hotel room was small, slightly run-down, but well appointed, and the soft feather mattress cradled her in warmth and contentment. Slocum's left arm, tucked beneath her neck and draped over her shoulder, his fingers stroking the swell of her breast, also helped.

"Girl," Slocum said, his voice soft and relaxed, "you do have a way of waking a man that no rooster could ever match."

"Thank you, sir. And, I might add, the way you come awake makes a woman wish it was yesterday evening all over again. I just *thought* bedrolls were fun."

Slocum grinned. "That reminds me. We haven't used that second bedroll too much lately. Think we should switch?"

"Nope. Yours is just fine. When we sweat it completely out, we'll switch to mine." Her fingertips drifted over his upper chest and firm belly muscles. "Do you feel like talking now? About your life, I mean? You did promise to tell me later what brought you out West and why you do—what you do."

Slocum sighed, raised his left hand, and stroked her thick, dark hair, enjoying the scent of rosewater and woman. "It isn't a long story. I grew up on the family farm in Georgia. I was the only one of my family to survive the war. When the fighting ended, I went back home and started putting the farm back in order. I hung up my guns and vowed I'd never use them again. It was a vow I couldn't keep."

"What happened?"

"Carpetbaggers and Reconstructionists." Slocum frowned at the memory. "One day not long after I'd come home, a federal judge rode up and told me he was taking over the farm. He said my father hadn't paid taxes on the land before he died. That was a damned lie. William Slocum never left a debt unpaid. I told him to get off my land."

"Did he?"

"For a few days. When he came back, he had a hired gun with him, a man who was supposed a lawman but had thief and killer stamped all over him. That's when I broke my vow about never taking another life. I went in the house, got my guns, shot them both, burned the house, barn, and crops, saddled up, and headed West. I've been riding one trail after another since."

"So you're a wanted man?"

"East of the Mississippi, maybe. I stopped worrying about it years ago. Nobody on the Western frontier gives a whit about some crooked judge and his henchman getting themselves shot in Georgia."

Lisa pressed her cheek closer against his chest. "That's as it should be." Her fingers traced the scar on his belly, touched the puckered bullet wound scar on his chest. "Looks like you've made an enemy or two along the way."

Slocum glanced down at the scars. "A few. The bullet hole's courtesy of Quantrill. He took offense when I tried to stop the butchery in Lawrence. A halfbreed down in Socorro gave me the belly scar. He had a big knife. He never used it on anyone else."

Lisa shivered. "Just the idea of a knife gives me the weeblies. Suppose Dan's up yet?"

"Dan's probably been up since before dawn. Weeblies?"

"Wobbly knees, crawly skin, wheezy breathing."

"Oh. Speaking of weak and wobbly knees, mine may be strong enough now to hold me up," Slocum said. "Hungry?"

"Famished." She gave him a maiden-aunt peck on the forehead. "You know me, Slocum. *Always* hungry. Now, roll out of the sack and get dressed before my nipples get hard again."

"They are already."

"Your fault. But you know the rules. You can't have any more until you feed me, you thoughtless cad." She pulled away, swung her feet over the bed, and plucked her new twill riding pants from the chair at bedside. "How long can we stay here?"

Slocum sighed. "I'm afraid our stay in Tascosa's over when breakfast is finished. It's back to bedrolls on the ground and trail camps for us. We can't spring any little surprises on Deschamp by lounging around Tascosa."

"Dear old Uncle June," Lisa said somewhat wistfully despite the sharp edge in her tone. "I sure hope he doesn't get bitten by a rattler and die before I get my hands on him."

Deschamp yanked at the reins as his gaunt gray gelding stumbled again and almost went down. He barked a sharp curse and tried to blink away the scratchy feeling beneath his eyelids. He twisted in the saddle to stare at the men strung out behind him.

He wasn't the only one in bad shape. The ten men behind him slouched in their saddles, half dozing, shoulders slumped in exhaustion. One, Dade, had his arm in a sling. Blood still seeped through the bandage over Ned's head. The two men barely had the strength to stay on their mounts. Deschamp had almost left the wounded pair behind, but at least they could still pull a trigger. And if they fell out of the saddle, he thought, he'd just take their horses and ride on.

The whole damn thing couldn't have gone worse.

Four of his best gunhands lay miles behind, three in Kiowa Canyon, one at Osage Springs. Two of them were his best men. Jenkins had taken a slug through the brisket on the charge up the canyon trail. Curly had died harder, with both kidneys blown out.

For their troubles, they'd shot up three dead men and a couple of horses. He'd started with the biggest band of tough men since Quantrill's days. And he had just ten—even if he counted Bud—left.

Now they limped along on worn-out, sore-footed mounts that couldn't break a trot, with only enough grub for half rations and maybe a half gallon of water apiece. No whiskey. Not even a decent bedroll. The buffalo gunner had dumped all their camp equipment in the deepest part of Osage Springs.

Nate Kimber had given them what he could spare—a couple of blankets each but no canvas groundsheets, a water skin, a skillet and coffeepot, a few tin cups, and half a gunnysack of grub. To top it all off, he and his men had less than fifty dollars left between them. Slocum and his partners had taken most every damn dime Deschamp had earned from the Lucas job.

Even their ammunition was running low. What they hadn't burned up blazing away in a wasted night fight had been sunk in Osage Springs. Two weeks ago they'd been rich men. Now they were broke. Deschamp knew he had no choice. He had to get to the Pease, to the army payroll buried there, then hightail it for Mexico. And if what the man Waggoner had caught and tied up like a branding calf said was right, Slocum and his partners would be waiting at the red bluff on the Pease.

Desperation, rage, and a touch of fear boiled in Deschamp's gut. Settling accounts with Slocum was proving to be a damn sight tougher than he'd counted on.

"June?"

Deschamp glanced at the man who rode beside him. "Yeah?"

Hake Horrel removed the Mexican hat from his oversized head and ran his fingers through a shock of thick, curly black hair. "How much longer to Tascosa? We gotta get our horses back pretty soon, or we're gonna be walkin'. These ponies we're on now are about wore down."

Deschamp peered at the hazy, blue-gray shape of a distant peak. The landmark shimmered behind heat waves, even though the sun wasn't that hot. "If we were goin' to Tascosa, Hake, we'd be there about noon tomorrow. But we're not."

"We're not? How come?" Horrel's bushy eyebrows drew into almost a single patch of fur above pale gray eyes so lightly colored a man had to look hard to see anything but the little black dot in the middle, Deschamp thought. Despite the big head, which looked even bigger on a skinny five-foot-four body, Horrel wasn't too long on brains.

"Because we been foxed, Hake. That damn Slocum and his

partners knew we can't claim those ponies in Tascosa. Hell, nearly ever one of them's stolen.''

''Can't we just go get 'em back anyway?''

Deschamp shook his head. ''Not unless you want to tangle with Jim East, Cap Arrington, and their men. I know I don't want any part of them.''

Horrel shook his head. ''Me neither. I reckon that Slocum knowed it too. He's pretty savvy, ain't he?''

The question stirred the smoldering embers of rage in Deschamp's gut. ''Got to give the devil his due,'' Deschamp said reluctantly. ''That damned Slocum *is* savvy. And he's good. Anybody can take down Wes Worden's hardcases and then catch Nate Kimber with his britches down ain't asleep in the saddle.''

Horrel tugged the sombrero back onto his head and stared into the distance for a moment. ''Sure wish Nate and the boys had come with us.''

Deschamp snorted in disgust. How in the hell could Nate have let just three people get the drop on the whole Slash Y outfit? And then have the balls to tell June Deschamp he was on his own, that not a Slash Y man would help him out?

''To hell with Nate,'' Deschamp snapped. ''We don't need him. There's ten of us and two of them.''

''Three, countin' the woman. I reckon a man oughtn't sell her short, June. What I seen and heard, she's a hardcase. Maybe as tough as the two men.''

Deschamp snorted. ''You ridin' scared, Hake? Of a woman, for Christ's sake?''

''Nope,'' Horrel said agreeably. ''Just figured a man might live longer was he a tad careful, that's all.''

''Careful my ass.'' Heat flared in Deschamp's cheeks. ''Slocum and that buffalo gunner's as good as dead. We'll save the bitch to play with a while before we cut her throat.''

Deschamp idly stroked the two scalplocks tied to his saddle strings. Fondling the thick black hair helped calm his nerves. He studied the distant blue-gray peak. The idea that had come to him a couple of hours ago firmed up in his mind, and brought the faintest hint of a smile to his lips. And Slocum wouldn't be expecting it.

''You just do what you're told, Hake, you and the boys. Leave the thinking to me. Fetch Bud. I got a job for him.''

''Sure thing, Boss.''

Five minutes later, Bud kneed his gelding alongside Deschamp's horse. "Hake said you wanted me." Bud's tone was surly. The kid was still mad about missing the fight in the canyon and the ass-chewing he'd gotten from the badlands scout.

"Yeah, Bud. You see that peak off yonder?"

"What about it?"

"That big bay horse of yours is the only one we got left that ain't half dead. I got a job for you—and this time, don't fuck it up like usual. Just do what you're told and get your butt back here."

"Dammit, June—"

"Shut up, boy!" Deschamp leveled a hard glare at his nephew. "Listen to me now, and listen good. You been so all-fired anxious to use that hogleg, now's your chance."

Bud's eyes brightened; his hand drifted to the butt of the Bisley Colt in his holster and the pout faded from his face.

"About a mile this side of that peak, where the country gets rough, you'll hit a dry creek with an old cottonwood that's been struck by lightning. Can't miss it. Follow that creek south by east about five miles, you'll top a rise and see an LE outfit line camp. That's where they pasture the horses they ain't usin'. Shouldn't be but one man, a line-camp wrangler, watchin' over 'em. You get a chance, kill him."

"You bet, June!"

"Now, don't go tryin' any fast-draw gunhawk tricks, dammit. Just bushwack the wrangler. Savvy so far?"

"I got it, June."

"Okay. Now, we'll be camped at a spring at the southwest base of that peak, in a stand of chinaberry trees. Bring a dozen LE horses, more if you can handle 'em, to us there. Reckon you can manage that?"

Bud pulled his revolver, spun the cylinder to check the loads, and holstered the weapon. Eagerness and excitement brought a flush to his cheeks. "I can handle it."

"Make damn sure you do. One more thing—if there's more than one man there, don't get et up by the stupids. Get your butt to that spring, and I'll send some help back with you."

Bud nodded and lifted the reins.

"Bud," Deschamp said coldly, "I mean it. Don't screw this up. We got to have fresh horses."

"Don't worry about me, June. I'll get the job done."

Bud kneed the bay into a steady trot. Deschamp watched until the young man was a quarter mile ahead, then grumbled, "I'll worry, Bud. Anytime you're on the job, I'll worry."

At least, he thought, if the kid got himself killed, no big loss; he'd only picked Bud for the job because he was the only man whose horse wasn't half dead—and the damn bay wouldn't let anybody but Bud ride him.

"Hake!" Deschamp called.

Horrel rode up. "Yeah, Boss?"

Deschamp nodded toward the peak. "You know that spring at the edge of the peak?" At Horrel's nod, Deschamp said, "Ride up ahead and scout it out. Make sure we're not ridin' into a bunch of guns."

Horrel nodded and spurred his exhausted horse into a semblance of a half trot.

Deschamp stared past the rider toward the peak. He couldn't shake the feeling something wasn't right. But he had no choice. That spring had the only good water and grass for miles, and there was game around the peak—mule deer, wild turkey, even mustangs. If Bud didn't screw up again, they'd be back on fresh horses and have meat in the sack for the last long ride to the Pease.

And if somebody *was* waiting up ahead, he'd know it. When they shot Hake.

# 13

"Company coming," Dan Waggoner called from his station atop the towering peak.

Slocum scrambled up the last few yards of the steep trail to the spot the Comanches and Kiowas had named Big-See-Place, and dropped to a knee beside Waggoner.

"How many?"

Waggoner peered through the long tube atop the barrel of the big-bore rifle. "Two. About a mile out, a couple of hundred yards between them. Here, take a look." Waggoner eased away from the rifle, its forestock resting across a folded blanket atop the rock outcrop.

Slocum settled his shoulder against the stock of the rifle and peered through the telescopic sight. It took him a moment to find the right eye-relief distance before the field of the scope snapped into focus.

The view through the powerful scope took some getting used to; inside the glass, the first rider seemed to be almost at the edge of the peak, but to the naked eye was barely a dark blot in the distance. There was no mistaking the lead rider, mounted on a tall, leggy black horse. Sunlight glittered from silver studs. Slocum lost sight of Bud as the rider disappeared beneath a rise.

Slocum spent a moment locating the other man in the glass. The magnification seemed to distort movement and distance. Then the crosshairs finally settled on the rider, a small man wearing a wide-brimmed Mexican sombrero.

"One out front's the dandy, Bud," Slocum said. "Don't

153

know the other jasper by name, but I got a glimpse of the sombrero and the horse during the Kiowa Canyon fight. Deschamp man.'' He leaned back from the telescopic sight and gestured for Waggoner to take over. ''How strong is that thing anyway?''

''Ten-power,'' Waggoner said. ''I found out by trial and error that's the best magnification for me. Anything higher magnifies even the slightest shake or quiver—'' He abruptly glanced up from the tube, then squinted again through the eyepiece.

''What is it?'' Slocum asked.

''Bud. He's turned away, up that dry wash by the old cottonwood. Looks like you called it.''

Slocum nodded. ''He's headed for the LE range, sure enough. And toward quite a welcome from the Reynolds hands. If he gets out alive, it won't be with any horses—there or anywhere else in the Panhandle or Llano Estacado.''

''Think the ranchers believed you, Slocum?''

''Monchy Russell did.''

''Who's he?''

''Manager of the LE. The other ranchers might not take the word of a drifter, but they'll believe Monchy. Cowboys who haven't packed a gun in years will have them cleaned and ready. Things are about to get tougher for Deschamp.''

Waggoner fiddled with a knob on the side of the telescope sight. ''Second rider's coming straight in. Another few minutes and he'll be in range. Should I drop him?''

Slocum eased his own rifle into place atop the rock outcrop. ''Don't pay him any mind, Dan. Let him come in closer. I'll take care of him when he's a couple hundred yards out.'' Over the open sights of the Winchester, the horse and rider looked like a sparrow from this distance. He raised his head from the rifle stock and peered past the lone horseman. ''The others are a quarter mile or so back. Pick one.''

Waggoner shifted his rifle slightly and grunted. ''I make it eight riders in the group,'' he said. ''Deschamp and another man are out front. Remember our deal?''

''Right,'' Slocum said. ''Don't kill Deschamp just yet. I've promised you and Lisa he's yours, alive. Take the man riding beside him.'' He turned his attention from the horsemen and glanced over his shoulder, down the hill. Lisa waited, holding the horses, in a bowl-shaped rockfall at the base of the trail below. An approaching rider couldn't see her unless he'd ridden to the top of the rockfall. Slocum was satisfied with the setup. He turned his attention back to Deschamp and his men.

The minutes seemed to drag into hours as the two men waited. It didn't bother Slocum, and he knew it didn't rattle Waggoner. A good sniper could spend three days in the same spot without moving, waiting for that one sure, clean shot.

"Say when," Waggoner said as he thumbed back the heavy hammer of the Creedmore.

"I'll time it so we've both got a clean shot," Slocum said. "Six hundred yards a problem for you?"

Waggoner fiddled with the scope knob for a moment, still peering through the instrument. "Not in the least."

The lead horseman with the big sombrero was within a few feet of the sage clump Slocum had picked as a range marker. The more distant horsemen had entered an exposed area. They'd have no place to hide. Slocum cocked his Winchester and lined the sights to allow for bullet drop.

"Might as well open the dance," Slocum said.

"You lead. I'll follow."

Slocum pulled in a deep breath, let it out slowly, and gently squeezed the trigger. The Winchester thumped against his shoulder; a half second later, the man in the sombrero jerked back in the saddle.

The crack of Slocum's rifle was drowned beneath the ear-numbing muzzle blast of Waggoner's long gun. Through the boil of powder smoke, Slocum saw the man riding at Deschamp's side lift from the saddle as though hit by a sledgehammer, hang in the air for an instant, then tumble over the back of his horse.

Deschamp and the rest of his men sat for a heartbeat as if frozen in time, then scattered for whatever cover they could find. Slocum raised the muzzle of the .44-40 high and levered a couple of rounds in their direction, knowing the flat-nosed pistol slug and its forty grains of powder wouldn't reach them. But it would give them something to think about.

Waggoner's big rifle boomed again. A horse went down, spilling the rider fifty feet short of a prickly pear patch. The man scrambled on hands and knees behind the scant cover. Through the ringing in his ears, Slocum heard the metallic clicks as Waggoner worked the action, ejected the spent cartridge, and slipped another round home in the Creedmoor.

"Damn," Waggoner said, "I sure hate killing that horse. Wasn't his fault. See where Deschamp went?"

"Off to the left, behind that rocky point. He's keeping his head down. Can't say that I blame him." Slocum racked another round into the Winchester, but didn't bother to fire. There was no need to waste ammunition at this range.

Waggoner swept the valley below with his scope. "No targets available. What's your pleasure, Slocum?"

A puff of powder smoke blossomed from behind the prickly pear patch, another from behind a fallen cottonwood tree. The slugs fell harmlessly a third of the way up the peak.

"How much ammunition do you have left?"

"Six rounds with me, about thirty more in my saddle pack."

Slocum nodded. "Spend one to discourage that gent behind the prickly pear."

Waggoner thumbed back the hammer, aimed, and fired. Prickly pear pads and dust flew; a moment later, a startled squawk drifted faintly through the echoes of the shot.

"That'll do for now," Slocum said, thumbing cartridges into the loading port of his Winchester. "Let them think it over a spell. I don't think Deschamp's dumb enough to try to attack us here. He knows we could cut his bunch to pieces if he did, but you can never tell what a desperate man will do. He's got to have water, and right now we control the only good source for forty, fifty miles. We'll stay until dark, just in case. Then we'll move out."

Waggoner nodded. "Sounds logical." He turned his attention from the scope long enough to pick up and pocket the spent brass for reloading later.

Slocum said, "In case nobody told you, Dan, you're a hell of a hand with that Creedmoor. Wish I'd had one like it back on the Round Tops."

"I'm most gratified that you didn't, Slocum. Wonder what's going through Deschamp's mind along about now?"

Slocum grinned. "I wonder what's running down his leg."

Deschamp pressed his body close against the rocky ridge, his bladder yelping and his mind swirling in confusion and disbelief.

One moment he'd been riding along beside Compton; the next instant, there'd been the sound of a heavy whack of lead and Compton's brains had spattered on Deschamp's cheek.

Compton was gone before anyone heard the shot that killed him. The sound had come an instant after Deschamp heard the lighter crack of a smaller-bore rifle. He hadn't seen Hake Horrel since.

Sweat poured down Deschamp's cheeks and soaked his shirt. Two men down, a horse killed, and he'd seen nothing but powder smoke way off on top of the peak.

"Boss!" The call from across the way was faint in Deschamp's ears. "You hit?"

"No—" Deschamp had to swallow before he worked up enough spit to manage more than a croak. "No, Sandy!" he called. "Get over here!"

"No way! I ain't crossin' no open spots! That bastard up there can flat handle a buffalo gun! I'm stayin' put!"

Deschamp bit back the urge to yell a curse at the dour man called Sandy. But he had to admit it was the same distance from here to there as it was from there to here, and June Deschamp had no intention of crossing open ground just yet either.

Deschamp started half out of his skin at the scuffle of boots behind him.

"Easy, June. It's Olan O'Malley."

Deschamp covered his yelping nerves with a dark glare at the the burly half-Irish, half-Choctaw owlhoot. "You ought to sing out, sneakin' up on a man like that, Olan," Deschamp growled. "Could have got yourself killed. Where the blue-eyed hell did you come from anyhow?"

O'Malley shrugged, pulled a plug from his pocket, and bit off a chunk. "Been following you boys for a spell. Looks like you're in a bit of a spot, June. Slocum's boxed you again. Chew?" Deschamp shook his head. He didn't have enough spit in his mouth to wet the tobacco. O'Malley's unexpected appearance had dried up what little he'd had to begin with.

"Where you been the last couple of years?" Deschamp asked.

"Here and there." The broad-shouldered halfbreed's presence calmed Deschamp's yapping gut a bit. He'd ridden with O'Malley for a time, and made money doing it. The man had been in tough spots before. The breed had been an army scout, and then a sergeant for the Choctaw Police in Indian Territory.

"They got the high ground on you, June," O'Malley said around his tobacco cud. "You can't get to the spring as long as they're up there. Not even at night. Slocum can see in the dark and shoot in the dark, and Waggoner can knock the eye out of a gnat at a quarter mile with that scoped cannon of his.''

"Tell me somethin' I don't already know, Olan," Deschamp growled.

The startlingly blue eyes in O'Malley's dark face showed no emotion. "You can't flank them, can't charge them, and can't outwait them. They've got water, you don't. Compton's dead. So's Hake. Saw him go down. If he wasn't dead when he got hit, he is now." O'Malley worked the chew and spat.

Rage and despair combined into a heavy lump in Deschamp's chest. "We got to pull back. Go around the peak. Where's the nearest water?"

O'Malley shrugged. "Palo Duro Creek, but it's likely dry. Hasn't rained around here in a spell. Long ride. Forty miles, give or take. What horses you got left are used up. They might get you there and they might not."

The mention of horses jolted Deschamp's mind into action. "Bud's bringin' new mounts. But if he does like he's told, he'll ride right into those guns up there. That wouldn't bother me so much, but I got to have them horses."

O'Malley didn't reply for a moment, working the chew, then lifted an eyebrow. "My grulla's fresh. I could catch up with Bud, but he won't have any ponies with him."

"What are you talkin' about, Olan?"

"Word's out that a gang of horse thieves is in the Panhandle. Every cowboy who can pack iron'll be carrying guns and watching the remudas like hawks. You won't get hold of a horse anywhere south of the Canadian, June."

Deschamp glared at the breed. "Olan, you ain't here out of the goodness of your heart or for old time's sake."

"Nope. Thought you might be willing to work out a deal."

"What kind of deal?"

"I get you out of this pickle barrel. Get you to the Pease. For half the army money you got stashed there."

Deschamp glowered at O'Malley. "What makes you think I need your help?"

"Because you haven't done so good on your own up to now." The pale blue eyes narrowed. "And I owe Slocum. He busted up a sweet deal I had working up in Nebraska a few years back. Damn near killed me in the process. Wouldn't hurt my feelings a bit to have that bastard in my sights. We'll iron it all out later. I better fetch that nephew of yours before he gets lost. Pull your men back a mile or so, out of sight of that peak. I'll meet you back there in a while.'' He rose and slipped away, keeping the cover of the ridge between himself and the peak.

Deschamp stared at the bluff some six hundred yards away. Christ, he thought, if I only knew what the hell Slocum and that buffalo gunner—it couldn't be anybody else up there— planned to do. Ride out? Stay and pick them off one at a time, like stabbing pickles out of a barrel? Come after them when the sun went down? He wouldn't put it past them to come hunting in the dark. The thought rewoke the worm of fear in his gut. ''Dammit,'' he muttered, ''those fellas ain't human.''

His mind refused to work. It kept bringing up the vision of the spring at the base of the peak, nestled in its grove of cottonwood and chinaberry trees, the clear spring waters, the rich grass. It might as well have been on the moon for all the good it was doing them.

The thought of fresh, cold water seemed to swell his tongue. He glanced at the mid-afternoon sun. It was going to be, he thought, one hell of a long time till sundown. . . .

O'Malley and Bud rode in just as the sun's rim touched the western horizon.

Deschamp glared at his nephew for a moment, then started to speak. Bud headed off the outburst.

''June, there wasn't a damn thing I could do. The LE remuda was right where you said they'd be. With six men watching, all of them packing rifles, handguns, and shotguns. I'm good, but not good enough to take half-a-dozen tough hombres. Remember, you told me not to get stupid. Don't get mad at me because I listened this time.''

Deschamp's flare of rage and disgust at his nephew gradually simmered to a low boil. Much as he hated to admit it, the kid was right. He *had* followed orders. Deschamp's anger flickered out under the unsolved problem—horses. ''Maybe we could try the LIT,'' he said.

O'Malley leaned from the saddle and spat. ''Don't waste your time, June. The other outfits are guarding their cavvies as close as the LE is, just like I said.''

''How do you know that? Go look?'' The sarcasm was heavy in Deschamp's tone.

O'Malley leveled a cold glare at Deschamp. ''Don't get

mouthy with me, June.'' He stepped from the saddle. ''I'm half Injun, remember? I slipped in close enough to hear a couple of the LE hands talking. You won't find a horse anywhere from the Canadian to the Pecos that isn't under gun guard. And it gets worse. I heard one of the wranglers say East has a dozen men guarding your horses. And Arrington's called in five of his best Rangers. They'll be coming after you. I don't have to tell you, that's one tough bunch of hombres.''

Deschamp barked a curse. ''That son of a bitch Slocum! Give me that grulla, Olan. I'm goin' after that bastard right now!''

O'Malley raised a hand. ''Can't do that, June. You'd get yourself killed. And you're the only one knows exactly where that army payroll's hidden.''

Deschamp's cheeks flamed. ''How the hell do you know about that in the first place?''

''People talk,'' O'Malley said with a shrug, ''and I used to tote a badge. Hand me two pair and I'll make four out of it. So, June, you want to talk deal, like I mentioned before?''

Deschamp's shoulders slumped. ''All right, Olan. You got a deal. What's your plan?'' Maybe, he thought, O'Malley's telling it straight. It wouldn't be that much of a problem to backshoot the breed after they got the money back.

O'Malley seemed to relax a bit. A slight smile touched his lips. ''Okay. June, I've chased bronco Indians and badmen from the Nations across this country more times than you've saddled a horse. I know it like the back of my hand, from here to the Arkansas River to the Brazos. I know where there's water. Where we can get fresh horses and enough supplies to see us through.''

''How about Arrington?'' Bud asked.

O'Malley spat out his used-up chew. ''He and everybody else will be looking for us south. So we go north.''

''North!'' Deschamp squawked. ''Dammit, Olan, you're not making sense. It'd take days, weeks—''

''No, it won't,'' O'Malley said calmly. ''You just get the boys together and follow me. It'll be full dark in half an hour. We'll move out then.''

Deschamp scowled at the halfbreed for a moment, then nodded. ''You better be telling it straight, O'Malley, or I'll skin you alive over a slow fire.''

"I'm the Injun here, June. Which brings to mind—I know what Slocum's after. And it isn't the money."

"Then what the hell *does* he want?"

"Tell you later. Right now, let's get ready to move."

Deschamp gathered the remnants of his once-formidable force. It didn't take long. And he was short one horse. Sandy's mount had gone down under the buffalo gun.

"Sandy, take Ned's horse. Guns, canteen, grub sack, and ammunition too."

The man with the bandaged head looked up, startled. "What?"

"Ned, you been seein' double since you caught that slug alongside the noggin back in Kiowa Canyon," Deschamp said. "You ain't worth a tinker's damn as a shooter. I need that horse."

"You—June—you can't just leave me here—like this! Good God, man, please! I can't walk—I'll starve to death!"

"No you won't, Ned," Deschamp said casually. "Shoot him, Bud."

The man called Ned flopped backward a second later, a dark, round bullet hole ringed with blood at the bridge of his nose. Bud, a pleased expression on his face, ejected the spent cartridge and reloaded.

Deschamp stared at his nephew for a moment, disgusted at the kid's smug look. "Bud, you're a hell of a gunhawk when it comes to cripples and old Injuns. One of these days, we'll find out how good you are when somebody's shootin' back."

Bud's face flushed, his jaw clenched. He turned to face Deschamp, the revolver still in his hand. "Dammit, June! One of these days you're going to rag me one time too many—"

"Shut up, you little pissant. You haven't got the balls to throw down on me and you know it." Deschamp sighed. "All right, boys, mount up. Olan's gonna lead us to the promised land. . . ."

Slocum knelt behind a rock outcrop at the edge of the camp in the Quitaque Canyon's labyrinth and tried to shake the feeling that something wasn't right.

The feeling had ridden with him for the last hundred miles.

He glanced over his shoulder into the curve of the rugged dry wash below. There was nothing going on there to account for the twitch in his gut.

The packhorses and spare mounts, now rested and with flanks distended from clean, clear water, cropped halfheartedly at the rich side-oats grama grass that grew along the creek in the narrow canyon. Slocum's sorrel palouse and Lisa's big bay had buddied up long ago. The two geldings didn't graze along with the others, but stood head-to-rump, tails flicking late-season flies from each other's heads.

Lisa and Waggoner sat close together on a bedroll near the evening cookfire, Lisa's finger moving over a page of the thin reader Dan had bought during their brief stop in Tascosa. Now and then, Waggoner would lean closer when she stumbled over a word. Slocum couldn't make out the quiet conversation, but it didn't matter. He had heard enough of the lessons before. Even learned a thing or two himself, when Waggoner had explained the history and often double meaning of a word.

Lisa was a quick learner, as Slocum had suspected all along. She struggled at times, but once she understood something, it stayed with her. Slocum liked the way her face brightened at each new word understood, every arithmetic problem solved.

He turned his attention back to the surrounding landscape.

For days, they had spotted no movement except for the abundant wild game and an occasional but equally wild cow. Not a sign of human life.

They had wasted a day and a half waiting at the first water hole along Palo Duro Creek, hoping to take down a couple more Deschamp men from ambush and deny them access to the water and grass. Deschamp had never showed. Waggoner had spent hours scanning the countryside with the rifle scope, and seen no sign of the gang.

The sound of the single pistol shot just before sundown at the peak lingered in Slocum's mind. It had to mean something, but to go check it out would have meant the possibility of riding into an ambush. He hadn't been about to take that chance. As badly hurt as Deschamp's bunch had been, they'd still had the upper hand in number of guns. It hadn't been worth the risk.

Three days out from Palo Duro Creek, Waggoner had suggested that maybe Deschamp had given up. Slocum didn't buy the idea. He knew Deschamp and the outlaw mind too well. Deschamp was under heavy pressure. Every Panhandle and Staked Plains rancher for two hundred miles was on the lookout for the band. Cap Arrington, a bulldog on the trail, would be hunting him.

Deschamp's horses had been all but dead on their feet days ago; without water and grass, the whole gang would be afoot in hostile country, facing the chance of walking into cocked weapons at every step.

Deschamp's only hope for survival now was to get to the money and head for Mexico. He'd keep coming until he was either dead or had recovered the payroll. But where the hell was he?

Slocum was still pondering the question at twilight, after supper. He leaned back against his bedroll, coffee cup in hand, his mind buzzing.

Lisa wandered down to the small pool for a bath. Slocum ran his hand across his stubbled chin and thought about going to share the pool with her. He decided that, this time, he'd wait until she returned.

Waggoner bent over the yard-wide stream that trickled past the camp, scrubbing the residue of the meal from tin plates and cooking utensils. Slocum topped off his coffee cup and squatted beside Waggoner. The lean Yankee glanced at Slocum, then went back to swabbing a skillet with a handful of fine sand from the creek bank.

"It appears our guerilla war isn't bearing fruit, Slocum," Waggoner said after a moment's silence. "I don't question your theory that Deschamp hasn't given up. Any idea where he might have gone?"

Slocum sipped at his coffee, then shook his head. "Not even a notion. But I've come to one conclusion. We've got to forget about jumping Deschamp somewhere along the way. It's plain enough we aren't going to get another crack at him so easily." He paused for a moment to roll and light a cigarette. "Dan, I can't shake the feeling that somehow, Deschamp has outfoxed us. That he's on his way to the red bluff on the Pease right now—and he just might get there before we do. If he does, we'll never see that army payroll. He'll grab it and head for Mexico."

"Then we'll go across the Rio Grande after him," Waggoner said as he rinsed the skillet and wiped it dry with a flour-sack towel.

"How much of that money do you think we'd recover once Deschamp's band scatters south of the border?"

Waggoner paused in the act of reaching for the Dutch oven. "I never thought of that. There's a lot of country in Mexico.

Outside of the Chihuahua region, I don't know an acre of it.''

Slocum dragged at his cigarette and let the smoke drift from his nostrils. ''I know some of it, Dan. But there's hundreds of towns, little and big, where gringos with cash money would be welcome. And more than a few where gringos would soon be relieved of that cash.'' He finished his smoke and ground the butt into the sandy soil. ''The only chance we have to put a quick end to this is to get to the Pease before Deschamps does.''

Waggoner finished up his camp chores and turned to Slocum. ''I agree. If I remember the lay of the land correctly, we're only a couple of days' ride from there.''

''We'll move out at first light,'' Slocum said.

Waggoner rolled himself a smoke and peered over the cylinder of tobacco at Slocum. ''Slocum, you're a hard man to read, but I feel I've come to know you rather well. You speak in terms of recovering the army payroll, but I sense your main concern in this hunt is for something more important than money.''

Slocum sighed. ''I like money as much as the next man, Dan, but you're right. I want Deschamp to pay for what he did up in the Nez Percé country. To pay for what he did to Lisa.'' He could tell from the expression in Waggoner's face that Lisa hadn't told Dan the whole story yet. ''Most of all, I want those scalplocks back. The thought of those scalps on Deschamp's saddle has eaten at my gut like gangrene, spreading by the day.''

''Was she—and her father—that special to you, Slocum?''

''Yes, Dan. They were.'' He stood and climbed to the ridge for one last look around, his gaze raking the empty horizon. His gut told him Deschamp had somehow outmaneuvered them.

He stared toward the Pease River, the sense of urgency growing in his gut. Slocum had learned to trust his instincts. For an instant, he thought he heard the soft, gentle voice of a young Nez Percé girl, calling his name. Logic told him it could only be the wind whispering through grass and brush. His heart told him otherwise.

Daylight couldn't come too soon.

# 14

Slocum lay between clumps of yucca on the south rim of the Pease River and muttered a bitter oath.

"I don't know how Deschamp got here first," Waggoner said, stretched out by Slocum's side and peering through the telescopic sight of his rifle, "but it wasn't long ago, judging from the looks of the horses. Still lathered and sweaty."

Slocum peered toward the men milling about at the base of the red bluff across the river. His hackles rose as his gaze settled on the burly, broad-shouldered man talking with Deschamp.

Olan O'Malley.

The halfbreed's presence complicated things more than a bit. O'Malley was a cutthroat, a thief, a gunhawk of the first order, and he should have been dead. But it helped explain how Deschamp had beaten them here.

Waggoner fiddled with the scope for a moment, then glanced at Slocum. "Every one of those horses is wearing the Rafter C brand. That ranch is across the state line up in Kansas, not far from Dodge City. They went north."

"And I know how they pulled it off," Slocum said bitterly. "Ever hear of a halfbreed named O'Malley?"

Waggoner frowned. "I've heard of him. One-time lawman up in the Nations who went bad."

"He's down there. The big man with long black hair, standing beside Deschamp."

Waggoner bent back over the tube of the telescopic sight. "I don't recall seeing him anywhere along the way. Not in Chama or anywhere else.''

''He wasn't with them before, Dan. I don't know when O'Malley hooked with Deschamp—he usually works alone— but it had to be since Osage Springs. Probably after the fight at the peak.''

''How do you know that?'' Waggoner asked.

''Because the three of us are still alive. That halfbreed's more than the best tracker in the Northern Plains. The son of a bitch can shoot. He's deadly with a rifle and even more dangerous with a handgun.''

''So I've heard. Think he's better than we are?''

''Don't bet the farm on the difference,'' Slocum said. ''I thought I'd killed the bastard up in Nebraska.''

''I gather there's no love lost between you two?''

Slocum nodded. ''We're both unfinished business with each other. But now I know how Deschamp got here so quick. Nobody but O'Malley knows every seep, every water hole, every isolated ranch house from here to the Canadian border.'' Slocum spat in disgust. ''If I had known O'Malley was hooked up with Deschamp, we wouldn't have wasted our time trying to ambush them. He's too smart for that. But even with O'Malley as a guide, they *couldn't* have covered that much country so quick.''

Waggoner looked up from the scope. ''They could—if they caught, or jumped, the southbound train from Dodge. The rail line from Dodge has been finished for two months. On a train, they could have covered as much ground in a day as we could in a week.''

Slocum nodded. ''That must be the answer. Nothing we can do about it now, Dan. We can't put whiskey back in the bottle. So jumping them when they ride in is out of the question.''

He turned his attention back to the camp. Almost three hundred yards away, across the thin ribbon of water that marked the main channel of the Pease, men went about the chores of setting up camp. Deschamp stood and stared up at the red bluff, Bud on his right, O'Malley on his left. Sunlight gleamed from the silver conchas of Bud's hatband and vest. O'Malley had his back to the bluff. He seemed to be staring straight at Slocum.

''We could drop a couple of them easily,'' Waggoner said. ''I could take off one of Deschamp's kneecaps. That would save him for questioning later." The comment was a question as much as it was a statement.

"No, Dan. We better sit tight a bit. We've got to rethink our strategy." Slocum drew a deep breath and glanced over his shoulder. Below the crest of the river bluff, Lisa stood beside a tangle of huisache brush, holding the leads of the horses, the .45-70 slug by a leather strap over her shoulder.

"They know we're here," Waggoner said, his scope trained on the men standing by the fire.

Deschamp had turned to stare toward the yucca. O'Malley and Deschamp talked for several minutes; then Deschamp said something to Bud, who bent to feed driftwood into the fire. The dry wood quickly flared into a sizeable blaze.

O'Malley swung aboard a coyote-dun mustang, pulled his rifle, and tied a strip of white sacking to the barrel. Then he kneed the mustang toward the bluff. As he rode, the men in camp scattered. Three climbed the steep, eroded bluff, and settled down behind cover of rockfalls or washes in the red earth. Another moved behind the drifted stump of what had been a huge cottonwood tree. Deschamp knelt beside his saddle, his back momentarily turned to Slocum. Bud stood in the open, exposed, and stared toward the yucca where Slocum and Waggoner lay.

"Looks like he wants a parley," Slocum said.

Waggoner didn't reply. O'Malley's horse splashed across the shallow stream. The man reined in at the base of the river bluff directly below them and seemed to look straight at Slocum.

"Slocum, you son of a bitch!" O'Malley's baritone voice carried well in the relative stillness of the clear mid-morning air. "I know you're up there! Come down and let's talk this out!"

Slocum felt Waggoner's hand grip his forearm. "Don't chance it, Slocum. I wouldn't trust that bunch as far as I could throw a horse."

"Don't plan to." Slocum raised his voice. "We don't need to talk, O'Malley! You and Deschamp know what we're here for!"

"You might want to think it over, Slocum, but don't take too much time making up your mind! Take a look at the fire!"

Slocum shifted his gaze. His heart sank.

Deschamp stood beside the fire. A dark mass dangled from his fingers above the flickering flames.

"Either you parley, Slocum, or June drops those two scalps right in the fire! You got one minute to decide!"

Slocum's lips tightened and his eyes narrowed. He couldn't seem to tear his gaze from the scalplocks dangling so near the twisting tongues of fire. Woodsmoke drifted upward, bathing the scalps in a gray mist.

"Slocum, don't—"

"I don't have a choice, Dan," Slocum interrupted, his tone tight. "If Deschamp drops those scalps in the fire, this whole hunt will have been for nothing. I've got to get them back. Dan, can you understand that nothing else matters to me?"

"I can."

"Time's up, Slocum! What's your call?"

"All right, O'Malley! You got the hole card for now! I'm coming down!" Slocum called.

Waggoner lowered his cheek to the stock of the Creedmore. "You know he's trying to sucker you into the open," Waggoner said urgently. "If O'Malley doesn't cut you down, any of that bunch will have a clear shot at you."

"Not for a while." Slocum had already spotted a way down the bluff that would give him cover most of the way. "I've got to go, Dan, and that's all there is to it. Get Lisa up here with that Springfield."

"Are you sure we should put her in danger like that?"

"She's in more danger if those bastards down there get past us and take her alive, Dan. If anything happens to me, drop O'Malley first, then as many of Deschamp's men as you can, and get the hell out if the tactical situation dictates. One thing, though—don't shoot Deschamp while he's holding the scalps over the fire."

Waggoner crabbed back from his lookout post, paused for a moment, and said, "Watch yourself down there, Slocum. Lisa and I will be ready." He strode toward Lisa.

Slocum stood, in full view for a second, both hands raised to shoulder height. "All right, O'Malley! I'm coming!"

Slocum worked his way down the steep bluff, careful not to expose himself to an easy shot, and at the same time stalling to let Waggoner and Lisa get into position.

A good quarter hour passed before Slocum stepped from behind a clump of junipers and stood facing O'Malley. Slocum kept his hands at his sides. The halfbreed on the mustang sat relaxed in the saddle, a half smile on his thin lips, the rifle muzzle with its truce banner still pointed skyward.

"So we meet again, O'Malley," Slocum said.

"I remember last time. I still ache some in the mornings from carrying your lead in my carcass." O'Malley's bright blue eyes and broad, swarthy face were calm but alert. A Colt revolver nested in a scarred holster at his side, the grips angled slightly forward for a faster draw. The holster rode high at the belt, not tied down in the style favored by would-be gunslingers who didn't know the off ox from a wild duck. The rifle, its butt propped against O'Malley's side, was a big-bore Winchester, probably a .45-60 or .50-90 caliber, Slocum figured.

"This isn't a personal thing between us, Slocum. Not today. It's about money I want. And two scalps you want," O'Malley said. "Where's your partners now, hoss?"

"They're around. You don't want to find out where."

O'Malley nodded. "Reckon you're right about that part. Now, June's just a tad pissed off at you, Slocum. He says it ends right here, right now. So here's the deal. June's nephew's been waiting for a chance to make a name for himself as a gunhawk. The man who takes Slocum down earns that name. You follow me?"

Slocum nodded. "Suppose Bud's not as good as he thinks he is. Then what?"

"Then you get the scalps. You and your partners get to ride out alive. We take your guns and horses and leave them ten miles or so downstream. By the time you hoof it that far, we'll be long gone."

Slocum shook his head. "I don't like bucking a stacked deck, O'Malley."

"Don't tell me you're all worried about Bud?"

"As a matter of fact, I worry about any man who packs a gun. But I'm more worried about you and Deschamp. I don't trust either of you."

O'Malley chuckled softly. "I don't trust June either, hoss. But let's turn that turtle on its back. Can we trust you?"

"You'd be a damned fool if you did."

"That's what I figured. In a way, hoss, I'm on your side. Being half Indian myself, I know what those scalps mean to you. So it's your call. You say no, I lower the muzzle of this rifle, and June drops the scalps in the fire."

Slocum lifted a hand. "That would make me real mad, O'Malley. You'd never make it back to camp."

"And you'd never make it back up that hill, hoss. Nobody'd win, except maybe old June over there. What's it going to be?"

Slocum sighed. "I said I didn't *like* to buck a stacked deck. I didn't say I wouldn't." Slocum leveled a hard gaze on the halfbreed. "Tell Deschamp he's got a deal. And that if he burns those scalps, I'll personally track him down and rip his guts out with my bare hands."

"Glad to hear you say that, hoss." O'Malley inclined his head toward Slocum. "Might be fun, watching you go up against Bud. The kid *is* fast, Slocum."

"Fast isn't always the answer, O'Malley. You're a shooter. You know that as well as I do. When?"

"Noon's good. That way neither of you'll have the advantage of the sun at your back." The breed started to rein the mustang around.

"O'Malley," Slocum said, "you've got my curious up. What's in this for you?"

O'Malley flashed a white-toothed grin. "The money that's hid over there, hoss. And the easy life it'll buy. I get half."

"If you live," Slocum said. "You know damn well Deschamp will shoot you in the back before he'll part with half that money. And somehow, Olan, I get the feeling you wouldn't be satisfied with half either."

O'Malley's grin widened. "You've always had something between the ears, Slocum. Since you brought it up, though, do us all a favor. If you get past Bud, don't kill June just yet. He's the only one who knows where that army payroll's hidden."

"No promises. But I'll keep it in mind."

The smile faded from the dark-skinned face. "Kill him, Slocum, and I'd have to kill you. Now, I wouldn't mind that so much, but then none of us would get any money. Like I said, this isn't a personal thing between us. It's business. Noon?"

"I'll be there."

"Dammit, Slocum, isn't there anything I can do to keep you from going down there?" Lisa pleaded, her hand clamped on his forearm. "They'll kill you for sure."

Slocum thumbed a sixth cartridge into the cylinder of his Colt. "They'll probably try. Everybody dies sometime, Lisa. The trick is to put it off as long as possible."

Waggoner stared at Slocum. "Lisa's right, you know. We could sit up here on the bluff and pick them off one at a time."

Slocum returned Waggoner's steady gaze. "We could. But then I'd never get the scalps back, you'd never find the army money, and Lisa wouldn't get to face Deschamp."

"Is it worth the gamble?"

"It is to me. And to two Nez Percé Indian souls." Slocum holstered the Peacemaker, pulled his spare handgun from the saddlebag, loaded its sixth chamber, and tucked it underneath his belt at the small of his back. "You two know what to do. Lisa, you've got the longest ride. You'd better get moving. Remember to aim low when shooting downhill. Leave Deschamp to Dan."

Lisa came into his arms for a moment, squeezing him tightly. "Live through this, damn you, or I'll never speak to you again," she whispered in his ear. She pulled away, mounted Duke, and rode away to the north, the .45-70 cradled in the crook of her elbow. She didn't look back.

"She's a good woman, Slocum," Waggoner said softly.

"I know that, Dan. If we don't pull this off, it's up to you to get her out."

"I'll do that. I don't want to lose a good student." Waggoner glanced at the sun. "I'd better move out myself if I'm going to be in position." He raised an eyebrow at Slocum. "Are you absolutely certain you want to go through with this?"

"I'm not," Slocum said honestly, "but I don't have a choice. Make sure of your aim, Dan."

"Always do," Waggoner said as he swung into the saddle. He leaned down and offered a hand. Slocum took it. "Watch out for O'Malley, Slocum. He may claim it's not personal, but don't bet the farm on it, as you say."

"I'll be on my toes."

Waggoner released Slocum's grip. "If it doesn't work out, Slocum, it's been good knowing you up close. If it does work out, I'll see you in a little while." He reined the black Tennessee-bred gelding to the east, riding just below the rim of the bluff overlooking the outlaw camp.

Slocum ran though the plan one more time. Lisa and Waggoner would have the high ground, Lisa on the north bluff overlooking the camp, Waggoner the south. They'd have Deschamp's bunch in a cross fire. The only flaw in the plan was that Slocum would be in a cross fire himself. That many guns weren't likely to miss. He could only hope that nobody got a slug into some part of him that wouldn't heal.

Slocum squatted beside Chief and rolled a smoke, waiting. The spotted-rump sorrel nuzzled Slocum's shoulder. Slocum didn't know if the horse was scratching an itch or showing friendship and encouragement. Slocum liked to think it was the latter.

Chief's shadow drew shorter by the minute, creeping beneath him. The sun was just short of overhead when Slocum snubbed out his second smoke, rose, and swung into the saddle.

"Well, Chief," he said, "we might as well get on with it."

The half-mile ride to the bend in the Pease, when Deschamp's camp would come into view, seemed to pass quickly but somehow slowly to Slocum. Every bush, stunted tree, driftwood chunk, and rock stood out in sharp relief before his eyes.

The tension drained from his shoulders, gave way to the relaxed, gentle peace that came to him before he rode into known danger. He loosened the Peacemaker in the holster before he rounded the bend.

Chief tossed his head, jangling the curb chain, as Slocum reined in a hundred yards from the red bluff camp and studied the field of battle.

Bud paced back and forth beside the fire, constantly jiggling the Bisley Colt in the black holster slung low and tied down on his right thigh. The kid was either nervous or anxious to make his name, Slocum thought, but it didn't matter. Twitchy men tended to make mistakes. He wasn't taking Bud lightly, though. The young ones were dangerous. A man never knew how quick their reflexes were, or how keen their eyesight, and they felt the immortality of youth.

O'Malley perched on a driftwood stump well away from the fire, outwardly relaxed, a tin cup in his left hand. O'Malley was the most dangerous gunhawk in the bunch. Slocum would have to keep the swarthy breed in his field of vision somehow.

Deschamp stood beside the still-flickering blaze, the scalps swinging idly in his left hand, his right gripping the receiver of his Kennedy rifle. The sight of the scalplocks brought a quickening of fury to Slocum's gut. He fought back the anger. An enraged man made mistakes too.

Slocum ignored the man standing at the base of the red bluff. His left arm was in a sling, his holster on his left hip. Not many men could handle a firearm equally well with both hands. He wasn't likely to be a problem. Slocum also ignored the four men he had spotted among rocks and washes on the bluff above. They weren't as good at hiding as they thought. He'd have to trust Dan and Lisa to take care of them if they opened up on him. Or more specifically, when, Slocum thought.

"Might as well open the dance, Chief," Slocum said as he kneed the palouse toward the camp. The sorrel's nostrils fluttered, ears perked forward. "I'm watching them, partner," Slocum said to the horse.

He reined in thirty feet from the fire and sat the saddle for a moment, his gaze on Deschamp's leathery face. A muscle twitched in the gang leader's jaw. At the edge of his vision Slocum saw O'Malley put down his cup and stand. Bud had stopped pacing. He stood with his hand on the grips of his Bisley, knees bent, a wild expression in his eyes.

"Well, Deschamp," Slocum said calmly, "I'm here."

Deschamp's gaze swept past Slocum. "Dammit, where's the buffalo gunner and the woman? You was supposed to come in together. That was the deal."

"Like I told O'Malley, I don't buck a stacked deck, June," Slocum said. "You've got men on the bluff to back your play. I've got people backing mine. So if you don't keep your part of the deal and cut me down, my people take you. What we've got here, June, is a standoff. If more than one man dies here, several will."

Indecision flickered in Deschamp's eyes. His gaze raked the bluffs on both sides of the river.

"You won't see them until the first bullet hits, June," Slocum said. "The way it works is, you give me the scalps. I ride out alive. You don't get the horses and guns. And I'll be on your trail like stink on a skunk as long as it takes."

"Damn you to hell, Slocum," Deschamp sputtered, "you gave your word—"

"Which, under the circumstances, is worth about as much as yours, June." Slocum stared at the outlaw leader, but kept most of his attention on Bud and O'Malley. The halfbreed sidled another step away; he was almost out of Slocum's field of vision now. Another step and he'd be out of sight. Slocum had read the expression in the breed's eyes the moment he rode in. O'Malley was going to pull iron. "Think back on it, June. Was the girl worth it? And the old man and the other Nez Percé you butchered on the Lapwai?"

Deschamp opened his mouth as if to speak. Bud cut him off.

"Chrissake, June! You promised me this long-legged son of

a bitch! You can't take that back now!'' Bud's voice quavered in the excitement of a killing craze. Slocum knew the kid was a heartbeat away from pulling his gun.

Slocum cut a quick glance at the young man. "What's the problem, Bud? You look like you're about to pee in your pants."

"Damn you, Slocum!" Bud's yelp was high-pitched, a touch on the quavery side. "Make your play!"

"Bud, no!" Deschamp yelped.

The yell was too late.

Bud was fast, but he wasn't Slocum's first target. Slocum whipped the Peacemaker from his holster, turned his right shoulder toward Bud, and hammered a slug into O'Malley an instant before Bud's hurried shot kicked sand at Slocum's feet. The six-gun spun from O'Malley's hand as the breed twisted under the impact of Slocum's slug. Slocum didn't fight the recoil; he cocked the weapon at the top of its buck, letting the weight of the gun pull it back into line. Bud frantically thumbed his hammer and fired wildly. The slug hummed past Slocum's ear. Slocum took half a heartbeat to line the sights and squeezed.

Bud staggered back, struggling to bring his revolver back into line. Slocum fired again, saw the puff of dust from the kid's shirt pocket, and threw himself to the side and rolled as Deschamp dropped the scalps and swung his rifle toward Slocum.

Slocum swung the Peacemaker toward Deschamp, slipped the hammer—and heard the dull click as the firing pin fell on a faulty cartridge primer. He braced himself for the bullet shock from Deschamp's rifle.

The shot never came. Slocum heard the heavy whomp of lead against bone. Deschamp's left leg flew up and back. His body spun and whipped to the ground as the blast of a big-bore rifle rattled the camp. Through the powder smoke haze, Slocum saw O'Malley struggle to his knees, starting to lift his handgun.

Slocum thumbed the hammer and drove a shot into the man's gut. O'Malley doubled over at the waist and dropped to his hands and knees.

Slocum felt a light blow on his left shoulder, heard the crack of a small-bore rifle from the cliff above, then the heavier whomp of Lisa's .45-70. A rifleman pitched from behind a boulder onto his face. A second later, another cried out and slid down the sandy shale as Waggoner's big rifle boomed again.

Slocum saw the muzzle of a rifle swing from behind a shallow wash upward toward Lisa's post on the rim of the bluff behind him. Slocum fired his last shot, saw dirt kick from the edge of the wash, heard the surprised squawk, and dropped the empty Peacemaker aside. He swept the second Colt from the small of his back and fired two quick rounds to keep the man pinned down. He had the hammer back for a third shot when the gunman suddenly pitched backward a heartbeat before the distinct blast of a .45-70 reached Slocum's ears.

The man with his arm in a sling threw up his undamaged hand. "I'm out, Slocum! Don't shoot!"

Slocum squirmed on his belly, looking for another target. Waggoner found it first. Slocum heard the wallop of lead on flesh, the bellow of the Creedmoor—then nothing except the echoes of rifle and handgun shots along the river breaks.

Slocum quickly reloaded the spent rounds. Through the ringing in his ears, he heard the moans of wounded men. He came to his feet cautiously, his Colt at the ready. One glance was enough to tell him Bud's gunfighting days were over before they had begun.

A thin, high-pitched scream of agony sliced through the whine in Slocum's ears. June Deschamp lay on his side, both hands clamped around his lower thigh. Blood gushed from the gory mess that had been Deschamp's upper shinbone. The Kennedy rifle lay well out of his reach.

Slocum strode to the man in the sling, lifted his revolver from the holster, and tucked it beneath his belt. He went to O'Malley's side and tossed the halfbreed's dropped six-gun twenty feet away.

O'Malley was still on hands and knees. He slowly raised his head. "Jesus, hoss—I reckon you—got the job done—this time." The halfbreed pitched forward, face down in the dirt. His boots cribbed at the soil in his death throes.

Deschamp's agonized screech faded into a thin, hiccuping whimper.

Slocum didn't bother to check the men on the bluffs above. He took the chance that the big-bore rifles that had put them down would keep them down. As he retrieved his other Colt and strode to Deschamp's side, Slocum realized the whole fight had lasted less than a minute.

He looked at the mangled tissue and shattered bone that had been Deschamp's shin, and made a clucking sound with his tongue. "Damn, June," Slocum said, "those forty-caliber Creedmoor slugs make a bigger mess than I'd thought."

Deschamp raised fear-lanced, pleading eyes. "For Christ's sake, man—help me. You got to—stop the bleedin'." Deschamp's face was pale, features twisted in agony and panic.

"Yep, I reckon you got that right, June," Slocum said. "Way your blood's pumping out, you might have another ten, fifteen minutes without help. And I just can't come up with a real good reason to lend you a hand."

Deschamp's breath whistled through clenched teeth. "God's sake—Slocum—there's money—"

"I know, June. The army payroll you stole."

"It's yours—I'll tell you where—just help me."

Slocum said, "Well, since you put it that way." He knelt, removed Deschamp's belt, and quickly whipped a tourniquet above the gory wound. The bleeding slowed to a trickle, then stopped as Slocum tightened the belt. He sat beside Deschamp and rolled a smoke.

"Water—God's sake, man—gimme water—"

"Maybe later," Slocum said. "When my partners get here." He fired the smoke and waited, ignoring Deschamp's whimpers of agony. He had finished his second cigarette before Dan and Lisa rode up after working their way down the bluffs on opposite sides of the river.

"So," Slocum said, "where's the money, June?"

Deschamp's tongue flicked across dry lips. "Thirty feet up the—bluff." He pointed to a wind-twisted and gnarled tree with a dirty, quavering finger. "Under—flat rock—by old juniper—" His voice was a hoarse croak. "Water—please—"

Waggoner's gaze flicked over the bluff and settled on the spot. He stepped from the saddle. "I think I see it, Slocum. I'll check it out."

Lisa, who had sat silently on her big bay during the brief exchange, dismounted and strode to Slocum's side. She stood silently and stared tight-lipped, her jaw set, at the huddled, whimpering form on the ground.

"Hello, Uncle June," Lisa finally said.

Deschamp raised his head and stared at her through pain glazed eyes. "Uncle—June? Who—you?"

"Maybe you don't remember me, Uncle June. After all, it's

been a long time. Do you recall all the times you came into my room back on the farm? The things you did to me—and made me do to you?''

Recognition filtered through the agony haze in Deschamp's eyes. ''Lis—Lisa?''

''That's right, Uncle June. It's Lisa. The young girl you had such a good old high time with. And whose life you ruined.'' Lisa fell silent for a moment, then shook her head. ''No wonder I almost didn't recognize you either. You're just a pitiful old man, Uncle June. Not the big, strong young bastard I remember—''

''It's here!'' Waggoner called from the side of the bluff.

Slocum glanced up. Waggoner stood beside the overturned rock slab, a heavy canvas bag in each hand. He started back down the trail, boots skidding on the shale slope.

''Lisa, please—'' Deschamp croaked. ''You gotta—help me. I'm sorry—what happened. I was young—drunk. Water—''

''I don't see why I should help you, Uncle June,'' Lisa said sweetly, ''but I will.'' She knelt, placed the .45-70 Springfield at her side, and strode away. She returned a moment later, at the same time Waggoner arrived. Lisa held a canteen. She twisted off the cap and handed it to Deschamp.

The outlaw gulped at the canteen for several swallows, then blanched. He turned his head and retched violently. Slocum, Waggoner, and Lisa waited until Deschamp's heaves stopped.

''Took too much too fast, Sergeant Deschamp,'' Waggoner said.

''Sarge—'' Deschamp's face paled further. ''I know—you. Lieutenant—Waggoner. Thought you—were dead.''

''You tried, Sergeant, but you didn't quite get the job done.'' Waggoner sighed and shook his head. ''You're in a bit of trouble, Sergeant Deschamp. You ruined my army career. You ruined Lisa in a worse way. And you killed some of Slocum's friends. Now we have to decide who's going to have the honor of executing you. In the least honorable way possible.''

Deschamp had to try twice before the words croaked out. ''God's sake—no! You got—to help me—doctor—''

Waggoner turned to Lisa. ''I suppose the honor is yours, Lisa, as Slocum and I promised. What he did to you was worse than what he did to Slocum and me. Do you prefer a knife, rope, or gun?''

Lisa stared at the crumpled, whining figure for a moment,

then shook her head. "I can't do it. I thought I could. It was the one thing that kept me sane all these years, my hate for June Deschamp. Now he's just a pathetic, whimpering old man." She glanced at Slocum. "I'm sorry. I can't kill him."

"Dan?" Slocum asked.

Waggoner shook his head. "I've shot men. More of them than I'd care to admit. Like Lisa, I can't do it in cold blood."

"I can," Slocum said. He pulled his revolver. "You see, June, I still remember all too well what you and your men did to a pretty young Indian girl. And her father."

Deschamp fixed a glassy gaze on Slocum. "Then—do it—put me—out of—misery."

"Sorry, June. You're not getting off quite that easy." Slocum eared back the Peacemaker and drove a slug through Deschamp's right instep. The muzzle blast of the handgun drowned Deschamp's yelp of pain and shock.

"Have yourself a nice long time dying, June," Slocum said. "I never met a son of a bitch who deserved it more." He turned to Waggoner and Lisa. "We can move on any time now. I don't want to camp here tonight. All that screaming and whimpering might keep me awake."

Waggoner glanced toward the one living outlaw. "What about him?"

Slocum shrugged. "Leave him with one canteen. We'll take their horses. If he can walk to the nearest town or ranch house, fine. If he doesn't, no big loss." Slocum paused near the embers of the fire, knelt to retrieve the scalps, and ran his fingers through the long, dark mane of Quill's hair.

"It's all right now, Quill—Joe. You'll not have to walk the darkness any longer." He strode toward the snorting sorrel palouse, mounted, and rode to Waggoner and Lisa.

"Let's move on," Slocum said.

Waggoner hesitated. "I hate to sound mercenary at a time like this, but four of these men have prices on their heads. Dead or alive. By my calculations, the rewards will total six hundred dollars."

Slocum thought about it for a moment, then nodded. "Like I said, Dan, I like money as much as the next man. Let's gather some horses and bundle them up. The sheriff at Vernon can verify their identity. It's only a day's ride, so they won't be getting too ripe before we get there."

"Deschamp's worth another four hundred."

Slocum said, "I got what I wanted from June Deschamp—the scalps. And the satisfaction of knowing he's going to hurt bad and for a long time before he dies. Let's get to work."

"Slocum, you're hurt," Lisa said.

For the first time, Slocum became aware of the sting on his upper left shoulder, the warm trickle of blood down his arm. He unbuttoned his shirt and stripped it down. A quarter-inch piece of flesh was missing from his shoulder.

"It's nothing serious, Lisa."

"I don't care how 'nothing serious' it is, dammit. I'll heat up some water and bandage it for you. Isn't that what women are supposed to do?"

"Personally," Slocum said, "I like a woman who can handle a Schofield and a forty-five-seventy."

"Go ahead, Lisa," Waggoner said. "I'll gather the mess here in the meantime. Police up the grounds, as we army officers used to say."

# 15

The two nights and a day in Vernon had been one of the most relaxing and comfortable times he had ever spent, Slocum thought as he snubbed the cinch on the spotted sorrel palouse and turned to the man and woman at his side.

"Slocum, are you sure you won't go with us?" Lisa said. Tears spilled unashamedly from her lids and trickled down the dark skin of her cheeks.

"I can't, Lisa. I've two mountain ranges to cross between here and the Lapwai. I need to get across them before winter sets in—" He grunted aloud as Lisa flung herself into his arms.

He stroked her long black hair. "I'll miss you, Lisa. I'd like to stay, but the days are already getting shorter. You'll do well in Fort Worth. Dan will have you writing, reading, and doing math with the best of them in a few more weeks. Tell Lou Calhoun at the Stockman's Bank that Slocum said if he doesn't give you a job, he's a bigger fool than I thought. And stay away from Hell's Half Acre."

Lisa pulled back, blinked at the tears, and managed a weak smile. "Don't worry about that, Slocum. That part of my life is history. I'm starting over now." She kissed him, long and wet, but somehow sad—not with her usual urgent, lusty ardor. When she pulled away, she said, "I'll never forget you, Slocum. Thank you for—for giving me something I never had."

He managed a wink past the tightness in his throat. "Some good man is going to be one lucky fellow, Lisa. I have to be on my way now. And your train will be along in an hour or so."

Slocum toed the stirrup and swung aboard Chief.

"You're forgetting something," Waggoner said. He held out a leather pouch. "Your share of the army money we recovered."

A wry smile touched Slocum's lips. "I'm not forgetting it, Dan. I have to admit I hate to ride away from that much gold."

"You earned it. Every dime."

Slocum held out a hand. "You said you plan to turn your share back over to the army. You know you won't get your commission back."

Waggoner took the proffered hand. "I won't get back in the army's good graces, but I'll get back in mine."

"That's all that counts, Dan. Add my share to what you turn in at Fort Richardson," Slocum said. "Besides, I've got a pocket full of money, thanks to June Deschamp's ability as a thief and the rewards on the heads of the men who rode with him. I'll make out." He released Waggoner's hand. "It's been good riding with you, Dan. You're a good man. I'm glad we didn't kill each other back on the Round Tops."

"As am I, Slocum. Are you sure you won't reconsider?"

"I'm sure." He reached down to again run gentle fingers along the smooth curve of Lisa's cheek. "Mind if I look you up the next time I'm in Fort Worth? Provided you're still single and available by then, of course."

"If you don't," Lisa said with a forced smile, "I'll be forced to hurt you. Real bad."

Slocum realized he had been stalling, unwilling to leave the company of two people he'd grown fond of over the last few weeks. But it was time to move on. Snow would be falling before long in the high mountain passes. He touched knees to Chief's sides.

At the end of the street, Slocum turned to look back. Dan Waggoner stood with his hand on Lisolette Barnes's arm. She waved with her free hand.

Slocum waved back, then settled into the saddle, ran his fingers through the thick black hair of the scalplocks tied to the pommel of his saddle, and kneed the spotted-rump sorrel into an easy trot.

"Let's get a move on, Chief," Slocum said softly, "it's a long ride from here to the Lapwai."

# If you enjoyed this book, subscribe now and get...

# TWO FREE

## A $7.00 VALUE—

If you would like to read more of the very best, most exciting, adventurous, action-packed Westerns being published today, you'll want to subscribe to True Value's Western Home Subscription Service.

Each month the editors of True Value will select the 6 very best Westerns from America's leading publishers for special readers like you. You'll be able to preview these new titles as soon as they are published, *FREE* for ten days with no obligation!

## TWO FREE BOOKS

When you subscribe, we'll send you your first month's shipment of the newest and best 6 Westerns for you to preview. With your first shipment, two of these books will be yours as our introductory gift to you absolutely *FREE* (a $7.00 value), regardless of what you decide to do. If you like them, as much as we think you will, keep all six books but pay for just 4 at the low subscriber rate of just $2.75 each. If you decide to return them, keep 2 of the titles as our gift. No obligation.

### Special Subscriber Savings

When you become a True Value subscriber you'll save money several ways. First, all regular monthly selections will be billed at the low subscriber price of just $2.75 each. That's at least a savings of $4.50 each month below the publishers price. Second, there is never any shipping, handling or other hidden charges—*Free home delivery*. What's more there is no minimum number of books you must buy, you may return any selection for full credit and you can cancel your subscription at any time. A TRUE VALUE!